*For my agent,
John White,
who kept his eyes on the far horizon*

Praise for *Me and Johnny Blue*

"*Me and Johnny Blue* is old-fashioned storytelling raised to the level of home-grown art, told in an American language that is almost gone."—Loren D. Estleman, four-time Spur Award–winning author of *White Desert*

"Wildly comic and darkly compelling."—Robert Olen Butler, Pulitzer Prize–winning author of *A Good Scent from a Strange Mountain*

"Real cowboys never lie ... except sometimes, and usually only to make a good story better. This rollicking big windy has occasional grains of truth, but not enough to keep it from being very funny."—Elmer Kelton, six-time Spur Award–winning author of *The Good Old Boys*

"*Me and Johnny Blue* is a tragi-comedy with the humor transcendent. It is an original, imaginative work. A delight. Do not miss this one."—Max Evans, Spur Award–winning author of *The Rounders*

"Take a pair of pugnacious cowboys who never saw trouble they didn't like, mix them with a fiendish villain and his diabolical filibusters, and the result is comic delight. Joseph West brings to this engaging novel an encyclopedic knowledge of the West. He keeps the body count sufficient to satisfy gluttons, frosts his cake with bawds, throws a few wolfers, a boxer, and a patent medicine huckster into the pot, rings in all the Western legends worth recounting, and seasons the stew with smiles."—Richard S. Wheeler, Spur Award–winning author of *Sierra*

Johnny Blue
and the
Texas Rangers

Joseph A. West

A SIGNET BOOK

SIGNET
Published by New American Library, a division of
Penguin Group (USA) Inc., 375 Hudson Street,
New York, New York 10014, U.S.A.
Penguin Books Ltd, 80 Strand,
London WC2R 0RL, England
Penguin Books Australia Ltd, 250 Camberwell Road,
Camberwell, Victoria 3124, Australia
Penguin Books Canada Ltd, 10 Alcorn Avenue,
Toronto, Ontario, Canada M4V 3B2
Penguin Books (N.Z.) Ltd, Cnr Rosedale and Airborne Roads,
Albany, Auckland 1310, New Zealand

Penguin Books Ltd, Registered Offices:
80 Strand, London WC2R 0RL, England

First published by Signet, an imprint of New American Library,
a division of Penguin Group (USA) Inc.

First Printing, June 2003
10 9 8 7 6 5 4 3 2 1

PUBLISHER'S NOTE
This is a work of fiction. Names, characters, places, and incidents either are the
product of the author's imagination or are used fictitiously, and any resemblance to
actual persons, living or dead, business establishments, events or locales is entirely
coincidental.

One

Boys, in the late summer of '88, me and Johnny Blue came hightailing it out of Arkansas, lighting a shuck for the Texas border. Behind us, not a pistol shot away, rode a determined posse with a hemp rope and a bellyful of anger.

Them rannies had followed us all the way from the fair town of Stonewall, and it didn't seem like they was about to give up the chase anytime soon, or at least not until they stretched our necks.

Johnny Blue, the brim of his hat flattened against the crown by the wind, galloped up alongside me in the highest state of agitation, his mouth all ready to spit spite.

"You just had to get drunk an' shoot the statue in their town square up the ass, didn't you?" he asked. He was bent low across the neck of his horse, because like me he was riding hell-for-leather.

Well, I was a mite offended, and I let him know it. "How was I to know them punkin' rollers figgered the old coot was some kind of hero?"

Johnny Blue shook his head at me. "Didn't you figger a ranny with a beard down to his belt buckle, a sword, an' a feather in his hat was somebody almighty important?"

I shook my own head right back at him. "Naw, I never figgered that."

"Hell, it said right on the base of the statue, 'Colonel Beauregard Maggs, the Tiger of Chickamauga and Honored Founder of Stonewall.' It said right there, 'Honored Founder,' so you must have knowed them sodbusters set store by him."

We were riding through open country, mostly low lying hills surrounded by mile after mile of summer-browned grass broken up here and there by ridges of volcanic rock. We reached a stand of ancient cottonwoods on the eastern bank of Bodcau Creek and I reined up my lathered horse. Johnny Blue's big American stud staggered to a halt beside me.

"You reckon they'll hang us if'n they catch us?" I asked, wiping sweat off the inside band of my hat with my fingers.

"Damn right they will," Johnny Blue said. "Them boys is a hair trigger lookin' for a finger."

I settled my hat back on my head. "Well," I said, trying my best to see the cheerful side, "me an' you, we've been hung afore. We're gettin' to be right good at it."

"Yeah, but I didn't much like it the first time we was hung, an' neither did you as I recollect," Johnny Blue said, stubbornly refusing to be cheered.

Scattered rifle shots rattled above our heads into the branches of the cottonwoods, showering us with leaves and chips of branch, and we again spurred our horses into a weary lope.

"I swear," Johnny Blue said, "if we get out of this alive, I'm gonna shoot you through the lungs my ownself. You jest ain't the same lunatic since you took a notion to plug folks up the ass."

I glanced anxiously over my shoulder as bullets split the air above my head, buzzing like angry hornets. "Johnny Blue," I said, "we got our tits caught in the wringer this time, sure enough. I reckon if you want to shoot me you'll have to wait in line until after I'm hung."

We followed Bodcau Creek for a mile, keeping to the short grass along the cutbank. It was just gone noon and the sun hung like a brass ball in the sky, relentless in that shadeless place and oppressively hot. Horizon and sky melted into one lemon-colored haze and the long grass was perfectly still, undisturbed by even the slightest breeze.

The posse was much closer now, though I reckoned that by this time their mounts must be as played out as our own. There were six of them, riding at a lope in a wide skirmish line, and they looked to be well-armed and determined men.

Boys, you know me, even back in them olden days my bravery was a legend throughout the West, but right at that moment I felt like a rabbit in a coyote's back pocket coming up for suppertime.

"They're closer," I said, kneeing my horse alongside Johnny Blue. "A lot closer."

"You think I don't see that?" demanded that dusky rider irritably. "You think I don't know that?"

"We could charge 'em," I said. "Maybe they'd turn tail an' run, being sodbusters an' married men an' all."

"Maybe, but if they don't run me and you won't care much because we'll be dead as a pair of wooden Indians."

"You just said a true thing, Johnny Blue," I allowed. "There are them as will run and them as won't. I don't think them fellers will run."

"Neither do I," Johnny Blue said. "But our horses are played out, so we got to do something."

We rode up on a low saddleback hill that was crowned by some jumbled rock and a scattering of stunted spruce mixed in with a few pines and scrub oaks, and Johnny Blue yelled: "Over there! We can make a stand among them rocks and maybe scare 'em off."

"But you just said they won't run. Suppose they don't scare, either?"

"Then," said Johnny Blue, "they'll have to shoot us or hang us, and when you get right down to it, I'd rather be shot than hung."

We reached the trees, bullets bouncing off the rocks around us with an angry *spaaang!* I quickly stepped out of the saddle and grabbed my Winchester from the boot and Johnny Blue did the same.

Well, those boys saw us up on that crest, rifles at the ready, but they kept on a-coming and it seemed to me that, punkin' rollers or no, they didn't scare worth a damn.

I cranked round after round into my Winchester and dusted the ground in front of those rannies. This time they got the message because they threw themselves from their horses and ran to an old buffalo wallow and from there they opened up on us.

I reckon them farmers had shot some in the past, because their fire was quick and accurate. One bullet chipped the rock where I was hunkered down and threw stinging chips into my face and I felt blood trickle down my cheek and into my mustache.

"Hell, where did them boys learn to shoot like that?" I asked Johnny Blue, wiping away blood with the back of my hand.

That reckless rider shook his head at me. "I don't know. Maybe some of them boys fought in the war and learned how to handle a musket gun."

A bullet ricocheted off a rock right close to Johnny Blue's head, whining its disappointment. "See what I mean?"

"Maybe we should run for it," I suggested. "If we stay here we'll be all shot to pieces."

"Those horses of ours won't take us far," Johnny Blue answered grimly. "They'd just catch up with us and then we'd get hung."

"Well, when it gets dark we could maybe just Injun out of here."

"Maybe. But I ain't going to count on it. Them boys down there seem mighty alert."

The firing from the buffalo wallow died away as the day progressed, and I reckoned the posse figgered to let the sun and thirst do their work for them.

Every now and then a bullet would strike the rocks around us, but for the most part our pursuers lay quiet, watching and waiting.

The heat settled over the hilltop like melting tar poured from a barrel, and me and Johnny Blue shared the last of our water and wished for a gallon more.

Johnny Blue rolled a smoke from tinder-dry makings and thumbed a match alight. "Wonder how long that posse is willin' to stay down there?" he asked. "I mean, don't they have fields to plow an' chickens to raise an' sich?"

I shook my head at him. "Seems to me, they'll stick it out as long as we do. I just can't imagine anybody getting so lathered up about some ol' general."

Johnny Blue just groaned and smoked his cigarette.

Right then I could tell he wasn't much in the mood for conversation.

As the day wore on, I finally decided to try to settle the matter with words, since bullets had failed.

I cupped my hand to my mouth and yelled: "Hey, you down there!"

"What the hell do you want?" answered a rough, angry voice.

"Listen," I hollered, "you rubes ride on out of here and go home to your sodbustin' an' sich. We won't harm you none."

"Oh Jesus," Johnny Blue whispered. "Now they're gonna hang us for sure."

"Nah, they won't hang us," I said. "You don't hang a man for shooting a statue up the ass. It ain't like it's real or nothing. We got nothing to fear."

"You sure?"

"Sure I'm sure."

"You up there!" This was a different voice, maybe softer and a sight more reasonable sounding than the first one.

"I'm listening," I hollered.

"I'm the Reverend Silas P. Odums and I advise you boys to come down here and take your medicine."

"What kind of medicine?" Johnny Blue yelled. "Are you aiming to hang us?"

"Not at all," the reverend said. "We plan on taking you back to Stonewall to face a judge."

"On what charge?" I asked.

There was a hurried consultation between the posse members but they were too far away for me to hear what they were saying.

Then the reverend spoke up again. "You boys will face

charges of malicious mischief and the desecration of a statue of a hero of the South, to wit, by shooting said hero up the ass with a murderous Colt's .44 revolver. Serious charges, boys. Serious charges indeed."

"What will the judge do to us?" This from Johnny Blue, who always tended to be a worrywart.

Again there was murmured talk from the buffalo wallow, then the reverend yelled: "Three months in the calaboose. Meals supplied."

"Meals supplied," I said to Johnny Blue. "That ain't too shabby. I like the sound of that."

In truth, we hadn't been eating regular since we left the employ of Judge Parker up in the Indian Territory and we were both ragged and skinny as bed slats.

Johnny Blue shook his head at me. "I don't like the sound of that pulpit pounder. Could be he's just sweet-talking us to get us to surrender on account of how he knows we could nail a few of them afore we got took."

"Johnny Blue," I said, "you have no faith in human nature, that's always been your problem. Do you recollect that time back on the old DHS when I put a scorpion in Tube Wilson's bunk an' it stung his pecker an' he asked who done it to fess up and said he wouldn't do nothing to him?"

"I recollect you didn't fess up and ol' Tube beat me to a pulp on account he figgered I was the guilty party," quoth my suspicious sidekick. "Afterward they had to pick me up with a sponge."

"That ol' Tube, he just wasn't extry keen on colored folks," I declared. "That was his trouble."

"An' what's all this to do with having faith in human nature? You sure as hell didn't have any faith in what Tube tol' you."

"Ah, but I learned my lesson. When I looked at you lying on the ground all bloody an' battered with your ears tied in a bow knot, squallin' like a stuck pig, I got to thinking."

"Thinking what?"

"That from then on I'd have faith in human nature. See, I should have believed ol' Tube and if I had, you'd never have been beat like a redheaded stepchild."

"That's right. He would have pounded on you instead."

" 'O ye of little faith,' to quote from the Good Book. I reckon you're sellin' ol' Tube mighty short."

"You wasn't the one gettin' pounded."

Boys, as you know, sometimes there's no reasoning with Johnny Blue, so I let the whole thing go. He could be a stubborn cuss when he had a mind to, and he'd argue black was white with a fence post.

"Anyhoo, I reckon we should take the preacher's word," I said. "It ain't like a man of the cloth to lie. Besides, if we stay up here, they'll nail us for sure if we don't die of thirst first."

"You sure about this?" Johnny Blue asked, his face troubled.

"Trust me," I said.

Two

Me and Johnny Blue were back sitting our horses among the cottonwoods by Bodcau Creek—only this time there was a hemp rope around our necks and a knot of fear in our bellies.

The posse surrounded us, and their eyes showed not the slightest suggestion of mercy. Four of the six were farmers with wide, untrimmed beards hanging down the front of their bib overalls and all had the typical sodbuster's sour and stingy look. But they handled their Winchesters capably enough and there was no give in them.

The sheriff of Stonewall, a man named Halahan, had the look of cow country about him. He was dressed in nondescript range clothes and rundown, high-heeled boots, and he sported a large and sweeping cavalry mustache that was almost as handsome as my own. But his eyes were mighty cold and he was handling the hanging in a real businesslike manner.

Of course by this time I knew why Johnny Blue hadn't trusted that hallelujah peddler, Odums. He was a pinched, stringy man with an oversized Adam's apple, and was dressed in a worn black frock coat and dirty, collarless shirt. He looked to me to be the calculating kind that says grace with one eye open so the kids don't beat him to the fried chicken.

He'd lied to us, that preacher, and we walked right into the trap he laid for us. I reckoned to blame Johnny Blue for not talking me out of surrendering, but one look at that rueful rider's face was enough to convince me that right now he had all the problems he could handle.

"Have you boys anything to say before you get hung?" Odums asked, holding his Bible high up on his chest with his right hand the way preachers do. "Your time is short an' it's time to make your peace with your Savior."

Johnny Blue, who was mad enough to kick a hog barefoot, told him he didn't see no sign of any savior here and he told the preacher to go to hell.

"How many poor black boys have you hung before?" he asked. "I'm bettin' on quite a few."

After Johnny Blue had his say, I let Odums know in pretty salty language that he'd sold me a bill of goods and that I should have known better than to trust a damned preacher not to lie anyhow.

The preacher's eyebrows knitted together. "As long as my breath is in me, and the spirit of God is in my nostrils, my lips will not speak falsehood and my tongue will not utter deceit," he said, denying everything with barefaced effrontery.

"Holy Scripture from the Book of Job. Young man, you are damned, not by my words, but by your own drunkenness and the vile stench of your fornication."

Odums pointed a skinny finger at me. "Did you not, in our fair town, consort with known harlots and loose women and indulge in whiskey? And did you not, in your lust and intoxication, proceed to fire your murderous revolver at the ass of our founder, the gallant Colonel Beauregard Maggs, the Tiger of Chickamauga?"

"Hell, it was only a statue," I said. "Don't hardly seem worth hanging a man for."

"Damned by your own words," Odums said ferociously. "The living image of a Southern hero is only a statue indeed! Now we may add desecration to drunkenness and fornication and thus have the complete and sorry catalog of your crimes."

He turned to Halahan and said: "He has judged the great harlot who has covered the earth with the power of her fornications. Now, Sheriff, you may do your duty and rid this land of the unholy shadow of these men."

Halahan nodded, and right about then that hemp necktie felt mighty tight. My big American stud had rested up some and I felt him move nervously under me.

The sheriff had a dog whip and he raised it to strike the rump of my horse, but a man's voice from the creek cutbank froze him in place.

"I wouldn't do that if I was you," the man said.

I turned toward the voice and my unbelieving eyes beheld the redoubtable figures of Doc Fortune and the Boston Mauler emerge from the cover of the cutbank and walk toward the startled possemen, rifles in hand.

Boys, two angels from heaven could not have been a more welcome sight.

Then two angels did appear—in the form of Doc's wife, Miss Georgia Morgan, and the Mauler's bride, Cottontail. Both ladies were also carrying Winchesters and their wary eyes and the careful way they walked left no doubt in the minds of those sodbusters that they were willing and able to use them.

Doc, his bald head shining in the afternoon sun, nodded at me and Johnny Blue. "You boys hangin' in there?"

"Like hair in a biscuit, Doc," I replied. "And I'm right glad to see you."

"The feeling is mutual, dear boy." Doc smiled, but the smile quickly slipped as he turned his rifle on Halahan and snapped: "Okay you damned star-strutter, cut them boys down."

"The hell I will," Halahan snarled. "I am a sworn officer of the law and I will do my duty and be damned to ye."

I'll give that lawman credit—he had sand. He went for his belt gun but Doc's rifle cracked first.

Then two things happened, one of them mighty unpleasant for me and Johnny Blue.

The sheriff went down, cussin' a blue streak with a bullet in his shoulder, and the excitable studs me and Johnny Blue were sitting took off like six-legged jackrabbits.

I felt the rope jerk tight around my neck, then my head seemed to explode into a million shooting stars, their searing light dazzling my eyes as the roaring blast of their passing echoed in my ears.

And after that there was no sound and no light, only darkness.

"Are you alive, boy?"

I opened my eyes and beheld Doc Fortune's round and shining face bent over mine. His blue eyes were clouded with concern as he—none too gently—slapped my cheek.

"Doc," I whispered. "Are we in heaven? Will I see mamma?"

That worthy shook his head at me. "Nah, you're still

in hell in Arkansas." He helped me into a sitting position. "You got yourself hung again, boy. I got to say, you're becoming a real expert at it. You got a way with gettin' hung that's just pure elegance."

"The posse?"

"Vamoosed. After I shot the sheriff them rubes got mighty disillusioned with the whole posse business." Doc was lost in thought for a moment, then he said: "That sheriff had sand and I'm right sorry I shot him in the shoulder. Of course, I was aiming for his head, but, at this juncture, that's neither here nor there."

I looked around and saw Georgia and Cottontail bent over the prostrate form of Johnny Blue. Georgia, a black woman of great size and strength, lifted that lanky rider like he was a day-old kittlin' and cradled him in her arms.

"Is he . . . " I began.

"Nah," Doc said. "He don't have a scrawny neck like you, so the rope almost done for him. Seems he was strangling a lot quicker. I thought he was a goner even before the Mauler cut him down."

The Mauler's battered face swam into my view. "Are you okay? I got to say, for a man who got hisself hung twice, you sure don't look too bad."

Using Doc's shoulder for support I struggled to my feet. "I'll make it," I said. "Though I feel like I was in the outhouse when lightning struck an' my neck burns like hell."

"You boys was real lucky you didn't have a drop like the last time you was hung," declared Doc, with the self-important air of a man who was about to impart some valuable knowledge. "The drop breaks your neck, you see. But if you slide off the rump of a horse you strangle to death, and that's how come we were able to save you in time."

Doc placed a forefinger against the side of his nose. "If'n you get hung again, you mind my words an' stay away from them trapdoors. Even I," he added, "couldn't save you then."

Johnny Blue gasped for breath, then turned away from Georgia and threw up a stream of green bile.

Cottontail said: "*Eeoow*, that's really disgusting," but Georgia shushed her into silence, then that huge, motherly woman hugged the retching Johnny Blue closer and asked softly: "Are you feeling better? For a poor, innocent colored boy, you sure get into some scrapes."

"*Gugga . . . lugga . . . lug . . .*"

"He's tryin' to talk," I said. "Ain't that a good sign after a ranny's just been hung?"

"*Lugga . . . lugga . . .*" Johnny Blue stammered, pointing a finger right at me. His face was swollen up and his eyes were almost popping out of his head. Boys, it was a horrible sight to see and it chilled my blood something fierce.

Johnny Blue shook his head then took a few deep, gasping breaths. "*Lugga . . .*" He took another breath and tried again. This time he got almost it: "Luggatic!"

"Blue Boy," I said, "I don't take your meanin'. You just been hung and you ain't thinking straight. What's a luggatic? I'm tryin' to help you here. Work with me."

This time he got it real good: "Lunatic!" he yelled. "You're a lunatic!" He went for the place where his gun would be, except it wasn't there. If he'd managed to put his hand on a hogleg he'd have shot me through the lungs for sure. That was always the trouble with Johnny Blue.

If'n he got the least bit worked up he was an unpredictable ranny, always hollering and shootin' at folks.

But my neck hurt like hell and I was a mite touchy my ownself, so I said right sharply: "Johnny Blue, you got no reason to be calling me a lunatic. How was I to know where that preacher's loop would land? He sold us down the river, sure enough."

Now, where this discussion would have gone I don't know, but then Doc said: "Ain't you boys the least bit curious how I found you?"

Johnny Blue stood, rubbing his neck. "You sure showed up at just the right moment, Doc."

"Hell, boy, I been eating your dust since you left Fort Smith four months ago," Doc said. "You rannies leave a trail a mile wide, mostly folks that are real mad at you for one reason or another."

I didn't want the conversation to swing back around to that statue in Stonewall, so I got in quickly: "Doc, I thought you was on the run from ol' Shanghai Pierce, on account of that hoss you stole from him."

"Stole," said Doc, "is such a harsh word. Let's say I acquired the animal. But, steal or acquire, there is no reasoning with a vengeful, violent man like Shanghai. He rightly believed that I took the horse but wrongly believed I still had him. I told you boys during our joyous reunion in Fort Smith that I sold the beast to a light-fingered gentleman wearing a frock coat and a pearl-handled Colt who had to get out of Texas in a hurry. Alas, little did I know that my simple act of charity would cause the relentless Shanghai to pursue me—and my poor family—almost to the Canadian border."

"And me and Cottontail with newborn babies," said Georgia plaintively.

"Ah yes," agreed Doc, nodding, as if this melancholy complication had been most adequately stated, "the fruit of the loins of myself and the Mauler, born not three days apart. The said little ones you will meet shortly, for I see the Mauler has gone to fetch our wagon, where the tykes even now sleep sound as angels."

An odd expression crept across Doc's face, as though he didn't really believe this was the case, but I let that go and said: "Ol' Shanghai ain't the kind of man to give up the chase. How come he never caught up with you?"

"Fate, dear boy—karma, kismet, God's chance, shuffle of the deck, call it what you will. Our most desperate hour was upon us and we were about to throw ourselves on the mercy of the wild Canadians and accept whatever hand was dealt us, no matter how dire. 'Dear God,' I pleaded, 'must we forever wander a foreign land like banished Cain?' But, on this matter, the Deity was most unfairly silent. Oh, many the time, possessed by the most exquisite melancholy, I thought about ending it all and freeing my family from the burden of my miserable existence."

"No!" exclaimed Georgia in a state of great alarm, adding most piteously: "My dear, I can't abide such a thought."

"My precious," said Doc, his eyes moistening, "your unquestioning love for me does you much credit." He dashed a hand across his face, took a deep, shuddering breath, then added: "Anyhoo, ere I could take the aforementioned dire step of self-destruction—to sleep, perchance to dream!—fickle fate shone her light upon us, and we were delivered from the very gates of a hell not of our own making. In short: Our bacon was saved before our goose was cooked."

"By a tooth," said Georgia. "We were saved by a tooth."

"To be exact, an upper right molar in the hairy jaw of one Shanghai Pierce," expounded Doc.

"He went back to Texas," said Cottontail, who had been busy picking up kindling to start a fire, since the day was now fast shading into night.

"Driven back by the need to find his dentist," Doc said. "The Assyrian came down like a wolf on the fold, but hightailed it back home with his tail between his legs and, I am reliably informed, his tormented jaw all bound up in a bandage."

As Cottontail and Georgia coaxed the kindling into flame, Doc studied me and Johnny Blue closely, then said: "It's just as well that Shanghai quit when he did. Otherwise I would have been too late to save you from the hangman's noose a second time."

"Sure enough, Doc," said Johnny Blue, his head crooked at an angle over his left shoulder. "We owe you."

Doc smiled, a knowing kind of smile that made me more than a mite uneasy. "You boys sure do," he said. "You sure enough do. . . . "

I heard the caterwauling from about a mile away—a terrible screeching that sounded like a ranch windmill crying for oil—and it set my teeth on edge.

"Ah, it's the babies," said Doc. "Our precious little ones are here."

The Mauler climbed down from the wagon, carrying a bundle in each arm.

"Lookee," he said as he walked up to the fire, turning the bundles toward me and Johnny Blue the better to display a couple of screaming little faces. "The kinda pink-colored one's mine an' Cottontail's; the dark-complected one with all that black hair belongs to Doc an' Georgia."

"Gee, I would never have guessed," Johnny Blue said sourly. He was still riled up about getting hung, and at the best of times he weren't real big on younkers.

"They're both boys," said Doc with a great degree of pride. "Ready to carry on our great family tradition."

Despite the infernal noise the babies were making, I tickled them under the chin and said, "Cootch-e-coo, cootch-e-coo," but that only seemed to make them cry all the louder.

"You leave them kids alone," Johnny Blue yelled at me above the din. "They know you're a lunatic an' that big red mustache of yours is scarin' them half to death."

Them babies were raising enough of a racket to jar pecans off a tree, and even Doc's eyes were rolling in his head at the noise. A couple of angry jays scattered out of the cottonwoods, chattering their displeasure, and somewhere a coyote yapped in alarm.

"Ladies, please!" yelled Doc. "Do your duty."

Thankfully Georgia and Cottontail bustled to the rescue, and soon both those bawling babies were each sucking on a breast and the blessed quiet of evening descended on the creek.

"Boys," said Doc, nodding toward the womenfolk, "regard, if you will, that tender tableau. How many times since the dawn of time have men stood in wide-eyed awe as their womenfolk, wives and mothers all, gave their offspring sustenance and nourishment from the bounteous wellspring of their own bodies?"

Truth to tell, I felt a mite uncomfortable, never having seen such a thing before, accustomed as I was to wild saloon women and rough company. But Johnny Blue took it all in stride. He declared that he hoped the women didn't get sucked dry anytime soon since it was apparently the only way them younkers would stay quiet, and between getting hung and the noise an' all, he had a headache and was feeling right poorly.

"That will pass, dear boy, said Doc. "It is quite natural for a man to feel a mite poorly after getting hung. And as for the headache, well, you can blame the constriction of the rope for that."

"Thanks, Doc," Johnny Blue said, rolling his eyes. "Now I feel much better."

As Doc and the Mauler made themselves busy around the camp, me and Johnny Blue went down the cutbank to the creek to bathe our bruised and rope-burned necks. There were women present, so I wet down my unruly red hair, parted it neatly in the middle and combed it down flat and shiny on either side of my head, and curled my mustache into two fine points. Despite my raggedy clothes and rundown boots, I know I made a right handsome appearance when I returned to the fire and greeted the ladies, who had put their sleeping babies in the wagon.

As night fell, Doc sliced salt pork into the pan and put coffee on to boil. The babies were silent, and as we ate we talked about old times.

I recalled how me and Johnny Blue had defeated the notorious rebel and killer Amos Pinkney—Georgia's father by a slave woman—and his Confederate guerrillas, and later how we'd saved the U.S. Army from destruction and then took time to bring law and order to the Indian Territory.

Doc had listened to all this with rapt attention, nodding

now and then to emphasize the fact that I'd made a good point or explained a dangerous situation extremely well.

When my account was over, Doc clapped his hands and cried: "Bravo!"

Then he poured himself some coffee and said: "But what you boys have done before, no matter how brave and stirring your exploits—and let me say here quite categorically that they are indeed brave and stirring—they are nothing to what you will do in the future."

"I know that, Doc," I said. "Me and him"—nodding toward the silent and surly Johnny Blue—"is off to jine the Texas Rangers. I call it the next logical step in our brilliant law enforcement career. See, what we're gonna do is bring law and order to the entire Lone Star State."

"Commendable, my young friend," said Doc, nodding wisely, "very commendable. And the Rangers, as fine a body of men as ever forked a bronc, will be very lucky to get recruits of your caliber. But as it so happens, your laudable ambition falls in very well with my plan for you."

"And what plan might that be?" Johnny Blue asked. Knowing Doc from old, he was wary and more than a mite suspicious. Ol' Doc was a snake-oil salesman from way back and at one time or another he'd scratched his name on *juzgado* walls from Texas to Kansas and beyond.

Doc spread his hands expressively and smiled, looking innocent and pink as a bald cherub. "Why, to make you boys rich men, is all."

Three

"**A**nd how do you propose to do that, Doc?" Johnny Blue asked. "We ain't robbin' banks, I can tell you that. There just ain't no future in it that I can see."

"Ah, bank robbing," said Doc in disgust. "That profession has gone all to hell, done in by the telegraph and the march of organized law and civilization across our fair land. Now, talking about civilization, that's what makes me cotton to you boys. See, you ain't even near civilized and ain't ever likely to be. In addition, you both have certain steady virtues, to which I can lay no claim my ownself, but that I much admire in others."

"So if it ain't robbin' banks, what is your plan, Doc?" I asked. I'd been screwed, blued, and tattooed by Doc before, and like Johnny Blue, I wasn't about to trust a man who was always on speaking terms with the bottom of the deck.

Doc nodded with an air of much gravity and purpose. "Yes, yes, I could tell you my plan. But better still, I'll show it to you."

He turned to the Mauler, who was sitting near the fire with his huge and muscular arm around Cottontail's shoulders, and I must admit she looked pretty as a speckled pup that evening.

"Mauler," said Doc authoritatively, "fetch the Flyer."

The Mauler did as he was told and returned a few moments later with a bright red . . . contraption!

"What the hell is that?" Johnny Blue asked.

Doc, in the highest state of exhilaration, sprang to his feet. "This, my boy, is called a bicycle and it represents an end to our present pecuniary difficulties. I have ascertained, on inquiry, that a year from now, because of this fine machine, we will no longer be eating salt pork"—here he toed away his empty (and licked-clean) tin plate with a great show of disgust—"but dining on steak and potatoes and champagne."

With a flourish, Doc waved an imperious hand toward the bicycle and announced in stentorian tones: "Boys, I give you . . . the Fortune Flyer!"

I was so enraptured by Doc's enthusiasm that I too rose to my feet, jumped up and down, waved my arms above my head, and yelled: "Huzzah! Huzzah!"

This so excited and gratified Doc that he ran forward and grasped my hand, saying over and over again: "Hear, hear! Hear, hear!"

"What," asked Johnny Blue from beyond the firelight, in no way sharing our excitement as he rolled a smoke, "is a bicycle?"

"This," replied Doc, slapping the machine, "is the modern successor to the horse. You never have to feed it, shoe it, or water it, and it will take you wherever you want to go. It is"—here his voice changed into a tone fitting something that he obviously considered deeply profound—"it is a *bike*!"

"Doc, if you think I'm about to give up my stud for that collection of scrap iron, you got another think coming," Johnny Blue said, rubbing his neck, which had been scraped raw by the rope.

"How does it work, Doc?" I asked.

"Show him, Cottontail," Doc said.

That young lady hiked up her skirts, revealing a great deal of slim and shapely leg, and straddled the bicycle. Then she unsteadily wobbled this way and that around the campfire.

"Huzzah!" I cried again, so impressed was I with Cottontail's skill.

"See," said Doc, "it's so simple a child could do it."

"Let me try," I said. "Please, Doc, let me try."

"Of course, dear boy," answered Doc. "Show us your balancing skills."

I got on the bike and sat on the seat—Doc called it a saddle, though that scrap of leather was like no saddle I ever saw—and pushed the pedals as I'd seen Cottontail do. It was amazing! I was propelled forward at speed and steered around the fire, narrowly missing Johnny Blue, who jumped out of the way, cussed a blue streak, and called me a lunatic.

As my speed increased, I circled the entire camp, yelling "Huzzah!" as I weaved and dodged between the trees, the bike responding a lot quicker than any horse.

But now I was going much faster—too fast in that confined space between the cottonwoods—and I called out to Doc: "How do I stop this thing?"

Doc shook his head at me and yelled: "I haven't worked that out yet."

I stopped pedaling and my speed slowed, but not enough to avoid the trunk of a cottonwood that loomed up out of the night. I crashed into the tree and went over the front of the bike, landing in a heap among the roots, the machine on top of me.

Doc ran toward me in a state of extreme agitation. "Is it all right?"

"Yeah, I'm fine," I said. "No broken bones."

"I'm not talking about you, I'm talking about the bike," Doc said.

Doc, his face a study of utmost concern, made a quick examination of the machine and ascertained that it was undamaged—a happy state of affairs he attributed to the superiority of its construction and the durability of its components.

I was still a bit unsteady on my feet, both from the hanging and the bike accident, and I implored Doc to find a way of stopping the machine just as quickly as he could.

"I'm working on that," replied Doc. "And have no fear, my young friend—a solution, if one exists, will be found."

Boys, looking back, it's just as well I didn't know it then—but having no way to stop or even slow the bicycle would thrust me and Johnny Blue into the greatest danger of our lives. The fault in Doc's design, if that's what it was, would very soon leave us at the mercy of a gang of murderous outlaws and cutthroats and in much fear for our lives.

But as we sat around the campfire that night, those doleful events were far in the future and we listened to Doc wax eloquent about the many virtues of the Fortune Flyer.

"The bicycle is a vast improvement on existing models and was made to my own design," Doc said proudly. "She was put together in just two weeks by a skilled mechanic who owns a machine shop in Springfield, Missouri." He waved a fond hand toward the bicycle. "Once mass production is up and running that fine artisan assures me we can turn out thousands of Flyers a year."

With the conspiratorial air of a man who has a great secret to impart, Doc leaned toward me and tapped a finger against the side of his large and bulbous nose. "My boy, there is a certain army officer in Springfield—let us call him Colonel X—who is very interested in the Flyer and most enthused over my idea of forming a crack brigade of bicycle infantry. But hush, keep this intelligence under your hat"—here he glanced over his shoulder as though a spy was hidden behind every tree—"since I have no wish to tip my hand to my competitors."

"Then why didn't you stay in Springfield instead of coming after us?" asked Johnny Blue—reasonably, I thought.

"Alas, a shooting scrape of a minor sort meant that I had to flee that fair city in a hurry, and my bold plan to mobilize the foot soldier and perhaps remount the entire United States Cavalry temporarily came to naught," replied Doc sadly.

Johnny Blue lighted a shapeless cigarette. "Who'd you drill, Doc? No offense, just curious."

"No offense taken, dear boy." Doc shrugged. "It was a ballet dancer."

"A what?" asked Johnny Blue, his jaw dropping in amazement.

"Yes," replied Doc, "a ballet dancer. It's a long story, you understand?"

"And a sad one," interjected Georgia.

"Indeed, my precious," declared Doc warmly, taking Georgia's plump hand in his own and staring into her eyes with a great show of affection. "It makes me sad even now to think on it."

Turning to me and Johnny Blue, Doc said: "Boys, that shooting scrape proved something I've known all along: If'n you plan on plugging somebody, for God's sakes make it some poor cowboy or maybe a gambler. You drill a cowboy and nobody much cares, figgerin' he was gonna get hung anyhow; same with a gambler or a dove on the line."

"That's so true," said Cottontail quietly, speaking from experience. "Ain't nobody cares much about a whore."

"'Cept me," spoke up the Mauler with great feeling. "I loved you when you was a whore an' I love you now when you ain't."

Cottontail gave a contented little sigh and snuggled deeper into the Mauler's arms as Doc continued: "But drill a farmer or a preacher or—in my particular case— put a ball into a ballet dancer's brisket an' there's sheer hell to pay."

"You just said a true thing, Doc," said I. "But I don't know why that should be."

"Womenfolk," stated Doc with great authority. "Respectable, God-fearing womenfolk. For some strange reason that eludes me, they set store by farmers an' ballet dancers an' sich an' that's why they'll clamor to get you hung. Since their husbands are sitting right there on the jury, wearing the aprons—well, boys, you're buckin' a losing game."

We all sat there in silence for a while, staring into the firelight as we contemplated Doc's words, and never were truer words spoke.

Me, I'd never plugged a farmer or a ballet dancer before, but Doc had given me something to study on if'n I ever got one or t'other in my sights.

Finally Doc broke the silence with a loud, drawn-out sigh, the firelight gleaming on his hairless head. "Well," he said, "times change and we must perforce change with them. As my family grows, and that of my adopted son the Mauler, we must provide for their future. And that," he added with finality, "is where you boys come in."

"Come in where, Doc?" I asked. Letting me ride his .bicycle was still no good reason to trust him.

"You will help me make the Fortune Flyer a success, and at the same time become rich in the doing of it." He turned an eye—bright and black as a bird's—on me. "Remember, success is not about the wishbone, it's about the backbone."

"Well, that's right nice of you, Doc," I said, "but, like I tol' you, me and Johnny Blue is off to jine the Texas Rangers, on account of how famous we've become as lawmen an' all."

"An' besides," said Johnny Blue, "we aim to find my little sister who was sold down the river when she was just a younker no older than them babies sleeping in the wagon there." Johnny Blue built another smoke and added: "She was took by Apaches after the War Between the States ended an' the last I heard she was down on the Texas side of the Rio Grande somewheres working in a saloon."

With surprising agility, Doc leaped to his feet again and clapped his hands delightedly. "But don't you see, this fits in perfectly with my plans! Oh, this is cracker-jack!"

"How come, Doc?" asked Johnny Blue, his eyes wary.

"Why," said that cheerful charlatan, "if you boys can

interest the Rangers in the Flyer, maybe the entire Frontier Battalion will give up their horses and take to the bicycle." Doc beat his chest, his eyes raised heavenward. "Yes, I see the Fortune Flyer propelling that brave band of stalwarts into the twentieth century! And"—here Doc bent toward me and tapped the side of his nose again— "making us a pretty penny to boot."

Well, boys, you know me, I was famous throughout the West in them days, not only for my handsome looks and great bravery, but for the fact that I was as smart as a tree full of owls. I looked at Doc's proposition—up, down, and sideways—but I couldn't see a catch or, more importantly to my mind, a con.

And if I didn't see a con, then there was none.

"Doc," I said, offering that highly excited worthy my hand, "me and Johnny Blue is your huckleberries."

Four

It was in Doc's mind that we ford the Red near Bois d'Arc Creek and head south to Dallas, where we could ride the Missouri-Kansas-Texas boxcars to San Antonio with his wagon and the horse that pulled it.

Doc said he had friends on the Katy—conductors and engineers and the like—and that they owed him a favor or three.

"With the little money I've put aside for a rainy day and the assistance of those friends of mine, I believe we have enough to make that epic journey along the rails," he declared.

It never paid to inquire too closely as to the origin of Doc's wealth. In addition to his goldbricking and patent medicine huckstering, he and the Mauler had never been loath to knock over a bank if it was in a rube town and loosely guarded. But his earlier melancholy observation that the bank-robbing profession had gone all to hell explained why he had—apparently at least—now turned to the honest industry of the Fortune Flyer.

"As I recollect, a large detachment of Company D Rangers is presently located in San Antonio, preparing to mount a major expedition into the Rio Grande country. Hell, you boys can enlist right away," he said.

A man in Doc's position always knew the whereabouts of the law—even the Rangers, who were then a restless, wandering breed, prepared at a moment's notice to go anywhere they were needed. Like the rest of the Frontier Battalion, the headquarters of Company D was wherever those gallant lawmen happened to spread their bedrolls and boil their coffee.

Even Johnny Blue agreed that Doc's plan was an excellent one, since a saloon somewhere along the Rio Grande was the last known location of our little sister. Most of you boys already know this, but for them as don't I should explain that me and Johnny Blue weren't kin, but we were blood brothers, so that's why I say "our" sister.

Johnny Blue was a black rider, but his kin were my kin and mine his, and there's the whole truth of the matter for them of you boys who've been asking.

That morning, as we took the wagon road to Dallas, Doc told us that the captain of Company D was a man named Frank Jones, who was known to be good with a gun and a bloodhound on the trail.

"Me and him have had, shall we say, dealings in the past," said Doc, "and he's a stern and hard man and not one to be trifled with." Doc, who was driving his wagon as I rode alongside, was silent for a while, his face troubled—and he scowled like a man dredging up old and unpleasant memories.

But then his expression cleared and he smiled at me. "But I guarantee he'll take kindly to you two boys, on account of how crackerjack lawmen is hard to find in his neck of the woods."

"An' that's a true thing, Doc," I said. "I'm willing to bet this Captain Jones feller has already heard of me and

Johnny Blue an' will swear us in right quick, then invite us to make ourselves to home."

"You said it, boy," agreed Doc, clucking at his horse. "Just remember to step light and mind what you say. If you do that, the way ahead will be plain sailing."

Boys, you've all been up the trail and you know the Dallas road was well traveled in them days. But as it happened, most folks gave us a wide berth on account of the caterwauling of them two babies. It seemed when they weren't at their feed or sleeping, all they did was squeal like piglets caught under a gate.

Johnny Blue, having no great love for younkers at any time, rode far to our rear and declared that he wouldn't come any closer until it was time for them papooses to put on the ol' nosebag—and even then he wouldn't feel right in his mind about it until they was both asleep, whenever that happened—if, he added dourly, it ever happened again.

Even when we stopped to boil up some coffee, that surly rider walked over to the fire, got his cup, and then retreated a fair piece out of earshot of them babies.

Later that first day Johnny Blue killed a deer in a dry creek bed on the Arkansas side of the Red and that night we had broiled meat with our beans for supper.

We'd made camp in a thick grove of oak that lay in the hollow of a shallow saddleback hill and when the babies were finally asleep, Johnny Blue came in and ate and then carefully built a smoke. Not looking up from the makings, he said casually: "Doc, you just done told us you only got about fifty dollars on you, ain't that right?"

"My boy," returned Doc with much feeling, "you indeed have the right of it. I wish it was otherwise, but that's the whole sorry truth."

"Then how," asked Johnny Blue, lighting his cigarette, "do you plan to get money enough to mass produce the Flyer? Fifty dollars ain't gonna go too far."

Well, I reckoned Johnny Blue had Doc there, but what Doc said next made me sit upright in surprise.

"Gold, my boy," he said. "Gold for the taking. Gold enough to get Flyer production rolling on a grand scale. Study on it, within a couple of years the entire nation will be in the saddle of the Fortune Flyer and we'll be rich beyond our wildest dreams. And all this will be achieved by gold!"

Johnny Blue, always suspicious as a goat eying a new gate, asked Doc how much gold and where.

"No banks, Doc," he added. "I done told you already, we ain't robbin' banks." He studied on that statement for a spell and then nodded, like he'd come to a decision. "Unless you been holdin' out on us an' know of one that shapes up to be real easy."

Doc shook his head at that doubtful rider. "No banks, you have my word on that." Doc took a deep breath and continued: "Listen, I'll tell you a story. About a year ago, a strongbox containing thirty thousand dollars in gold coin was stolen from the Laredo to San Antonio stage by a Mexican bandit named Pablo Olguin—close kin to an even worse bandit named Severio Olguin, him that runs wild down in Mexico's Tres Jacales country.

"Olguin was pursued closely by the *rurales* of Porfirio Díaz, the leader of the Mexican Republic, sometimes called the Strongman of Chapultepec. Now, this Olguin feller hid the strongbox in the Sierra Madres afore he was caught and killed."

Doc poured himself coffee from the battered, blackened pot that sat on the coals of the campfire and continued: "Olguin made a map of the location of the box afore he was shot, and one of them *rurales* got to his body first and took the map.

"This feller made a copy of the map for his ownself and sold the original to another Mexican bandit by the name of Clemente Perez, a ranny known to me. I am told, by reliable sources, that only a couple of weeks ago Perez was heard boasting in a saloon in Rio Bravo that he was leaving to go after the gold."

The Mauler, who was sitting by the fire with Cottontail in her customary place under his arm, spoke up: "You boys might recollect that Perez ran with John Wesley Hardin an' them down on the border country."

"We've heard of him," I said. "Seems we was told he's a widow-maker an' right good with a gun."

Doc nodded. "Perez is a ruffian and a rogue, quick to kill and very dangerous. They say he has a score of notches on his gun, some of them women and children."

"Twenty-eight, last I heard," Johnny Blue said.

"Ah yes," agreed Doc, "Clemente is something of a late bloomer. Even in these modern times the border is a haunted and parlous place and no man knows what dangers tomorrow will bring. Clemente and his gang of cutthroats play a major part in all that uncertainty."

Doc told us that the copy of the treasure map changed hands many times until it fell into the clutches of a tinhorn gambler who ran a penny-ante poker table in Springfield.

"This gent and I engaged in a game of chance, and the upshot was that I won the map from him, more or less on the square."

"On the square?" interjected Georgia. "Doc, you was

pulling aces out of your sleeve fast as a hen chasing a grasshopper."

"Indeed, beloved," smiled Doc benignly, as though his spouse's observation had been most fairly stated, "but if the rube couldn't afford to lose he couldn't afford to play. Even so, he shouldn't have bet an Arkansas straight against four aces."

"So now you have the map, Doc," I said, stating the obvious, but with Doc you never knew.

"Indeed," he replied. "And now only two people know the location of the gold, me and that blackhearted devil Clemente Perez. That's why I must beat him to it."

"Hell, Doc, you don't need no damn bicycle," said Johnny Blue. "If you get to the thirty thousand afore Perez you'll be on easy street."

"Chicken feed, boy," returned Doc heatedly. "Look around you, if we split the thirty thousand six ways, we'll each get five thousand. I can spend that in a week. No, we've got to think big. If we use the money to fund the production of the Flyer, we'll be rolling in millions—millions I tell you. We'll all be as rich as Midas."

I nodded. "I've heard of that Midas feller. Doesn't he own a ranch out Californy way?"

"Ah yes," said Doc. "Something like that."

Johnny Blue shook his head as though trying to clear his thoughts. "Doc, I don't get it. Where do me an' the lunatic come in? You got the map, you got the time, now go an' get it."

I opened my mouth to make a right sharp comment to my *compadre*, but Doc cut me off. "This here is my plan and I believe it to be sound: Me and the Mauler will leave our dear wives and the babies in San Antone and go fetch the gold," he said. "You two will take care of the ladies and their precious bundles until we return. You will then use the authority of your Ranger stars to see that we get out of Texas with the loot. I don't want any waters muddied, you understand. The gold will be in our wagon and will remain secret, safe from prying eyes—and I mean both the outlaw and damned government kind."

"Seems fair to me, Doc," I said. "But you jest be careful of that Perez feller. If he knows you have the other map, he could do you harm—an' I mean shoot you through the lungs for sure."

"That is a chance I'll have to take," returned Doc. "By this time I'm sure he knows I have the other map, for"— Doc smiled mysteriously—"like me he has spies everywhere. But no sacrifice is too great, no peril too extreme when it comes to the welfare of my family." And he ended on the triumphant shout: "I will do or die!"

On this unhappy and somewhat alarming note, Georgia wailed and exclaimed: "Oh no, I am quite undone. My poor, poor husband."

"Be assured, dear lady," said Doc, taking his wife's hand as he darted me a hard look since I was the one who brought up the shooting possibility in the first place, "that we will have the gold afore Perez even knows we're in the Sierras."

"Still," said Georgia, dabbing her eyes with a small lace handkerchief, "it would be a comfort to know that you've a little something laid by, Doc. Maybe a small bank account I'm not aware of, or some stocks and bonds squirreled away that could support me in my—oh, woe is me, I can hardly bear to say it—grieving widowhood?"

"Alas, beloved, I have no such thing," said Doc in the greatest state of anxiety. "Apart from the fifty dollars that will take us to San Antone, I'm down to my last chip."

"Right, well," said Georgia, dry-eyed as she speared the last piece of bacon in the pan, "in that case just make damn sure you get back with the thirty thousand, Doc."

After this somewhat overwrought exchange, a silence descended over our camp, Cottontail and the Mauler clinging even closer together. But after a few minutes Johnny Blue spoke up and said: "Say, Doc, I've been meaning to ask, how come you plugged that ballet dancer? Jest don't seem like your style."

Doc thought for a moment, then replied: "It's a sad story, tragic really, and a violent one, dear boy. I warn you, it's a tale to freeze the very blood in your young veins. It's a story no man should ever be made to relate."

"Still, relate on," said Johnny Blue, quite unfazed by Doc's apparent horror. "Rannies who have drilled ballet dancers are kinda rare around these parts."

"Well," began Doc, "how it come up, after I won the map and an additional forty-seven dollars to boot, we four celebrated with Mumm's all round, then decided to attend the local theater to see a ballet—or such it was billed.

"Unfortunately," he continued, "that cheap tinhorn gambler followed us." Doc turned to his wife. "As you will recall, my dear, he stood in the street, a large and murderous revolver in his hand, and called me out. I mean, sweetheart, he called me out in front of the whole town. What could I do?"

"That's right, he did," agreed that plump lady. "He called you out for all to hear. Plain as day. There was nothing you could do but meet him."

"I was quite scared," said Cottontail, shivering. "That gambler was a mean and nasty man."

"Lucky I was there to protect you," the Mauler said,

giving his wife a peck on the cheek. She smiled and cooed something and snuggled deeper into his arms.

"Anyhoo," said Doc, "I stepped onto the boardwalk and cocked my piece, telling the tinhorn he was a scoundrel and a low person and to clear off at once or face the consequences.

"Now, at that very moment the ballet-dancer feller walks between us, all dressed up in—my dear, what was the name of that little frilly skirt-thing he wore?"

"A tutu," supplied Georgia.

"Yeah, that was it—a tutu. Very fetching actually."

"Wait a minute, Doc," I said. "I thought you said he was a feller."

"He was," said Doc. "But he was a mighty peculiar feller. Well, he remonstrates with me an' the tinhorn, telling us that we're uncouth Western barbarians and to cease and desist, stuff like that. But then I sees the tinhorn extend his arm, raise his Colt to his right eye, an' get ready to cut loose, so I thumbed off a quick shot. As luck would have it, the ballerina, or whatever he was, stepped into my line of fire an' the ball from my old Dragoon took him right in the brisket. You boys recollect the hair trigger on that Dragoon of mine. It's not a weapon to be trusted."

"It was terrible," observed Cottontail, her eyes wide. "That dancer was a right nice feller. He went to church reg'lar and would pick up a woman's dropped hanky even if she wasn't pretty or nothing."

"Yes," said Doc after a moment's silence, "it was a terrible sight for any man to see. That poor artiste—for that's what he was boys, a bona fide artiste—went down squealin' like the springs on a fat woman's bed an' he took to chawin' up the ground and kicking his legs, all done up in them pink tights of his. Oh," declared Doc fervently, clutching at his shirtfront, "it was truly heartrending."

"Poor, sweet, dear man," observed Georgia, dabbing once again at her eyes. "Lying there all gut shot—and him dressed up an' painted real nice for the ballet."

"Indeed, my love," declared Doc. "That ballet-dancer feller was more suited to the next world than this'n." Doc contemplated on this statement for a few moments, joined his hands as though in prayer, turned his eyes heavenward, and added: "Hell, maybe it was just as well I hastened him into it."

"Yes, he's in a better place now," said the Mauler reverently. "I sure hope they let him wear his tutu. He looked real nice in it when he was prancing around the stage."

"Did you manage to drill the tinhorn?" asked Johnny Blue, who was always interested in such matters.

"Nah," replied Doc. "When he saw what had happened, he took off runnin'. By the time I stepped over that dancer it was too late—though I did manage to put a couple of balls through the tail of his coat."

Five

A week later, missing our last three meals, we arrived in Dallas and Doc insisted we head straight for the Katy train station where he had friends.

Well, it seemed to me that those friends held out their hands, palm upward, pretty damn quick when Doc asked them if they could make room in an empty boxcar for his wagon and the horses. There was very little of his fifty dollars left by the time we got the wagon and horses loaded and took our places, sitting on hogsheads of sardellen destined for the free-lunch counters of the San Antonio saloons.

You boys will recall sardellen—I'm sure you've eaten them enough—them big sardines pickled in brine, with head, tails, and guts still intact. Well, pretty soon, in that hot, stuffy boxcar they began to stink to high heaven.

Add to that the caterwauling of the cranky babies, who had to be changed constantly; the smell of sweaty humans and horses; the clatter of the rails; and the red-hot cinders that found their way through every opening, no matter how small; and pretty soon our boxcar became a rolling, swaying annex of hell.

At one point, midway through our journey when the noise and smell was at its worst, Johnny Blue declared he was going to end it all by blowing his brains out. And maybe he would have, had the engineer not been forced to water the locomotive every thirty miles or so, giving that rueful rider a chance to go outside long enough to stretch his legs and get away from the noise and the stench. We were all of us dirty, thirsty, and bedraggled by the time the train pulled into the adobe station in San Antonio and we unloaded our horses and the wagon.

The city is located at the headwaters of the San Antonio River in Bexar County and in that year of 1888 it was the center of the Texas cattle industry.

As me and Johnny Blue rode into town flanking Doc's wagon, a keening wind was blowing off the northern plains—a chill warning that fall was cracking down fast. The streets were crowded with people: blanket-wrapped Indians, dark-eyed Mexicans, and lean, hard-bitten horsemen—veterans of the cattle country—men who had ridden the dusty trails north and had fought the Comanche and Kiowa.

San Antonio was a city with snap in them days, and right off I knew it suited me and Johnny Blue down to the ground. Once we were Rangers—something I reckoned would happen within the next couple of hours— we'd soon bring law and order to here and elsewhere in Texas.

A few inquiries revealed that a company of Rangers under the command of Captain Frank Jones was camped to the east of town near Salado Creek.

The bearded old-timer who gave us this information—an old buffalo hunter and Indian fighter in stained buckskins—warned us that the Rangers were in no mood to receive guests.

"Them boys is a mite touchy an' liable to shoot first

an' ask questions later," the oldster said. "If'n I was you, I'd holler plenty afore I rode up to their camp."

"And why," asked Doc, "is that intrepid band of brothers in such a foul mood?"

The old man shifted his chaw in his jaws, spat, then wiped his mouth with the back of his hand. "Damned if I know." He shrugged, smoothing down his gray mustache and beard with a gnarled hand. "I hear tell they've been ordered to the Rio Grande an' got no mind to go there."

"Me an' him," I said, nodding toward Johnny Blue, "is here to jine the Rangers, an' the Rio Grande country will suit us just fine."

"Your funeral," the old man said, then he turned on his moccasined heel and walked away.

Doc, who'd had dealings with the Rangers before—much to his detriment—suggested that me and Johnny Blue ride to the Ranger encampment while he and the others followed at a discreet distance.

"We'll camp on the creek well away from those lawmen, and you boys can join us there," he said.

Doc reached into his coat pocket and brought out a canvas wallet I hadn't seen before. There was paper money inside and he counted it in silence for a few moments. "Eighteen dollars," he sighed. "Slim enough pickings, but at least we'll eat tonight."

"Where did you get that wallet, Doc?" I asked suspiciously.

Doc smiled. "Providence, my boy. Remember when we first rode into town we stopped a rube in a striped vest an' plug hat who told us he didn't know where the Rangers was an' couldn't care less?"

"Yeah, I recollect," I said.

"Well, when I accidentally bumped into him—you recall that, too, I guess?—his wallet just jumped into my hands. By the time I recovered from the shock and tried to call him back, he was lost in the crowd."

"Doc is the soul of honesty," Georgia said without apparent irony. "He tried to call that rube back, so this little bounty was the will of God."

"Indeed, my dear," agreed Doc. "But, you understand, a dryness in the throat made it impossible for me to holler too loudly. Indeed," he pondered, shaking his head, "the Deity works in strange ways, His wonders to perform."

"You get his watch, Doc?" asked Johnny Blue, quite unimpressed by Doc's piety.

Doc fished in his pocket again and brought out the timepiece—a gold railroad, by the look of it.

"I got to hand it to you, Doc," said Johnny Blue admiringly. "You sure know how to fleece the rubes, an' that's a natural fact."

"It's also an excellent reason to put some distance between him and us afore he finds what's missing," Doc said. He pointed toward the east. "Onward, my brave lads. There waits your destiny—and mine."

Me and Johnny Blue rode on ahead, Doc and the others stopping to pick up some coffee and bacon and other supplies.

Boys, as we rode I looked at us and I didn't cotton to what I saw. We were both ragged as a sheepherder's britches, and the soles of our boots were so thin, if we'd scratched a match on them we'd have set our socks on fire—not that there was much of them left, either. We were skinny as smoke from not eating regular, and on the trail we'd only been able to roughly curry our hair and shave with Johnny Blue's case knife.

"We don't look real good to go meetin' them Rangers, Blue Boy," I said. "We're a couple of right shabby punchers, an' that's a natural fact."

"You speak for your ownself," replied that dusky rider. "Me, I look jest *'esta bien.'* "

We rode in silence for a few moments, then I said: "We don't smell too good, either."

Johnny Blue reined up his horse and turned to me, an exasperated look on his face. "What the hell's the matter with you? We're joining the Texas Rangers, not gettin' duded up from the Sears an' Roebuck catalog to go to a church ice-cream social."

"Still, the next ranch house we see, maybe we could stop an' get cleaned up some."

Johnny Blue sighed. "Whatever you say, only don't expect me to take a bath. Hell, we had one just a couple of months ago an' my hide still ain't recovered."

"I didn't say we'd go that far," I replied defensively. "I just said we'd clean up some, not all over."

Ten minutes later we rode into the yard of a small ranch house and when the owner—a bearded man with a Sharps .50 in his hands—heard our story he nodded toward the barn.

"There's a water trough right there, some lye soap, an' a piece of mirror," he said. "He'p yourself."

We turned to walk our horses toward the barn, but the man stopped us. "You boys wait right there," he said.

He ducked inside his cabin and appeared a few moments later, a small purple bottle in his hand.

"My woman done walked out on me a spell back, but she left this behind." He studied the label on the bottle.

"It says right here 'Eau de Lavender.' You boys splash some of this on and you'll show them Rangers a thing or two. Me," he added, "I got no use for it on account of how I don't have a woman no more an' nobody to impress."

"Man needs a woman," I said, taking the bottle from him. "At least, from time to time."

"Yeah, well, she just up an' left me," the rancher said. "Took my best mare, too. Me, I was good to her an' didn't beat her but oncet a month—an' then only when she deserved it. She was a fat woman, but she kept me warm in winter and give me plenty of shade come summer."

Johnny Blue shrugged. "It takes all kinds. A woman jest don't know when she's lucky."

"An' ain't that the truth," the man said, walking back into the house, his head hanging.

That ol' boy sure missed that woman of his, but he hadn't broke that filly to the halter real good, and that was his big mistake.

Well, boys, me and Johnny Blue washed our face and hands and tried to straighten up our ragged shirts and pants as best we could. I still had some of that hair pomade Silas Bramwell had given me while I was waiting to get hung up in the Territory, so I put it on thick, then parted my hair in the middle and plastered it down on each side, smooth and shiny as a new mint penny. Then I put the pomade on my mustache and twirled the ends into two fine points that stuck out a good four inches on either side of my face.

Me and Johnny Blue used up that whole bottle of Eau de Lavender between us, and when we was finished we both made a handsome and gallant appearance and we

smelled real good. Then we saddled up and found the
Ranger camp while it was still full daylight.

I hollered: "Hello the camp!"

After an answering yell to stay the hell away—which
me and my stalwart companion boldly ignored—we
bravely rode toward the Ranger campfire.

And into a heap of trouble.

Six

Boys, them were some pretty riled up Rangers.

One tall, lanky ranny wearing two guns in cross-belts and a couple more under each shoulder leveled his Winchester at us as we rode into the camp.

"Are you boys deef?" he asked. "I just done tol' you to stay the hell away."

The muzzle of that rifle was pointed right about where my hair parted, and it made me more than a mite uneasy, but when I spoke my voice was steady enough.

"Me and him," I said, nodding toward Johnny Blue, "is famous lawmen an' we've come all the way from the Territory to jine the Rangers."

"Yeah, well, this ain't the time," the man said. He chewed on his mustache and looked over his shoulder toward a group of about ten men who were standing around the fire. Them rannies were all armed to the teeth and their faces were bright red like they'd just had a major fallin' out.

"You boys come back another time—maybe next year," the Ranger said. "Like I tol' you, now ain't the right moment, if'n you get my drift."

"Now, lookee here," I said, getting angry myself.

"We're famous lawmen an' Indian fighters an' we won't be treated this way. We have friends in San Antone."

The man's rifle muzzle moved down maybe an inch so that it was now pointing right in the middle of my forehead. "Mister," he said, his voice low, hard, and flat, "am I gonna have trouble with you?"

"No trouble," Johnny Blue said quickly. "See, my friend here is a lunatic an' he doesn't know what he's saying half—or maybe most—of the time. He shoots folks up the ass just for fun, so that will tell you what kind of a lunatic he is. Oncet he took a notion to shoot everybody's hoss an' he left the whole Montana Territory afoot. He should be locked up."

"Well, maybe so," the Ranger said, but his rifle didn't waver an inch. "You can tell me how tetched in the head he is some other time. Right now I'm warnin' you boys to ride on out of here afore you get hurt. I won't tell you a second time."

Remembering how Doc spoke when he wanted to get the better of some obstinate ranny, I stood in my stirrups and said: "Now see here, my good man, I—"

"Well, that tears it!" the Ranger yelled, and his Winchester came up to his shoulder fast and smooth as a striking snake.

"Slim, no!"

A tall, bearded man ran toward us, waving his arms.

He skidded to a halt, pushed down on the barrel of Slim's rifle, and yelled: "Hell, man, ain't we got enough trouble arguing among ourselves without you blowin' holes in a couple of saddle tramps?"

His face getting redder by the minute, Slim yelled: "I told them to leave an' they didn't. Am I on guard duty or not?"

"Ease up, Slim," the bearded man said in a more reasonable tone of voice. "This Mexican thing has us all on edge." He looked at me and Johnny Blue with the coldest gray eyes I ever seen in a man. "What the hell do you boys want?"

"Me and him," I said, trying to keep my voice steady because I was a tad shook, "is famous lawmen an' we've come to jine the Rangers."

Slim said: "I tol' them, not today, Cap'n."

Captain Frank Jones—for that's who he was—shook his head at us. "Like Slim said, this isn't a good day. You boys ride on home an' come back some other time an' maybe we'll talk."

"Me an' him," I said desperately, "we saved the United States Army an' then we cleaned up the Indian Territory for Judge Parker. We're right famous—maybe not in these parts, but in some parts."

"An' we got to be goin'," said Johnny Blue.

Captain Jones waved a hand at us. "Some other time, boys."

He started to walk away, then stopped and slapped the side of his head with his hand. "Hell, what am I doing? I knowed you two must be famous lawmen the first time I ever set eyes on you."

The other Rangers had walked from the fire and were now clustered around their captain, so I puffed up a little and said: "We don't make a boast of it. Me an' him, we ain't big talkers an' little doers. I guarantee that."

"Never thought for one minute you was," Jones said, smiling. "Why, when I saw you boys ride up to our camp I turned to the rest of the Rangers here an' said, 'Lookee there, them boys is true blue.'"

One big Ranger with a black beard and a knife scar on

his cheek was looking at Captain Jones like he was loco. But then his face cleared and he grinned like a mule eating cactus.

"Beggin' your pardon, Cap'n, but you said 'gold dust.' I recollect exact. You said to me, 'Corporal Svenson, them two boys a-ridin' toward us, looking so brave an' tall in the saddle, is pure gold dust.' Strike me, if'n I haven't hit the nail on the head."

Another Ranger—a tall, skinny galoot with hair so long it fell over his shoulders in waves prettier than any woman's—said: "Maybe you allowed that these two boys was gold dust, Cap'n. But I do recollect you also sayin' they was true blue."

"And that's what you young men are—true blue in my book," Captain Jones said, beaming up at me and Johnny Blue. "The wilder the colt, the better the horse, is what I always say. Now you boys step down an' come to the fire. Seems to me the coffee's biled."

Well, them Rangers slapped our backs and smiled and said we was *mucho hombres* and they said they knew right off that we couldn't be stampeded, and one or two even gave a "Huzzah!"—though at the time I couldn't figger why.

From being a bunch of angry, gloomy Rangers they was suddenly walking around three feet off the ground, and I reckoned maybe it was because they was so proud to have a couple of famous lawmen and Indian fighters join their brave Frontier Battalion.

Boys, if'n I'd known the real reason for all them grins, I would have jumped back on my bronc and lit a shuck for the Texas border. But I didn't—at least not then—and there's no use crying over spilt milk. A man can't start choppin' till he's treed the coon, and that's a regular fact.

Well, Captain Jones poured our coffee his ownself and spiked it with some good Kentucky bourbon from a bottle he carried, then said: "I got to tell you plain, you boys smell real good." He turned to his men. "Don't they, boys?"

A murmur of agreement came from the Rangers and Captain Jones said: "Now, why don't you tell me about yourselves and your great exploits as famous lawmen an' Injun fighters."

So I told him, missing out nothing. I recounted how we'd saved our great Republic by routing a whole Confederate army plus the entire Blackfoot Indian nation, then how—just in the nick of time—we'd rescued the United States Army from desperate bandits, and finally I told about riding for Judge Parker and cleaning up the Indian Territory.

"We made that wild and untamed land safe for the forward march of civilization," I said, then added, dropping my eyes to my coffee cup: "Judge Parker tol' me that his ownself."

After I'd finished, Captain Jones rose to his feet and led the Rangers in three cheers, their loud huzzahs setting the roosting jays to scattering out of the cottonwoods.

"True blue!" exclaimed that excited lawman. "That's a powerful story, an' you can put more kindlin' on that particular fire anytime you have a mind to." He shook my hand and then Johnny Blue's. "Damn me, but I never get tired of shakin' you boys' hands."

"Likewise," said the longhaired Ranger, and then the rest crowded around and shook our hands so often my knuckles ached.

After the excitement had died down a little, we all sat around the fire again and Captain Jones leaned toward me. "Since we're all being confidential here, I'll say what's on my mind. I'll give it to you straight." He poured another shot of whiskey into my cup and did the same for Johnny Blue. "In brief, it ain't easy to join the Texas Rangers, an' that's a natural fact."

I allowed that I'd been looking around at his brave band of stalwarts and that this was obviously the case, and that he'd put the matter—as the English say—in a nutshell.

"Then," said Captain Jones, "taking a clear view of things, I ask myself this question: How can I best get these two gallant boys into my company? An' the answer came to me in a flash of inspiration—in a word, that flash was: smallpox!"

At this, Johnny Blue looked up real quick and said: "Beggin' your pardon, Cap'n, but that's not a flash I care for, an' no mistake."

"God bless your soul, an' why should you?" Jones asked. "Smallpox is nothing to be messed with, an' that's why I'm turnin' to you boys. You're going to get rid of an epidemic of it for me."

The captain immediately sprang to his feet, shook his head, and waved his hands at his Rangers. "No, no, boys, quiet! For pete's sakes let's have no petty jealousy, if you please!"

Now, them Rangers hadn't been making any noise that I could hear, in fact they'd been mighty silent, but I let that go.

"I know you was all arguing about who would have the honor of fumigating them Mexican *jacales* down on the Rio Grande, but since these two famous lawmen rode into camp, my mind's made up," Captain Jones said.

"Aw c'mon, Cap'n," said one big Ranger in a cowskin vest, "you promised me I could go."

"An' me, too," said another.

"This don't hardly seem fair," growled a third sulkily.

Captain Jones looked at me and shook his head again. "Do you see what I have to contend with? They know this noble task will make them famous all over Texas, an' that's why they all want to do it."

"Seems to me," said Johnny Blue, rolling a cigarette and looking stubborn, "you should let them."

"Yes, I could," allowed the captain, "but I won't be railroaded. I'm keeping that job open for you boys. It's what's known in the Rangers as . . . as . . . " Jones thought for a few moments, frowning. Then his face cleared and he said: "It's known as a TOR."

"What's that?" I asked.

"Why, it stands for Test of Resolve. In other words, young feller, if you volunteer for this job, it means you really want to be a Ranger. An' after it's over and done proper, you come right back here to San Antone an' I'll pin stars on you." He turned to his men again. "Ain't that right boys?"

"Sure enough," said Cowskin Vest. "We all had to pass the TOR an' no mistake."

I studied on this for a few moments, then said: "Cap'n, you want us to ride down to the Rio Grande an' fumigate Mexicans. Do I have it right?"

"Right on the button." Jones beamed. "You're sharp, boy, mighty sharp. See, every year at this time, smallpox breaks out in the villages along the river, an' the federal government, in its wisdom, has given the Texas Rangers the job of stamping it out. That's why we're all so eager to go, as you can see.

"Now, if you boys take on the task, you ride southeast of here as the crow flies an' you reach the village of Santa Alana on the U.S. side of the river. As villages go, it ain't much—maybe a dozen *jacales*, adobes with tar-paper roofs mostly, a cantina, and some horse corrals. But that's where the most recent smallpox outbreak started. You boys fumigate them *jacales* an' the cantina real good an' then ride back here an' become true-blue Texas Rangers."

"Huzzah!" said one man, but he was sniggering behind his hand and I figured it was a pretty weak cheer.

"What do we fumigate them places with?" I asked. "Me an' him,"—I nodded toward Johnny Blue—"know nothin' about fumigatin'."

"An' we don't want to know nothin' about fumigatin'," observed that surly rider.

"What's to know?" Jones said. He reached behind him and dug into a bulging burlap sack. He held up a flat canister with a paper fuse on the top and said: "This is what's called a formaldehyde fumigation bomb. You just light that there fuse, then toss the bomb through a window or door. Nothing could be easier."

"That's all?" I asked. "We just throw them bombs in the *jacales*, fumigate the Mexicans, an' then ride on out of there?"

Captain Jones nodded. "That's it. You're a right smart ranny ain't you? Catch on quick."

Johnny Blue rose to his feet and crooked a finger in my direction. "Come here. I want to talk to you," he said. "In private."

"That's right, you boys discuss things among yourself." Jones smiled. "Just don't be too long, because"—he placed a lot of emphasis on his next three words—"*your fellow Rangers* is green with envy an' rarin' to go. Boys, strike me, I don't think I can hold 'em much longer."

There was a murmur of agreement among the lawmen as me and Johnny Blue stepped away a few paces, then stopped.

"I don't like the sound of this," said my suspicious sidekick. "You recollect back when we was ridin' for the ol' DHS when smallpox hit them so'diers at the fort. It started with one or two an' then dozens of them came down with it. I recollect they buried upwards of twenty men afore it was over. Smallpox," Johnny Blue added, "is catchin'."

He looked over at the Rangers sitting around the fire, and those friendly lawmen waved and smiled, and one said, "True blue," and another, "Fine fellows."

"And another thing," Johnny Blue continued. "Them Rangers don't look too cut up about not going down there to fumigate the *jacales*. Could be the Mexicans want to be left in peace to enjoy their smallpox undisturbed."

I shook my head at that perplexed puncher. "Johnny Blue," I said, "you have a suspicious nature and that's always been your problem. You heard Cap'n Jones say *'your fellow Rangers.'* He said it plain as day an' that means we're as good as wearin' a star already. Why we're—"

"Like I said," Johnny Blue interrupted. "Smallpox is catchin'."

"Hell, we won't have time to catch it," I said. "We ride in there, toss the bombs into the *jacales*, an' hightail it out again. Seems to me it will only take a few minutes. And besides," I added, throwing in the kicker, "we can't sell the Flyer to the Texas Rangers until we become Rangers ourselves."

"Are you sure about the smallpox—I mean us not being in the village long enough to catch it?" Johnny Blue asked.

"Sure, I'm sure," I replied, slapping that doubting Thomas on the back. "Trust me."

Well boys, when we told them Rangers we'd take on the job, they made a big fuss of us and told us we were true blue and sich, and Captain Jones dug into his own pocket and gave us ten dollars to cover expenses on the trip. Then he loaded up a burlap sack with fumigation bombs and tied it to my saddle horn.

"When you boys come back, we'll have us a shindig," the captain said. "An' don't be surprised if the governor of Texas, ol' Lawrence Sullivan Ross himself, arrives to pin on your Rangers' stars personal."

It came to me then that those Rangers looked mighty relieved that me and Johnny Blue was going and not them. But at the time I just put it down to the fact that they badly wanted us to join Company D and were rooting for us to pass the TOR.

I was wrong on both counts, but I didn't discover that till much later—and by then it was way too late.

Seven

When we met up with the others and told them about our plans, Doc said that suited him just fine. He and the Mauler would await our return from the Rio Grande, since they were planning to goldbrick some of the rubes that hung around the San Antonio saloons, and he figgered to use at least some of the resulting profits to recruit some gun help for their dangerous trip into the Sierras.

"Doc is always a man of business," Georgia said admiringly. "And a wonderful provider."

"Indeed," agreed Doc, nodding his shiny head. "I am a flowing river to my family."

That flowing river then quickly relieved us of five of our ten dollars, saying he needed the cash for supplies and for walking money to work the goldbrick.

A few minutes later, after much hugging and tears from Georgia and Cottontail, me and Johnny Blue resolutely turned our horses southwest; two stalwart, handsome, and determined men—and already Texas Rangers in all but name.

The village of Santa Alana, where we were heading, lay on the north bank of the Rio Grande near Eagle Pass in the shadow of the Piedras Negras peaks of the high Sierras. That was wild and remote desert country in them days, relieved now and then by gently rolling hills studded with prickly pear cactus, tough blackbrush bush, and mesquite. It was a land that offered nothing to the traveler, and just a few years earlier the Apaches, under Victorio and later Geronimo, had often raided there.

We headed southwest for four days, keeping the Nueces Plains to our south, riding almost parallel to the Balcones Escarpment to the north. By the time we crossed Elm Creek at noon on the fifth day our money was gone and so was our bacon and coffee.

We camped that night at Jacob Springs, a couple of miles east of Santa Alana, sharing a stale biscuit and even staler alkaline water from the sluggish stream that gave the place its name. Johnny Blue—now that his tobacco sack was empty—was in a foul mood and grumpily refused to talk about fumigating the *jacales*, claiming that the whole thing was all my idea and he'd never wanted to be a goddamned Texas Ranger anyway and for sure he was going to die of smallpox and he'd never find his little sister . . . and on and on.

But I'd prepared for such an emergency and dug into my saddlebags and found the sack of tobacco I'd stashed there before we left San Antone. I'd learned from bitter past experience that if my *compadre* didn't have his smokes there was just no being around him.

After he'd rolled and smoked three or four cigarettes, Johnny Blue's mood improved considerable and he allowed how being a Ranger maybe wasn't such a bad idea after all. That's how much power tobacco has over a man. I reckon it's worse than whiskey or even women.

We rode into Santa Alana early next morning. As Captain Jones had told us, the village wasn't much—even for that neck of the woods. There were maybe eight adobe *jacales* clustered around a central square with a dry fountain in the middle. The cantina—the biggest building in town—was to our right as we rode in, and we dismounted and tied our horses to the hitching rail.

A few Mexicans were walking this way and that across the square, heads down and disinterested, and a skinny hound lay outside the cantina, moodily watching a small lizard warming itself in the sun after the cool of the evening. Chickens pecked for bugs in the dusty street and from one of the *jacales* came a woman's voice protesting loudly in Mexican—then a slap, followed by the urgent squeal of bedsprings.

"Don't look like a town with a smallpox epidemic to me," Johnny Blue said doubtfully. "You sure we're in the right place?"

"Sure, I'm sure," I replied. "Cap'n Jones said we should ride southwest an' that's just what we done. This is got to be Santa Alana. Trust me."

"Maybe we should ask somebody," Johnny Blue suggested.

I shook my head at him. "Ask, hell. We don't even speak Mexican. Nah, this is the place all right. Maybe a lot of them already bought the farm."

"Could be. But it don't look right to me."

"Johnny Blue," I said, untying the sack of bombs from my saddle, "quit arguing an' shuck your rifle. We got a whole heap o' fumigatin' to do."

"Why the rifle?"

"In case they don't want to be fumigated."

Well, boys, as it turned out, them Mexicans cooperated real good.

At first.

We rounded up all the men in the square and sent them back to their *jacales*. They took one look at our Winchesters and our determined, unshaven faces and began jabbering and smiling at us, and I guessed they knew—even though we didn't speak their lingo—that we were there to do them some good.

Once the Mexicans were all inside, including a few in the cantina, I showed them by gestures that I wanted them to close their doors and shutter their windows real good.

Now that they were all inside, I took Johnny Blue aside and said: "See, there's nothing to it. Now open each door and toss a bomb inside."

"Are you sure about this?" Johnny Blue asked, his face troubled. "That Ranger captain said we was to fumigate the *jacales*."

"Yeah he did, but he didn't mean just the *jacales*. Study on it. The *jacales* don't have smallpox, it's the Mexicans who have smallpox. Captain Jones told us to fumigate the village an' end the epidemic an' this is the only way to get it done."

"I guess you're right," said Johnny Blue doubtfully. "I suppose it's the only way."

"Trust me," I said.

Well, we got the burlap sack and one by one opened each *jacale* door wide enough to throw in a fumigation bomb, its fuse sputtering, then slammed the door shut right quick.

It was quick, it was easy, and as it turned out, me and Johnny Blue was real good at it.

But then all hell broke loose.

Them Mexicans—men, women, children, and dogs—

came pouring out of the *jacales* coughing and wheezing, tears streaming down their faces. They was screaming out stuff like "*Madre de Dios*" and "*Mercy, por favor,*" and that much else that we couldn't understand.

"No, no," I yelled, "you got to get back inside an' get fumigated. You all got the smallpox and the Americans are here to cure you."

I guess they didn't understand, because they crowded into the square, bent over and coughing, the younkers caterwauling and throwing up, while the good ol' U.S. fumigation bombs were smoking away and going to waste inside the *jacales*.

"Back inside!" Johnny Blue yelled, gesturing with his rifle. "You ain't even near fumigated yet." But them Mexicans ignored him.

"Right," I yelled, "that's it!"

I cut loose with my rifle, dusting the ground around the villagers' feet pretty good, and you should have seen them scatter as they all ran back into their homes, wailing and moaning and screaming that "*Madre de Dios*" stuff and causing all kinds of fuss and bother.

Pretty soon the square was quiet again, but it didn't last for long.

No sooner were they in, than they were back out, hollering and staggering and carrying on even worse than before. This time about a dozen of those people collapsed onto the street, hacked their guts out, and then they didn't seem to care to move much after that.

"Well," I said to Johnny Blue, "judging by what I can see, I reckon these folks is fumigated real good, else they wouldn't be chokin' an' gaspin' so much."

That dusky rider nodded. "I guess we done the job we was sent to do right enough."

"Captain Jones is sure to make us Texas Rangers now," I said. "Hell, Blue Boy, he might even give us a gold medal."

"Sure enough," agreed my *compadre*, nodding as he rolled a cigarette. "I reckon we're gettin' mighty good at this fumigatin' business."

But then something happened that spoiled everything.

How it come up, me and Johnny Blue climbed up on our horses and I rode into the middle of the square and I made a patriotic little speech to them puking and wailing Mexicans. I told them how I didn't expect any thanks— since fumigating was all in the line of duty for a Texas Ranger—and was only too happy to have helped. And then I said God bless America and that I had to leave them now but to remember me and Johnny Blue always with gratitude—"And *adios muchachos!*"

I'd just finished speechifying when a party of about two dozen horsemen splashed across the river from the Mexican side.

"Hell, those are *vaqueros*," Johnny Blue said. "I guess they heard your shooting and have come to thank us for ending the smallpox plague an' all."

"That's a true thing you just said, Blue Boy," I allowed. "Them boys is here to give thanks where thanks is due."

The *vaqueros* rode into the square and some of them dismounted and went to the people lying on the ground and I heard a lot of excited jabbering back and forth in Mexican.

"Listen," I said, "the villagers are telling them boys how much we've helped them."

The man who seemed to be the leader of the *vaqueros*—a huge *hombre* with thick black eyebrows, a knife scar on his cheek, and crossed ammunition belts over his chest—rode up to me and Johnny Blue on a buckskin pony and I greeted him most civilly.

"I no speakee Mexican," I said. "But anyhow, I'm right glad to make your acquaintance."

A split second later I'm looking down the muzzle of Eyebrows' Colt and he's got the hammer eared back, ready to cut loose. A dozen of his *vaqueros* rode up and rifles began to get shucked and levers cranked.

"What the hell did you do here?" the bearded man asked angrily.

Boys, right about then I began to feel a mite uneasy, but I said steadily enough: "We fumigated this village for smallpox. We are here on official Texas Ranger business and must not be interfered with."

The big man's eyes hardened and his knuckles whitened on the handle of his gun. "There is no smallpox here," he said.

"Excuse me," said Johnny Blue mildly. "But is this the village of Santa Alana?"

"No, this is Santa Domingo," the *vaquero* said. "Santa Alana is six miles to the south. Everyone there is already dead. I think."

"Then we threw our saddle on the wrong hoss," I said, smiling. "But it was an honest mistake, so I'll bid you a very good day an' we'll be on our way."

"No, so fast, you," the man said, real thin and mean. Then he did a strange thing. He didn't even move his head—keeping his hard black eyes on me the whole time, he said to the *vaquero* beside him: "Manuel, get a rope."

Now, you boys will recollect that me and Johnny Blue had already been hung twice and although we was getting real good at it, I didn't fancy being strung up a third time.

There's a time for talking and a time for doing, and I realized the time for talking was past.

I let rip with a Rebel yell, gave my horse the spur, and charged into the bearded man. My big American stud, a Montana-bred horse all of sixteen hands high, hit his mustang hard. The little buckskin—he couldn't have weighed more than eight hundred pounds—screamed and went down, but as he fell the man dropped the hammer on his Colt and it went off next to my ear and I smelled my hair burn. Another *vaquero* cursed and swung at me with his rifle barrel but missed.

Then I was through them, riding fast across the square. Somehow or other, maybe because I'd surprised them, Johnny Blue got through the *vaqueros* and was riding hell-for-leather beside me.

Rifle and revolver shots split the air above our heads, so I unlimbered my Colt, turned in the saddle, and cut loose. A revolver isn't much on accuracy at the best of times and even worse when you're shooting off a horse's back, so I couldn't determine if I'd done any execution among the oncoming horsemen.

But what was mighty plain was that those Mexican riders had recovered from their shock and were coming after us in a most determined manner, yelling and cursing in American that they was going to cut off our *cojones* then hang us.

At a spanking gallop I swung between two *jacales* and into the flat country beyond. We were headed due north, back into the scrub desert, and I let my stud stretch out his neck and run.

Beside me Johnny Blue was cussing a blue streak. "You're a lunatic!" he yelled. "I swear you should be locked up."

"How was I to know it was the wrong village?" I asked. "All them places look alike."

Johnny Blue opened his mouth to yell at me again, but he closed it right quick when a dry creek bed suddenly yawned wide in front of us. My horse hesitated just a split second, then plunged down the cutbank, kicking up a thick cloud of dust, sand, and shale as he hit the flat, then climbed the other bank.

Johnny Blue wasn't so lucky. His horse stumbled as he went down into the creek bottom, throwing that reckless rider over his neck and into the side of the cutbank, where he hit with a sickening thud, kicking up a thick cloud of dust.

I swung my horse around, trotted back to the creek, and shucked my Winchester. The *vaqueros* were about a hundred yards away but they were coming fast. I cranked a round into the chamber, fired, then fired again. The horsemen split into two parties, one heading to the north of us, the other to the south. They meant to flank us and come at us from two directions, but this was the shallowest part of the dry creek, the banks rising rapidly higher on either side. The *vaqueros* would be slowed up by the steepness of the cutbanks or else they'd have to ride back to this point and face our rifle fire.

Johnny Blue rose unsteadily to his feet, favoring his left leg, and caught up his mount. He climbed up slowly with a horrible groan, but this time his big stud took the bank with ease and he rode up to where I sat my horse.

"They'll be slowed by the cutbanks," I said. "Let's light a shuck."

We swung our horses to the northwest and set the spurs to them. The ground was flat and level, hard and dry after the long heat of the summer, and we made good time.

After about fifteen minutes I turned in my saddle and checked our back trail. There was a faint cloud of dust a long ways behind and I reckoned those *vaqueros* had no hope of catching up to us on their short-legged mustangs.

I reined my lathered horse into a walk and Johnny Blue did the same.

"How's your leg?" I asked.

"Broke," Johnny Blue replied sulkily.

"Take your foot out of the stirrup an' see if you can bend it," I said.

That peeved puncher did as he was told, and although he winced in pain, he managed to bend his leg at the knee.

"If you can bend it, it ain't broke," I said. "An' that's a natural fact."

Johnny Blue merely grunted in reply, obviously still blaming me for fumigating the wrong Mexicans, so I said: "Know something, Blue Boy, there's just no accounting for folks. You try to help them and this is all the thanks you get for it. Study some on what I just said an' let me know your feelings on the subject."

"I don't have to study on it, I can tell you what my feelings is," replied Johnny Blue, eager to get something out that was sticking in his craw. "My feelings is that you're an idiot an' a dangerous lunatic an' I don't want to talk about it anymore."

"Well, suit yourself," I said. "But name-calling won't get us anywhere."

We rode in silence for a few moments, then I shook my head and said: "Them was the most ungrateful Mexicans I ever met in all my born days."

* * *

Two days later, missing our last six meals, I shot an antelope and we holed up a day eating steaks while we smoked the rest of the meat over a mesquite fire.

Around noontime a cavalry regiment rode past at a fast gallop headed for the river, a cannon bouncing behind them. A few minutes later another party of horsemen appeared in the distance, headed in the same direction.

Johnny Blue rose to his feet and shaded his eyes with his hand. "Hey," he said, "ain't that them Texas Rangers?"

I looked, but the riders were too far away and riding too fast in a cloud of dust for me to make them out.

"Nah," I said, "them aren't Rangers. The Rangers is still in San Antone."

"I wonder what's going on down there on the Rio Grande?" Johnny Blue said. "Hell, the way them so'diers was ridin', it looked like they was goin' to a war."

I had a piece of broiled antelope on a stick and I took a bite, then shrugged. "I dunno, but it's got nothing to do with us."

Eight

Three days later, we rode into San Antonio and went directly to the Ranger camp. It was deserted.

"I tol' you it was them Rangers I saw," Johnny Blue said, kicking at the cold gray ashes of their campfire.

"Well, this isn't good," I said. "How can Captain Jones make us Rangers if'n he ain't here?"

Johnny Blue shook his head at me. "Beats me. Maybe he won't make us Rangers anyway, on account of how we fumigated the wrong village."

"Nah, that was just a little misunderstanding. Water under the bridge. He won't let something like that stand in the way of swearing in a couple of famous lawmen like us."

We mounted up and rode to where Doc had been camped, and to my relief he was still there. As we were greeted like long-lost kinfolk, I noticed that Cottontail and Georgia were wearing new dresses and both Doc and the Mauler looked sleek and well fed—and that's something I couldn't say about me and Johnny Blue.

"Between poker and goldbricking the rubes, we've been making out all right," Doc said, and I noticed that he wore a fancy silver watch across his flowered vest and an emerald ring on his left pinkie finger.

"Glad to see that you're standing pat, Doc," I said. "Me and him"—I nodded to Johnny Blue—"is back to ridin' the grub line until we can catch up to Captain Jones an' become Rangers an' all."

Doc frowned like something mighty unpleasant had just come into his mind and he motioned toward the fire. "You boys set and drink some coffee, because I'm afraid I have dire news to impart."

We sat and Georgia poured us coffee. She put her hand on my arm—her round, motherly face concerned. "You poor thing," she whispered. "You poor thing."

Well, boys, about then I started to feel more than a mite uneasy, so I said: "What's this all about, Doc?"

Doc sat next to me, his face grave.

"My boy," he said, "the telegraph lines have been burning up for days between here and Laredo and all the way up to the Big Bend country. It seems you and your companion have been branded with the mark of murderous Cain and are doomed to wander as despised outcasts in this harsh and unforgiving Texas land. In short: You're both wanted dead or alive."

Johnny Blue was rolling a smoke, but his hands stopped in mid-motion and he asked nervously: "On what charges, Doc?"

"Well, my boy, where to begin?" Doc scratched his bald head. "Ah yes, now I recollect. The army wants you for fomenting rebellion against the United States, high treason, and attempted murder. The penalty: Death by firing squad. The Texas Rangers want you for impersonating officers, attempted murder, high treason, and the robbery of the Katy Flyer—they just threw that one in on account of how they have to blame somebody. The penalty: Death by hanging. The Mexican government wants you for the attempted murder of its citizens by poison gas and for firing on *rurales* who were investigating said offense. The penalty: Death by hanging or life imprisonment at the judge's discretion."

"So that's where those so'diers were going," Johnny Blue said. "They were after us."

"Not quite," corrected Doc. "Indeed, they would have gladly shot you, had they found you, but their main purpose was to quell major riots along the Rio Grande that began in the village you . . . er . . . accidentally fumigated. Boys, you set the whole border aflame. One of the more dramatic incidents was an artillery duel between Mexican and U.S. troops near Carrizo Springs in which a gallant American general was wounded and three Mexicans killed." Doc shook his head sadly. "Dire tidings, boys, dire tidings indeed."

"Doc," said Johnny Blue, motioning toward me with his still unrolled cigarette, "is there any chance they'll go light on us if'n they know he's a lunatic?"

Doc shrugged. "Lunatics have been hung afore. I am told, on inquiry, that even as we speak upwards of three thousand men—soldiers, Rangers, Mexican troops, and bounty hunters—are actively seeking to apprehend or shoot you."

After that gloomy observation we sat in silence for a while, then I said: "Doc, you won't turn us in, will you?"

"Me play the Judas role for thirty pieces of silver?" demanded Doc. "Never, I say."

"That's not Doc's way," said Georgia. "He is a man of honor."

"Although I must admit, the sum of five thousand dollars is being bandied about as reward money," mused

Doc. "Any way you add it up, that is considerably more than thirty pieces of silver."

I didn't want Doc nibbling any longer at that particular worm, so I said quickly: "Doc, we'll go with you into the Sierra Madres after the hidden gold. That way we can steer clear of posses an' sich."

"That is a possibility," said Doc. "But I fear your value as drummers for the Fortune Flyer has been badly compromised. The army will shoot you on sight, as will the Rangers, and those two are both potential customers."

Again the camp was plunged into gloom and even Johnny Blue was silent for once, smoking his cigarette with an expression of the deepest misery and apprehension on his face.

"On the other hand," Doc said cheerfully at last, "a couple of extry guns on this dangerous quest might not go amiss. My rival for the gold, the bandit Clemente Perez, is not to be taken lightly."

"We're your huckleberries, Doc," I said quickly, choosing that ruthless rogue as very much the lesser of two evils.

"Well," said Doc, stretching out his hand, "let's shake on it."

This we did, though I made sure I counted my fingers afterward.

After a few moments' thought, Doc said: "Now, since you boys is wanted men and can no longer help me market the Flyer I will pay each of you fifty dollars when we get the gold out of the Sierras and back into Texas. After that, we part ways—possibly forever."

Well, boys, it wasn't much of a deal, but right then it was all we had or could expect.

"Sounds good, Doc," I said. "We'll stand with you, never fear about that. An' if things go downhill fast an' become as difficult as shovelin' sunshine an' this feller Perez ever looks like gettin' the upper hand, I'll shoot you through the lungs my ownself and put you out of your misery."

Doc was so moved by this token of my loyalty and friendship that he insisted we all link hands around the campfire and sing "Auld Lang Syne," or as much of it as we could remember:

Should old acquaintance be forgot and never brought to mind?
Should old acquaintance be forgot and the days of old lang syne?
For old lang syne my dear, for old lang syne,
We'll take a cup of kindness yet for the days of old lang syne.

After the song staggered fitfully to an end, there wasn't a single dry eye around the fire and the Mauler, overcome with emotion, embraced first me, then Johnny Blue and vowed never to forget us.

"Not once," he declared with much feeling, "was I tempted by the five thousand dollars' reward money—no matter what you might otherwise hear from sneaks, cheats, and all manner of low persons, including dance-hall loungers and razor grinders."

For his part, Johnny Blue told us that he'd often thought about shooting the Mauler through the lungs just on general principles, but that those days were over—especially since the Mauler was now a family man with a lovely wife and a wee baby.

This tender declaration, so sincerely meant, sent us all to crying again, and Cottontail allowed that this was the happiest day of her life since she'd quit whoring—and maybe even for a time or two before that.

Georgia, her round, brown face shining in the firelight, dabbed at her eyes with her handkerchief and made little sobbing noises. Doc was so touched by this tender display, he ordered another verse of "Auld Lang Syne," though he admitted that he had no clear idea of what "old lang syne" meant. But he declared he was content, in his own mind at least, that whatever it was, it had been shared and enjoyed in the past by one and all here present.

As we sang, the long day shaded into night and the first sentinel stars appeared—but so enraptured were we that we never even noticed.

Later, the womenfolk cooked supper, being in so mellow a mood they made flapjacks to go with our salt pork, something they weren't often inclined to do. After we ate, Doc produced a bottle of good Kentucky whiskey and we each poured a liberal dash into our coffee.

Doc lit a cigar, settled back comfortably against Georgia's great bosom, and said: "I have yet another surprise to impart to you boys and—hark!—just in time, I believe I hear it approach."

A few moments later a magnificent white stallion galloped into the circle of the firelight and for the first time in my life my wondering eyes beheld: the Gunfighter.

"I got him cheap," said Doc by way of explanation, "on account of how there ain't too much call for his kind anymore. His is another profession that's going all to hell."

The Gunfighter walked up to the fire and just stood there, the better to let us view his splendor. He wore a short jacket of buckskin, almost white in color, and under this a silk shirt of vivid scarlet, a black bandanna knotted loosely around his neck. He wore skintight riding breeches tucked into English riding boots, and around his slim hips were crossed gun belts, each carrying an ivory-handled Colt. His blond hair was perfumed and hung in gentle waves over his shoulders, and his mustache was trimmed and well cared for. His hands were long and slender and very white—the hands of a man who'd never done a day's hard work in his life. A jet-black mole—the kind women call a "beauty spot"—adorned his right cheekbone, and his eyelashes were very long and dark.

He was the prettiest man I'd ever seen in my life. In fact, he was the prettiest man or *woman* I'd ever seen in my life, and even Cottontail's vivid beauty paled beside that of the Gunfighter.

"The Gunfighter will add his Colts to our own when we enter the Sierras," Doc said proudly. "He's a known and named man and not one to be trifled with."

Johnny Blue looked the Gunfighter up and down and slowly raised his coffee cup to his mouth. "If'n you ask me," he said quietly, "this ranny is a mite too dainty to be shootin' at anybody."

It happened in an instant—so fast I almost didn't see it.

The Gunfighter went for his guns in a single blurred motion. The Colts came up blazing and knocked Johnny Blue's cup out of his hand. The Gunfighter then set the cup bouncing into the darkness, hitting it with every shot. until his guns were empty.

The whole thing took only about a second, and when it was over the Gunfighter spun his Colts—their ivory handles and silver barrels flashing in the firelight—then each landed with a thud back in its holster.

As our ears became accustomed to silence after the racketing roar of the guns, Johnny Blue contemplated all that remained of his cup—the bent handle that he still held in his hand.

"I stand corrected," he said.

The Gunfighter seemed to harbor no ill will toward Johnny Blue and he acknowledged that rueful rider's apology with a slight incline of his glossy head. He stretched his right hand out, palm down, and studied it for a few moments, then swore. "Damn it," he said, "I've broken a fingernail."

Unfortunately, the roar of the guns had wakened the babies and their screeching cries rang through the timber. As Cottontail and Georgia ran to the wagon to succor the little ones, Doc sprang to his feet in a state of great alarm.

"Between the shootin' and the babies, we could have alerted every posse, army patrol, and Ranger in Texas," he said. "I suggest, gentlemen, we pull out right now and travel through the night. The darkness will be our cloak."

Doc then told me and Johnny Blue to ride in the back of the wagon and tie our horses behind. When I protested this plan, he sadly shook his head and said: "Boys, I was tryin' to keep this from you, but now the die has been cast and we are determined to embark on this great adventure, it is better you know."

And so saying, with a dramatic flourish he produced a crumpled sheet of paper from his pants pocket and thrust it into my hands. "Behold," he said, "the wages of sin."

It was a Ranger dodger, offering a five-thousand-dollar reward for me and Johnny Blue for attempted murder and high treason. The words that caught my attention right away were big letters that said WANTED DEAD OR ALIVE.

Although there were no pictures on the dodger, it described Johnny Blue as a "tall, lanky Negro, surly and uncommunicative with a habitually scowling expression. He is much addicted to tobacco and smokes it in the Mexican fashion, rolled in paper."

About me it said: "Small and self-important. Talks a great deal. Nondescript in appearance but for a large red mustache that he fashions into points."

Then the final kicker: "Both men are unemployed drovers, carry one or more murderous pistols of the largest kind, and present a ragged, shabby, and desperate appearance. They use lavender parfume profusely and can be identified at a long distance by smell."

I studied the dodger for a few moments longer, then asked Doc what the word "nondescript" meant.

"Son, that means you ain't much to look at," said Doc. "It means you're the small end of nothin' whittled down to a point."

"Well, Doc," I said, "I got no quarrel with attempted murder an' high treason, but callin' a man nondescript is a low blow and not to be tolerated."

"Sticks in a man's craw, don't it?" said Doc. "But nevertheless you boys is now marked men and wanted by the law, an' that's why you must travel in the back of the wagon."

"With them babies?" asked Johnny Blue, horrified.

"Can't be helped," said Doc. "Parlous times make for strange bedfellows."

Johnny Blue groaned, but he didn't argue, seeing the right of Doc's argument.

And so it was that me and Johnny Blue traveled under a canopy of stars into the endless night in the back of the wagon, sharing what little space there was with them squallin' infants and the hard steel of the Fortune Flyer.

And once again we were poor, hunted creatures, fearful fugitives with every man's hand turned against us—and once again it was through no fault of our own.

Nine

Boys, I won't describe the stifling, jolting misery of that trip to the border, because even now, after the slow turning of the long years, it is still too painful to recall.

We traveled by night and holed up in hidden places by day, sleeping and eating what little food we had. We saw plenty of deer and antelope, but couldn't shoot them for fear of bringing the Rangers or the army down on us.

The women held up remarkably well, though the Gunfighter complained endlessly about not being able to keep up with his toilette—especially his hair, that he usually washed every single day. Cottontail kept his flagging spirits up by talking endlessly about women's fixin's, like how big the bustles were being worn by women of fashion in Dodge and Denver, and how small the hats. She let the Gunfighter wear one of her red dresses a time or two during the heat of the day, and this always seemed to make him feel better.

Johnny Blue watched all this with scowling disapproval, but, remembering how the Gunfighter used his Colts, he kept quiet about it. As he whispered to me: "If'n you don't stay friends with the devil, you could end up on his prong."

Meantime Doc studied his map day and night and figgered to cross the Bravo del Norte into Mexico south of
Laredo, the better to avoid attracting unwelcome attention. We'd head into the rugged peaks of the high Sierras
and strike west toward the Sabinas, crossing the river at
Juan Miguel's Ford twenty miles south of Juarez. From
there we'd head northwest into the wild Picacho de
Zozaya mountain country where the treasure was buried.

We would be leaving the rainy pine-and-oak–covered
slopes of the southern Sierras behind us to ride into wa-
terless desert country. This was a stark world that seemed
like God had stood it on end—the ancient, craggy peaks
rising to almost three thousand feet, casting their blue
shadows over wide, flat-topped buttes and mesas. It was
a land that offered nothing except unforgiving mountain
ridges cut through by narrow valleys, deep canyons, and
treacherous ravines harboring a hundred different ways to
kill a man.

This would be wild, lonely country: a sun-hammered
wilderness of buzzards, rattlesnakes, tarantulas, and scorpions, where everything that moves bites and everything
that grows has thorns. The air in that part of the Sierra
Madre Oriental lays across the hard-baked landscape like
a blanket—thick, heavy, and hard to breathe—and the
brackish lukewarm water we'd carry in our canteens
would be the difference between life and death.

But hunted men that we were, me and Johnny Blue
would be well away from the clutches of the law. The
only law in the land where we were headed was the law
a man makes for himself with his rifle and six-shooter,
and it sized up to be a good move for us until all the fuss
died down.

As it happened, things didn't quite turn out that way,

because of a violent incident that sowed the seed of future tragedy.

How it come up, we'd crossed the Rio Grande just south of Laredo as we'd planned and were heading for the village of La Lajilla. The town was described by Doc as a general store and a few adobe houses huddled among the cactus-covered foothills of the Sierras—a nothing place on the edge of nowhere.

"But I have friends there," Doc said, "who might extend us the credit needed to buy supplies." Me and Johnny Blue were now riding and we were scouting about a hundred yards ahead of the wagon in the drowsy heat of the late afternoon. Georgia rode in the wagon on the seat next to Doc and Cottontail, and the Mauler walked alongside. The Gunfighter on his white horse was talking to Cottontail. He was wearing one of her hats—probably the result of one of their endless conversations about female fashion—and for once the babies were asleep and mercifully silent.

"Quiet, ain't it?" I said to Johnny Blue.

That reckless rider didn't get a chance to reply, because right then a bullet split the air above my head, followed by half a dozen more. I swung my horse to get back to the wagon and saw Cottontail go down, a bright scarlet flower suddenly blossoming on her dress.

Then things happened very quickly.

The Mauler roared in anguish—a terrible thing to hear—and ran to his fallen wife. Bullets thudded into the wagon and Georgia, fat as she was, threw herself backward off the seat, trying to reach the now screaming babies.

Johnny Blue shucked his rifle and slammed some shots into a jumble of volcanic rock and stunted cactus to the right of the trail. I couldn't see anything, but drew my Colt and thumbed off a couple of shots in that direction.

Doc had jumped from the wagon and was yelling, "Murder! Help! Murder!" as he ran around in frantic circles like a man demented.

They came at us then.

There were four of them—big, bearded men on good horses, each firing at us with their murderous revolvers.

I fired, missed, fired again, missed.

Beside me Johnny Blue's rifle barked, but his ball did no execution as the riders thundered closer.

A bullet tugged at my sleeve and I felt the hot splash of blood on my arm, then Johnny Blue clutched the side of his head, his rifle spinning away from him, and fell to the ground with a horrible cry.

Then the Gunfighter showed us all what being a trained, professional *pistolero* was all about. He stepped out from behind the wagon—still wearing one of Cottontail's little flower-trimmed straw bonnets on his head, tied under his chin with a big pink ribbon—and cut loose with both Colts.

One of the bushwhackers went down, falling back over his horse's rump—then another and another. The fourth man reined up and shoved out his Colt at arm's length, steadying himself for a shot. He never pulled the trigger. One of the Gunfighter's balls took him right between the eyes and his whole head seemed to burst asunder, the back of his skull shattering into a fan-shaped mess of blood, bone, and brain.

As the racketing of the guns died away I beheld a scene of the utmost horror.

All four bushwhackers were down and two horses lay wild-eyed and screaming, kicking in their death agony.

The Gunfighter walked to the wounded horses and triggered them out of their misery.

"Are they Rangers?" asked Doc in a terrible state of anxiety. "Oh my God, are they Texas Rangers?"

The Gunfighter untied his bonnet and let it dangle by its ribbons from his steady fingers. "Nah," he said, the glittering toe of his riding boot turning over the last man he'd shot. "I know this ranny. This here is Jeb Bodine an' he rode with Frank an' Jesse an' them back in the old days. Last I heard he was marshalin' a cow town up Oklahoma way."

The Gunfighter nodded his head and smiled, a gesture of admiration from one professional to another. "Ol' Jeb, he killed his share an' he had sand, I got to give him that. I guess marshalin' got too tame for him so he just naturally turned to the bounty-hunting profession."

Johnny Blue was sitting up clutching his head and seemed dazed, but mercifully the bullet had just grazed him, leaving a burn across his scalp but little blood.

I did what I could for him—no more than a few words of encouragement and a pat on the shoulder—then walked over to where Cottontail lay, surrounded by the sobbing Mauler, Doc, and Georgia, who was holding a hollering baby in each arm.

"How is she?" I asked above the noise of the younkers.

Doc looked up at me with bleak eyes. "It's bad. She took a ball in her thigh an' it's still in there. She's losing blood fast."

"Doc," I said anxiously, "you got to get that ball out of there. You know how. You took one out of me one time."

Cottontail was unconscious and very pale. Even her lips, normally so red, were almost white—and to me, she suddenly looked very small and at least twenty years older.

"We'll put in her in the wagon and take her to La Lajilla," Doc said. "Maybe they got somebody there who knows something about doctoring."

"You know about doctoring," I said. "You cut more bullets out of more rannies than I can count on my fingers."

"Not this time," Doc said, his face lined with misery. "The bullet's too deep. There are major arteries down there. If I even nick an artery, she'll die."

"Doc," the Mauler said, his battered prizefighter's face stricken, "if'n you don't get it out she'll never make it to La Lajilla an' she'll die just the same." He put a huge hand on Doc's narrow shoulder. "We been through a lot, me an' you, an' I never asked you for much afore, but I'm askin' you now. No, I'm begging you—save my wife. Doc, I ain't what you'd call a feelin' man most of the time, but I never loved anything in my whole life like I love this woman. She brought light into my darkness. You got to bring her back to me."

"Mauler," Doc said, and I could hear how he was struggling to make his voice as steady as he could, "an operation like this . . . there just ain't no guarantees."

The Mauler shook his head. "You do it. I trust you, Doc."

"Then God help me," Doc said.

We carried Cottontail to the wagon, and by the time Doc began his operation twilight was already painting the slopes of the surrounding hills pale blue, filling in the gullies and ravines with a deeper purple shade. The persistent sun still hung like a gold coin low in the sky to the west, though it would soon drop behind the towering peaks of the Sierras.

Cottontail was still unconscious from loss of blood, and this was a mercy.

Since I was small and skinny, Doc ordered me into the wagon and everyone else out. I held the lantern, splashing orange light onto Cottontail's white thigh and the open, scarlet lips of her terrible wound. Despite the growing cool of the desert night, beads of sweat hung on Doc's forehead and he stopped every now and then to dash them away with his forearm.

"Goddammit, boy, hold that light closer," he whispered.

I noticed that his hands were unsteady but his chin was hard and set, jutting out from his face in deep concentration.

A bowie knife, even one as sharp as Doc's, is not a precise instrument for surgery, and Doc mangled Cottontail's leg pretty bad as he dug deep for the ball.

It took maybe ten minutes of digging to find the bullet, and by that time the interior of the wagon was full of black, greasy smoke from the coal oil of the lantern, so that I could hardly see what was happening.

Doc's hands were red to the elbows with blood by the time he held up the .45 ball, studied it closely, and then tossed it out the open flap of the wagon cover.

"It didn't hit bone," he said. "That will make a difference."

Georgia, her round face drawn and strained, thrust her head into the wagon: "How is she, Doc?" she asked.

"She'll live," replied Doc. "I didn't touch the artery." He laid a hand on Georgia's arm. "Bind up the wound, my dear," he said. "I'm going to get drunk."

The Mauler, a baby in each arm, sat with Johnny Blue and the Gunfighter and when I climbed out of the wagon and walked to the fire, he looked up at me. "How is she?"

"She's fine," I said. "She'll be just fine."

But I stood there, a forced smile on my face, recalling how badly mangled was Cottontail's leg, and I was filled with a nameless dread—not about the present, but about what the future might bring.

I'd seen wounds less severe than hers get poisoned before.

Ten

Come morning we had neither the time nor the inclination to bury the dead. The Gunfighter took this hard, saying as how he always buried his dead decent, with a headstone and the prayers said over them and all.

"We ain't got time," Doc said. "I want to get Cottontail to La Lajilla real quick."

The Gunfighter let his displeasure be known in no uncertain terms, but in the end he compromised by placing a silver dollar in the mouth of each of the four dead men, saying it would pay for their burying should someone chance by that way on the trail.

"And even if someone don't, when them rannies reach the Pearly Gates the good Lord will see their dollar and reckon they was standing pat," observed Doc. Then we rode out of that terrible place and didn't look back.

By the time we reached La Lajilla Cottontail had regained consciousness, though she was very weak and the Mauler was beside himself with worry. He never left her side in the wagon and over and over again told her she had to get well, both for him and their baby son.

Doc hadn't exaggerated the godforsaken nature of the town of La Lajilla.

It consisted of a row of a dozen or so adobe *jacales*

fronting a single dusty street. There was a small white-washed church at one end of the street, a cantina at the other. Set apart from the rest, a corral and barn behind it, there was what looked like a trading post and the name MICHAEL O'SHAUGNESSY, PROP. painted on a warped pine board above the door.

About the only interesting feature in the town was a gallows that Doc said had been erected twenty years before to hang some bandit or other and for sentimental reasons had never been taken down. The villagers had painted the beams in various hues and draped them with garlands and potted plants, and a life-sized statue of the Madonna dangled from a rope where the bandit had once hung.

"The outlaw allowed that he saw a shining vision of the Virgin while he was standing on the trapdoor," Doc explained. "He said the Holy Mother had forgiven his sins and absolved him of all guilt for a lifetime of murder an' rape an' robbery. Maybe he was hopin' to be freed, but if'n he was, it didn't work. They strung him up anyhow."

Doc nodded toward the hanging Madonna. "Ever since, the people here have venerated Our Lady of the Gallows, an' they say she's a very powerful Madonna—a lot more influential up there in heaven than even the golden Madonna in the Mexico City Cathedral."

"Well, what do you know," said Johnny Blue. "I been hung my ownself so often, maybe I can ask her for some help, because we surely need it."

In fact, Doc was torn between taking Cottontail back to Texas for proper medical treatment and going on into the mountains after the gold. Although he dickered for credit with O'Shaugnessy—a big, profane Irishman with a brick-red face and beard—I could see his heart wasn't in it.

Doc told me that he feared Cottontail wasn't up for the Sierras in her present weakened condition.

But Cottontail insisted she was feeling better and that her leg no longer pained her so much. "Besides, Doc," she said, "all our futures are tied up in them gold sacks. If we go back now, we'll lose our chance of a better life forever."

It seemed to me that Doc was much heartened by this, and renewed his dickering with the Irishman with fervor.

The result was that we left La Lajilla with enough bacon, beans, coffee, and flour to last several weeks if need be. And me and Johnny Blue was wearing new shirts and pants and I even managed to talk O'Shaugnessy into letting me have a jar of Dr. Benbow's Hair and Mustache Pomade for Gentlemen—the very best there is, since it says right on the label that it's made from bear fat.

We headed west toward the Sabinas, but this time the Gunfighter insisted on taking the point, relegating me and Johnny Blue to the swing on either side of the wagon.

"I seen you boys in action," he said, "an' so far you haven't shown me much."

As Doc had planned, we crossed the Sabinas at Juan Miguel's Ford, then headed northeast into the fastness of the Sierras. Cottontail was much improved, though Doc said her wound was still inflamed and showed little sign of healing.

Our progress into the mountains was slowed by the wagon, especially when the Mauler insisted we stay away from bad going so that Cottontail didn't get jolted too much.

We were now well among the mountains. The bald,

rocky peaks surrounded us on every side, their monotony broken up by towering flat mesas and slender spires of standing rock carved into all kinds of fantastic shapes, the result of millions of years of erosion. Unlike the greener southern Sierras, watered by rains from the Gulf of Mexico, this was a barren, inhospitable land, harsh and unforgiving.

Because of the wagon, we kept to the boulder-strewn valleys between the mountains, more often than not taking dried-up streambeds that promised smoother going but seldom delivered on that promise, being rocky and treacherous underfoot. Down here in the valleys and canyons there was no breeze and the air lay hot and still, and the big American studs me and Johnny Blue rode, not being bred for mountains, began to suffer.

When I asked Doc if he reckoned we were getting close to where the gold was hidden, he just smiled and shook his head. "Closer, my boy, but not close."

We rode on the alert, knowing that Clemente Perez might also be in the mountains following his own map, but of more immediate concern was Cottontail.

She was much weaker and was running a fever, and her leg—when I rode close enough to the wagon to notice—was beginning to smell.

Doc used our precious water to bathe the wound. It looked angry and inflamed and her whole leg was taking on a blue color.

But every time Doc mentioned the possibility of turning back, Cottontail told him she was doing just fine and that we must press on to the gold.

She had plenty of sand, that young lady, but I reckoned if she didn't get proper medical care soon, her time was fast running out. I'd seen a leg like hers once before on a poor cowboy up in Montana's Milk River country. A steer drug him along a barbed wire fence and it opened up his right leg from ankle to hip. The leg turned black and began to smell and a doctor cut that rotten leg off of him but it didn't do no good. The poison from the leg had spread all over his body, and that was another poor cowboy we buried, though he was scarce eighteen years old.

I didn't want the same thing to happen to Cottontail, and it worried me so much I felt like the frog who found himself in the frying pan.

Come noontime on our third day in the mountains, Doc camped under a jutting shelf of rock that gave the wagon some shelter from the sun. There was a small water tank there, a natural hollow worn in the rock that allowed seepage to collect from the rain that occasionally fell on these mountains. The water was green and brackish, but the tank was about half full, enough for the horses and our canteens.

Doc called me and Johnny Blue over to him. "I want you boys to see something," he said. He beckoned us to follow, then scrambled up the side of the rock shelf and onto the flat top. For a man of his age, Doc was right sprightly when he had to be.

Me and Johnny Blue dismounted and scrambled up the slope beside him.

"You boys see those peaks over there?" Doc asked, pointing to a couple of mountaintops that were almost lost against the hot blue haze of the sky.

I took off my hat and wiped my sweating brow with my forearm. "I see them, Doc," I said. "That's quite a ways."

Doc nodded. "You're right, it is quite a ways. But

that's where the gold is hid an' that's where we're headed."

"We'll never make it hauling a wagon and a sick woman," Johnny Blue said, building a smoke.

"We won't be hauling a wagon," replied Doc. "I'm sending the Mauler back to La Lajilla with Cottontail and my own dear wife. That big mick O'Shaugnessy traded with the Apaches in the old days an' I'm told he knows something of doctoring. If he doesn't, he'll be able to find them as does."

"Doc," I said, "you ain't goin' nowhere without a hoss."

"I've got the Fortune Flyer," Doc returned proudly. "It will take me anywhere in these mountains I wish to go and it will still be going strong when them big studs of yours is dead from thirst."

Doc said he'd let Cottontail rest up in the shade for a couple of hours, then send the Mauler back. In the meantime, he told me and Johnny Blue to check the trail ahead of us and search for any sign of water, but above all to keep our eyes peeled for Clemente Perez and his *desperadoes*.

"He's here," Doc said. "I can feel his presence. And boys, that vile killer is very close."

With those reassuring words, Doc dismissed us and me and Johnny Blue mounted up and headed into a narrow canyon that split a flattop mesa about a quarter mile beyond the rock shelf. It was incredibly hot and stifling in the canyon and our stirrups occasionally scraped along its sides, so narrow was it in places. Here and there cactus and stunted, dwarf juniper grew from ledges higher up the canyon walls, and above us the cloudless sky looked like a streak of pale blue paint.

After an hour's riding, the canyon gradually opened into a shallow bowl of bluish-gray volcanic rock about one hundred yards wide, the floor littered with broken rock amid stands of saguaro cactus growing as high as a man on a horse. The sides of the bowl were about twenty feet high and we couldn't see its end from where we stood our horses.

"Lookee," Johnny Blue said. "Up there."

I followed his pointing finger to the sky where a passel of vultures glided in lazy, effortless circles.

"Dead animal, most likely," I said. "There ain't nothin' human in these mountains 'cept for us an' maybe Clemente Perez."

"Let's go look anyhow," Johnny Blue said.

I shucked my Winchester then kneed my horse next to his. We started across the bowl, which narrowed noticeably the farther into it we rode, and I figured it would end in yet another canyon.

The vultures seemed to be congregated over the wall of the bowl to our right, so we headed over that way, riding close to the rock-strewn base of the wall itself. It was very hot and hemmed in, as there was no breeze.

My stud picked his way along the base of the wall for maybe a dozen yards, then I happened to glance up at the wheeling vultures—and that's when I saw him.

He was a white man with gray hair and he was hanging head down from the rim of the wall, a rope tied around one ankle. His face was red from the blistering heat of the sun and his lips were swollen and cracked. The height of the wall at this point was about twenty feet, and no question that ranny had got himself in a mighty precarious position.

I reined in my horse and looked up at him. "Howdy," I said.

"Likewise, I'm sure," the man croaked. "Hot today."

I removed my hat and wiped the sweatband with my fingers. "Yeah, it gets mighty hot in these canyons—hot enough to melt leather and it still being on the cow, as my ma used to say."

"Very true," the man said. "Oh my yes, no doubt about that at all."

There was a few minutes' pause when nobody could think of anything neighborly to say, then the man said: "My name is Gray, Sir John Gray, late a surgeon lieutenant colonel of Her Britannic Majesty's Fifty-third of Foot." The hanging man waved a sunburned hand. "I think things go so much better when one is properly introduced, don't you?"

Johnny Blue, who was rolling a cigarette and up until now hadn't shown much interest in the proceedings, suddenly perked up. "Her Britannic Majesty. Do you mean old Queen Vic?"

"Victoria, yes," Sir John said.

"You ever have tea with her?" Johnny Blue asked. "And them little fairy cakes?"

"Yes, I had that honor, but only once. It was at Buckingham Palace in the spring of seventy-nine."

"Well, I'll be," Johnny Blue said. "See, I've never had tea in all my born days. Well, I had it once from a Chinaman but I was shot through an' through at the time an' don't recollect it too good. Didn't have no fairy cakes though."

"Tea is nice," said Sir John. He flicked his tongue over his dry lips. "Thirst quenching, you know. Very." The Englishmen looked around, which isn't easy when you're hanging head down. "I half expected to have seen a native or two by this time, but there seems to be none around."

"You mean the Apaches?" I asked. "They're long gone. None of them in the Sierras anymore."

"I'm afraid I don't know anything about Apaches," Sir John said. "But I was with the Fifty-third when we fought the Zulus in Africa. Brave warrior, the Zulu—very—and quite a personable chap when you get to know him and meet the wife and kids."

Once again there was a few moments' awkward silence, so I said finally: "Well, been right nice talking with you, Sir John. But me and Johnny Blue here, we got to be ridin' on, so we'll say so long."

"Oh yes, well, cheerio," said that unfortunate Englishman.

I kneed my horse forward, but Sir John's voice stopped me. "I say," he said, "I hate to be such an infernal nuisance, but I've been trying for the last three hours to free myself from this rope—without much success, I'm afraid. Before you go, would you chaps mind awfully helping me down from here?"

"Oh sure,"-I said. I raised my Winchester and drew a bead on the rope just above Sir John's ankle and I cut 'er loose. It wasn't too difficult a shot to make and the bullet severed the rope clean as a whistle. The Englishman wailed and seemed to fall for a long time before he crashed to the rocks at the bottom of the cliff.

"Hell," Johnny Blue said, "why didn't you just shoot him? You've done broke his neck for sure."

But that Sir John feller was one tough old bird.

He rose shakily to his feet and began to dust himself off. He was wearing a tan shirt tucked into corduroy pants of the same color and he had what looked to me like army boots on his feet and laced-up leather gaiters.

Now I saw him the right way up for the first time, I took him to be about sixty years of age. His hair was gray, like his name, and he had brown eyes, bright as a bird's. He seemed to be in good shape for an oldster and he had the erect bearing and square shoulders of the professional soldier.

"I hope I wasn't too much of a bother to you chaps," he said. "It's deuced difficult to ask total strangers for help. Not quite the British thing to do, if you know what I mean."

"Hell, you was no trouble," Johnny Blue said. He swung off his horse and handed Sir John his canteen. "Here," he said, "you look like you kin use this."

The Englishman drank deeply, wiped his mouth with the back of his hand, and returned the canteen to Johnny Blue. "Thankee," he said. "I was just about dying of thirst. If you lads hadn't happened along when you did, I'm sure I'd have been a goner very soon."

"What you doin' in this neck of the woods anyhow?" asked Johnny Blue.

Suddenly Sir John's face looked stricken. "They took her, you know. I mean my beloved Agatha."

"Who took her?" I asked.

Sir John said that he and his bride of just six weeks— "Agatha is thirty years younger than me," he said, almost apologetically—had ventured into the Sierra Madres to study the Monarch butterfly.

"That's how Agatha and I met, actually," he continued, "at the annual meeting of the Royal Moth and Butterfly Society in London. She'd just become an honorary member of the RMBS in deference to her father, the late—and let me add, great—English moth expert Lord John Montescue."

"All them butterflies an' sich are in the Sierras way east of here in the oak forests," I said. "Ain't nothin' up this way but vultures, scorpions, and buzzards."

"I know that now, but since this was my first visit to the colonies, I didn't know it when we arrived in Laredo a week ago. I put it out that I needed a guide to take me into the Sierra butterfly country and this Mexican chap stepped forward. Agatha told me she didn't like the look of the man, that he kept undressing her with his eyes, but I put her fears down to that natural hysteria found in the fairer sex and hired this man as our guide."

"Seems to me he should have knowed there was no butterflies here in the Sierras up near the Big Bend country," Johnny Blue said.

"Oh, he knew all right—to my terrible cost," said Sir John, his face bleak. "This morning, at dawn, our guide and his men made off with our mules and supplies. And he took my poor Agatha with him. Before he left, he tied a rope around my ankle, made fast the other side to a rock, then tossed me over the cliff, where you found me. I begged him not to hurt my wife, but he just laughed and made a profane gesture with his fingers."

"This guide," I said, "what was his name?"

"He called himself Perez," Sir John said. "Clemente Perez."

Eleven

Sir John begged me and Johnny Blue to loan him a canteen and a rifle to go after Perez and free his bride. But I pointed out that the odds were stacked against him and that we should return to camp and ask Doc's advice.

"Doc?" the Englishman asked. "Is he a medical man?"

"Sorta," I said. "He knows a sight about doctorin' and medicines."

"Then I'll talk to him," Sir John said. "But I fear he'll be about his own business and be little concerned about mine."

"Doc's all heart," I said, "an' smart as a bunkhouse rat. If anyone knows how to get your wife back, it's Doc."

I didn't mention the buried gold, since I figgered Sir John had enough problems to think about already, but I said: "We got a sick woman at camp, an' since you were an army surgeon an' all, maybe you could take a look at her."

"Of course," said Sir John without hesitation, "but I will agree only to assist, since she's already being treated by a competent physician."

"Oh, Doc's competent all right," said Johnny Blue, rolling a smoke, "but I think you're going to have to do more than assist."

"We'll see," returned Sir John. He pointed to Johnny Blue's cigarette with an accusing finger. "That, young man, is an unhealthy habit and I fear it will one day bring you to grief."

Johnny Blue shrugged, grinning. "Hell, Colonel, life is too long as it is."

We made our way back to Doc's camp under the rock overhang and met Georgia as she stepped out of the wagon, her round, brown face splashed with tears.

"She's worse, much worse," she sobbed. "She's delirious and running a high fever and I don't think she'll last till nightfall."

After I made some hasty introductions, Sir John asked Doc if he required any assistance.

"My dear fellow," declared that cheerless charlatan, "I need more than assistance, I need a miracle. She's got a bullet wound in her right thigh that ain't gettin' any better. In fact, it's getting a sight worse."

"Might I be allowed to see your patient, Doctor?" Sir John asked. "I don't mean to intrude, but perhaps I could consult? I treated many bullet wounds when I was with the Fifty-third of Foot in Africa."

"By all means, go ahead," urged Doc. "Cottontail is sinking fast."

Sir John raised his right eyebrow at the patient's name, but being an English gentleman he kept silent as he stepped up to the wagon and looked inside.

"Oh my God!" he roared, wakening the sleeping babies, who immediately began to caterwaul. The Englishman staggered back from the wagon and rounded angrily on the hapless Doc. "You have the impertinence to call yourself a physician! You, sir, are a disgrace to the medical profession!"

Doc hunched his shoulders and seemed to shrink under Sir John's verbal barrage.

"Didn't you know the leg was gangrenous?" Sir John demanded. "Damn it all, man, you'll have to amputate right away. There is no time to be lost!"

Miserably, Doc hung his head and in a small, defeated voice whispered: "I'm not a doctor."

"Not a doctor?" Sir John cried. "Then what kind of creature are you, for God's sake?"

"I sell snake oil . . . er, patent medicines—that's why they call me Doc. It's . . . it's the only reason."

Suddenly Doc looked twenty years older and very small and vulnerable, and for the first time since I'd known him I really felt sorry for him. Trying to make things better, I said: "Doc took a bullet out of me one time. Saved my life."

"I suppose even the most incompetent humbug can have his moments," Sir John said. He took a deep breath, then added: "I have to operate right away."

He turned to Doc. "I don't suppose you have any instruments?"

At this, Doc's face brightened. "I do! I do! Turns out I do. I have an amputation set I won at poker from an army doctor up in the Montana Territory a few years back."

"I'll bring it," Georgia said. "Then I have to feed them babies."

Sir John glared at Doc the whole time Georgia was gone, and for his part, Doc continued to wither under his disapproving gaze.

Georgia, a baby at each huge breast, returned with a flat wooden box, the lid secured by tarnished brass hinges.

Sir John opened the box, said "Harrumph" deep in his

throat, then added: "I've seen an amputation set like this before. It's an ivory presentation set by the New York maker George Tiemann and it's one of the very best." He glanced at Doc. "That army surgeon must have owed you a great deal."

"He didn't owe me nothin'," said Doc. "He just put all his faith and all his money on a pair of queens."

Sir John's look became even more scornful. "My dear man," he told Doc, "if you were in the British army I'd have you shot." He closed the lid on the amputation set and declared steadfastly: "Now, to my patient."

Cottontail was very sick. She lay in the back of the wagon, the distraught Mauler hovering beside her. She'd been taken by the fever, but was still conscious, though now and then she'd babble about stuff that happened a long time before. Her leg, where Sir John had bared it, was swollen and black from toe to thigh, and it smelled horribly.

"Can you hear me, my dear?" the Englishman whispered, taking Cottontail's small hand in his.

Cottontail nodded and replied weakly. "I hear you."

"Then listen to me. I must take your leg off. If I don't, you'll be dead before dawn."

The Mauler looked at Sir John, his scarred, battered face looking empty and sick. "Is there no other way?"

Sir John shook his head. "No. And I fear it may be already too late. The gangrene has spread very rapidly."

"I don't want to live with just one leg," Cottontail whispered. "No matter what happens, you ain't taking my leg." She turned to the Mauler and her fevered eyes softened. "I reckon my whorin' days are over."

The Mauler traced the line of his wife's cheek with a

thick forefinger. "Honey, I loved you when you was a whore, an' I'll love you still when you ain't."

"Whiskey," Sir John said sharply.

Doc, eager to please, ran to the front of the wagon and returned with a bottle of Anderson's rye.

The Englishman uncorked the bottle and held it to Cottontail's lips. "Drink this, my dear," he said. "It will help ease the pain."

But Cottontail weakly pushed the bottle away. "Bring me my baby," she whispered.

The Mauler glanced at Sir John, and the Englishman nodded. "Do as she says."

A few moments later Georgia—tears streaming down her face, and two damp patches on the front of her dress from the milk she'd produced—handed Cottontail her baby.

The young woman took the child from Georgia and laid his soft little cheek alongside her own.

"Good-bye, my son," she whispered. "You grow up tall and strong and always take care of the Mauler. Your daddy is a nice man but he ain't too smart, and people take advantage of him, an' that's a natural fact."

"Cottontail," Sir John said, using her name for the first time, "I must amputate now. If we wait much longer it will be too late."

From somewhere deep inside her Cottontail summoned up the strength to say sharply: "Doctor, you're not taking my leg. Right now I'm in no pain an' I feel kinda warm an' drowsy. You cut off my leg an' I'll die screaming. Ain't that the truth?"

For a few long moments Sir John was unable to answer. Then, his voice shaking, he said: "There will be pain. And shock. Considerable shock."

"Then let me be," Cottontail said. "Let me die in my own way an' in my own time."

She handed the baby to the Mauler. "Raise our son well," she said.

For his part, the Mauler took the child and nodded dumbly, tears staining his face.

"You'll stay with me?" Cottontail asked him. "You won't leave me?"

Again the Mauler nodded, unable to speak

All this I saw through the open canvas at the back of the wagon.

I turned and walked back to the fire. The Gunfighter sat in silence, his face buried in his hands. He and Cottontail had grown very close in the past weeks, always talking about women's fixin's and laughing when she painted his face and let him try her hats and bloomers and sich. Now and then he'd open his hands and glance over at the wagon like he expected Cottontail to step out of there, pretty and giggling and well again, like he remembered her.

When I walked up to the fire, the Gunfighter looked up at me expectantly, a faint glimmer of hope in his eyes. Me, I just shook my head at him because there was nothing to say.

Johnny Blue, who always had strange little ways of surprising me, sat beside the Gunfighter and put an arm around his shoulders. The Gunfighter did not move. He just took his hands from his face and both men gazed into the fire, not speaking, two very different rannies bonded only by their grief.

Slowly the day shaded into evening, the evening darkened to night, and at seven minutes past two o'clock in the morning by Doc's watch, Cottontail gave up the fight and died.

We buried her at first light in a quiet place near the rock overhang, piling up rocks to make a cairn. There was wood aplenty, mostly dry juniper branches washed down the canyons and creeks by occasional flash floods, and from these we fashioned a cross.

The burying words fell to Sir John because none of us had the will to say them. The Englishman talked about death and resurrection and eternal life and then sang a hymn for those in peril of the sea and afterward even Johnny Blue allowed that he'd done a right good job.

The Mauler took it hard.

He stepped up to me, his face white and empty of all expression. "Cottontail's gone, ain't she?" he said. "I mean, she's there, under the ground and she's never coming back to me."

I didn't have the words. "Mauler," I said, "I don't know what to say. I don't know what to tell you."

The Mauler studied my face for a long time like he expected to find the answer to his question there. Then he turned on his heel and walked away from me. I watched him go and kicked the dirt under my feet with the toe of my boot and silently cursed myself for not being able to say what I felt inside. Boys, you know I've always been a talking man, but now, when I needed to talk most, I was suddenly struck dumb.

How do you explain that? I don't know. And from that day to this, no one has ever been able to tell me.

Doc and Georgia found solace in each other, but the Gunfighter and Johnny Blue stood apart, each with his own thoughts, having no one to turn to for comfort and too proud to seek it from each other.

Doc looked old and small and defeated. He finally stepped away from the sobbing Georgia and held up his hands. "Listen, everybody," he said, "this quest is now over. It's already claimed one life and I won't let it take another. There ain't enough gold in the world worth Cottontail's life."

"What's your plan, Doc?" I asked.

"We're going back to Texas," Doc replied. "Beyond that, I have no plans."

"The hell you haven't, you old scale-thumber!"

This from the Mauler, who stood there with his fists clenched, his face blazing.

"You heard what Cottontail told you," he said. "She said all our futures was tied up in that gold, and that includes the future of my son, and yours. We're not stopping now. Cottontail would have wanted us to go on and do what we came here to do. I won't see her die for nothing. Doc, you take a step back down that trail and I swear I'll kill you."

"Now see here—" Doc began, obviously shaken, but the Mauler cut him off.

"An' another thing. This man here"—the Mauler nodded toward Sir John—"lost his wife to Clemente Perez and his bandits. Are you just going to stand by and do nothing?"

"Sir John," said Doc, turning to the Englishman with a little bow, "I have a Sharps .50 caliber in my wagon that is both wife and child to me. Take it, it's yours. Go rescue your lady wife, and good luck to you."

The Mauler shook his head. "Too thin, Doc, way too thin. He can't do it on his own."

"Mauler," said Doc sharply, "out here a man makes his own road or he falls by the wayside."

"Listen to him," the Mauler said, turning to the rest of us. "He thinks the sun comes up just to hear him crow."

"That may be so," declared Doc, his face set and hard, "but I am determined to return to Texas."

"Do that, Doc, and my wife will have died for nothing," the Mauler said. Then he added in a thin, mean voice I'd never heard him use before: "I'm not about to let that happen. Try to turn that wagon around and by my wife's grave I'll shoot you right off the seat."

Doc was taken aback, and it showed. The Mauler had never spoken to him like that before, and he was stunned into speechlessness.

Sir John, seeing how things lay between Doc and the Mauler, quickly stepped into the breach.

"Thank you for your kind offer of the rifle," he said. "I accept it willingly and in the spirit intended. 'Pon my soul, yes."

Johnny Blue then took a pace forward. "Doc, there's nothing back in Texas for me but a rope. I'm for going on."

"Me too," I said, though nobody paid me much attention.

The Gunfighter, who had been standing hat-in-hand by Cottontail's grave, now walked up to Doc. He pointed at the grave. "That little lady died for the gold, so it seems to me she has a claim on it that she's now passed down to her child. If you don't want to go, give me the map. I'll get the gold my ownself." He turned and waved a hand toward me and Johnny Blue. "Me an' these two."

"Doc, without the gold the Fortune Flyer is a dead

duck," Georgia said. "You owe it to me and our son to make the Flyer a success."

Scowling, Doc stood there thinking for a few moments, then he said: "No babies. I'm not taking the little ones any farther. It's too dangerous." He looked at the Mauler. "You will take Georgia and the babies back to La Lajilla and wait for us there." Doc's face softened a little. "You ain't going to be thinkin' straight, boy. You'd be too much of a liability."

The Mauler opened his mouth to object, but closed it again when he realized the logic of Doc's argument. There was just no way we could take them younkers any farther into that wilderness, and Georgia couldn't be left alone. After a moment he said: "One other thing, Doc, you got to help Sir John find his wife. We've lost one wife on this trip, we don't want us to lose another."

Now, Doc would have strongly objected to this course of action had not the Gunfighter said: "Hell, we'll get his wife back an' maybe at the same time I can settle accounts with that rat Perez and leave us a clear path to the gold."

"Then it's decided," said Doc. "I will argue no further." He looked at the Mauler and was suddenly overcome with the deepest emotion. "My dear boy, can you ever forgive me?" he pleaded.

"There ain't nothin' to forgive, Doc," the Mauler said. "You did your best, so what's done is done an' there's no goin' back."

The two men then embraced and wept copiously and all present later agreed that it was a poignant and touching scene.

After that there was nothing left to do but join hands around Cottontail's grave and sing that grand old hymn

"Nearer, My God, to Thee." And that was how we finally took our leave of her.

Boys, she's still up there in the high Sierras, buried near an overhanging shelf of rock. If you look close, you can still make out Doc's initials carved into the edge of the stone as he had a habit of doing whenever he found himself in a new place: D.F. 1888.

Just tread lightly round Cottontail's grave, and if you have a mind to, wish her well from me.

Afterward, I gave the Mauler my arm and we walked to the wagon, where I took leave of him with many an embrace and fondest wishes for the future. One by one, the rest of us did the same, then we stood and watched as the wagon carrying Georgia and the babies rocked and lurched down the dry creek bed then around the wall of a low mesa until it was finally hidden from view.

"My wife," Doc said, wiping a tear from his eye, "has taken all this hard. I fear she'll never be the same again."

From somewhere far off I heard a coyote bark his terrible hunger at an uncaring sky and a premonition of death hung heavy on me. Despite the heat of the dawning day I shivered. And when I glanced at Johnny Blue he was standing perfectly still, watching the cloud of dust that had been stirred up by the wagon. His face was expressionless, like it was carved from stone.

Twelve

Me and Johnny Blue, the Gunfighter, Doc, and Sir John filled our canteens and bravely rode farther into the mountains in search of the gold and the unfortunate Lady Agatha.

Only three of us were mounted; Doc pushing the squeaking Flyer and Sir John tagging along on foot.

We rode through the basin where we'd found Sir John and into another narrow canyon. After an hour's ride, the canyon suddenly opened up into a valley about a mile across, its sandy floor broken up by cactus—including prickly pear and the vicious-thorned jumping cholla—large boulders, and clumps of mesquite.

The air was thick and still here between the mountain slopes and nothing moved except our own shadows under the white-hot glare of the relentless sun. The sky above us was so pale blue it was almost transparent, the sun hanging over us like a twenty-dollar gold piece.

The Gunfighter—who was a very strange ranny, especially to those who didn't know him well—had hung his wide-brimmed white Stetson on his saddle horn and wore the little straw bonnet Cottontail had given him, its pink ribbon tied under his chin in a perfect bow.

He had a little jar of some kind of cream or other and

he kept smearing little dabs of it on his cheeks and nose. When he caught Johnny Blue looking at him, he said by way of explanation: "It's so my face doesn't get dried up by the sun."

Johnny Blue raised an eyebrow but said nothing. Like me, he reckoned the Gunfighter was one peculiar ranny but he was too good with a gun to tease. That was one dangerous line I'd no intention of stepping over—not now, not ever.

Shortly after noon we found some shelter in the shade of a huge bell-shaped rock, boiled coffee over a handful of mesquite twigs, and ate cold salt pork with some stale tortillas.

Nobody was inclined to talk much, Cottontail's death and the heat making each of us content to sit with his own thoughts.

Johnny Blue rolled a cigarette, smoked it, and then we mounted up again.

There was no sign of Perez and his bandits and I began to think they'd taken the woman and gone directly after the gold. If that was the case, they were well ahead of us and it was very unlikely we'd catch up, especially with two men on foot. Strictly speaking, Doc wasn't on foot but he didn't make much headway riding the Flyer. For one thing, he was an uncertain and wobbly rider and for another, the wheels kept bogging down in the soft sand of the valley.

The Gunfighter, as was his inclination, scouted ahead, studying the ground for sign.

We'd been in the valley maybe two hours when we saw him up ahead, waving his white Stetson at us to come on. Me and Johnny Blue rode up to the Gunfighter, and Doc and Sir John hoofed it after us.

"Tracks," the Gunfighter said. "They cross the valley here and angle toward that mesa over there."

"How many men?" Doc, who'd finally caught up, asked breathlessly.

The Gunfighter shook his head. "I don't know for sure. Ten, maybe twelve. One horse is being rode double, probably carrying Perez and Sir John's wife."

"Then we're close to Agatha?" asked Sir John, his face alight with hope.

"Very close," the Gunfighter said. "I think Perez is camped on that mesa somewhere. Outlaws ain't early risers, especially if they've been pleasuring themselves with a woman all night."

Sir John flinched as though he'd been struck, and the Gunfighter said: "Sorry, don't mean to be cruel, but that's the way things are out here."

The mesa was about half a mile away, its flat top crowned by scattered juniper and mesquite. The gradually sloped sides looked to be covered in loose sand and shingle, and here and there the white bones of dead trees stuck out. It was not a place that favored a sneak attack, and I doubted that our horses could take the slope at any kind of speed if they could get up there at all.

"Lookee there, to the southern slope of the mesa," the Gunfighter said.

Straining my eyes, I saw a thin trail of smoke tie a gray ribbon in the air. Unlike the northern end of the mesa, this side wasn't a continuous slope. It rose straight up from the valley floor for about thirty feet to end in a narrow ledge or plateau of rock about twenty-five feet deep before again rising very gradually another hundred feet or so to the top of the mesa.

"That's where Perez is camped," the Gunfighter said.

"On that ledge of rock." He turned in the saddle and beckoned to the others. "We've got to get out of here. We're out in the open and if they see us they'll light out and we'll never catch them."

Sir John's knuckles whitened on Doc's Sharps rifle and I knew his inclination—a result of his long association with the British army—was to charge headlong at the mesa into the heavy and accurate rifle fire of Perez and his bandits.

The British won a lot of victories that way, but they also went down to a lot of bloody defeats, and I told the eager Englishman this wasn't going to be another of them.

In the end, Doc's cooler head prevailed and we swung wide to the north, planning to scale the side of the mesa away from the bandits and then attack from its summit, pouring our fire down on the unsuspecting bandit camp.

"Your plan seems strategically sound, Doc," agreed Sir John, who seemed to have forgiven Doc's botched surgery on Cottontail. "I suggest we put it into operation with all haste."

It took us an hour to get into position, and by that time the sun was hanging right above us in the sky and it was scorching hot, hammering the landscape into motionless submission. Johnny Blue, rolling a smoke as he sat his horse, looked down from the saddle at Sir John, who walked beside him, white-lipped and tense.

"Back in the olden days, when I was cowboyin' on the ol' DHS an' it was hot like this, we used to feed the chickens cracked ice so they wouldn't lay hard-boiled eggs," he said.

The Englishman glanced up at that reckless rider in surprise, perhaps sensing a big windy.

"The deuce you say," he declared. " 'Pon my soul, but that's passing strange."

Johnny Blue nodded, then lit his cigarette. "Strange," he agreed, "but a natural fact."

My *compadre* was always exaggerating about stuff like that, since we didn't have no cracked ice on the ol' DHS. We fed them chickens cold water and it worked just as good. Leastways, them hens never laid any hard-boiled eggs that I knew of.

I left Johnny Blue and Sir John to talk about hot days and chickens they'd known and rode ahead to follow the Gunfighter and Doc to the base of the mesa towering above us, the slope all loose sand and shingle, slippery and treacherous.

"We can't get the horses up there," the Gunfighter said, stating the obvious. "We'll have to leave them here and climb up on our own."

Doc agreed how this was an excellent plan but I quickly improved upon it.

Boys, you know me, I've always been smart as a tree full of owls and right about then I had me one of those brilliant ideas that later made me a legend all over the West.

"Hosses can't get up there," I said, "but the Fortune Flyer can."

"What's your drift?" asked Johnny Blue, who had just joined us.

"Listen," I said, "first we get the Flyer up the slope to the top of the mesa."

"So far, so good," Johnny Blue interrupted suspiciously. "Then what?"

Boys, you'll recollect that Johnny Blue was always

wary of my ideas, mainly because he never had any good ones his ownself.

"You gents is gonna love this," I said. "It's brilliant."

"Spill," snapped Doc. "Don't keep us in suspense, boy."

"I'm the best bike rider we have," I said, and Doc nodded in agreement, giving me encouragement to continue. "Well, I pedal the Flyer an' Johnny Blue here gets up in front of me. I'll give him my pistol an' then we go chargin' down the side of the mesa, me pedaling an' Johnny Blue a-hootin' an' a-hollerin' an' blazin' away with two Colt Armies, knocking them surprised bandits down afore they even know we're there. Then you boys open up from the top of the mesa an' nail the rest."

Johnny Blue opened his mouth to speak, but I held up a hand to silence him. "Then we rescue Sir John's bride, go snag the gold, an' we're home free an' happy as pigs in a peach orchard."

"The strategy does seems sound," observed Sir John pensively. "But it is indeed a desperate endeavor and not one with a guarantee of success."

"Maybe so," declared Doc thoughtfully, "but I have a suggestion that could improve our odds. Since the Gunfighter is our best shot I suggest he ride on the handlebars of the Flyer."

"Not me," the Gunfighter exclaimed, horrified. "I want nothin' to do with that contraption."

"Do I get a say in this?" asked Johnny Blue, who had been opening and closing his mouth like a stranded fish.

"Speak your piece," I said, "an' welcome."

"Well, first off, this plan was concocted by a known lunatic." I made to object but Johnny Blue shushed me into silence, so I bit my tongue. "And secondly, this known lunatic's plans have gotten me shot three times afore an' hung twice. An' thirdly, since I can't hardly hit nothin' with a Colt when I'm standing still, how the hell am I gonna hit anything when I'm movin'?"

"Sound objections, my boy," said Doc. "Yet, despite your lack of skill with firearms, you are the only one here qualified for the job, being young an' limber an' all."

"A job we'd better get to damn quick or them boys up there on the ledge will be long gone," said the Gunfighter sourly. "It's time to quit jawin' and start doin'."

Seeing how the land lay, Johnny Blue reluctantly agreed to my plan, though he seemed less than pleased about the whole scheme.

As we started to climb the steep incline of the mesa slope, he pulled me aside. "Afore we get up there, I'm gonna warn you about somethin'."

"Warn away, Blue Boy," I said. "Your words won't fall on deaf ears."

"Just this," declared that surly saddle-warmer, "you know how you are, so don't you go shootin' folks up the ass. Them boys is gonna be plenty riled at us as it is, stampedin' down on them an' all like you plan. You start shootin' them up the ass an' they're gonna get mad enough to bite a bullet in two."

"Relax," I said. "You're the one that's gonna be doing the shootin', remember?"

"Just so you know," Johnny Blue returned. "I've said my piece."

"Trust me," I said.

It took us twenty minutes to climb the slope of that mesa, me pushing and dragging the Flyer and having a hard time of it. When we reached the top we paused for breath and drank a few sips of water from our dwindling canteens.

The southern rim of the mesa was maybe two hundred yards from where we stood. The top was mostly flat, broken here and there by jutting slabs of rock and a number of shallow depressions. Cactus grew in every nook and cranny among the rocks, and a few juniper trees, dwarfed from thin soil and lack of rain, raised skinny limbs to the white-hot iron of the sky.

It was a stark, unwelcoming place, a massive anvil for the ferocious hammer of the sun, and it was a place where none of us cared to linger.

I pushed the Flyer toward the edge of the mesa and the others followed. When I was about twenty yards from the edge, I took off my hat and Injuned up to the rim and looked over.

About a dozen bandits sat around a fire, apparently drinking the last of the coffee, because their horses were saddled and ready. The men were mostly Mexicans wearing wide sombreros and crossed ammunition belts on their chests, but there were a couple of renegade Anglos present, including one who had the confident, arrogant look of a gunslick, a Colt stuck in the waistband of his pants.

Sitting a little apart was a slender, blond young woman, her chin on her knees. She was half naked, since her blue dress had been pulled from her shoulders and hung in tatters around her waist. Even at a distance I saw that she was cut and bruised, a huge black-and-blue welt on the swollen cheek that faced me.

The woman was Lady Agatha, no doubt about that, and Perez and his gang had obviously had their way with her—though, judging by her bruises, she'd fought hard for her honor.

The slope from the top of the mesa to the bandit camp was a lot steeper, now that I saw it up close, and because of the prevailing wind it had been blown free of sand and shingle, being now mostly smooth, bare rock.

I didn't know how fast the Flyer could go, but reckoned the shelf of rock where the bandits were camped was wide enough to slow it down so I could turn the machine away from the cliff edge beyond their campfire and bring it to a halt.

The smooth going down the slope would also help improve Johnny Blue's doubtful marksmanship, so overall, my plan still seemed an excellent one.

How wrong I was.

As some poet or other once said: "The best schemes of mice and men aft gang agley."

And how right he was.

Thirteen

When I got back to the others I communicated my intelligence, though I omitted to tell Sir John the melancholy details of his wife's captivity, contenting myself to declare that she was alive and seemed in good health.

That served to bolster the Englishman's resolve, and he insisted that our daring and desperate rescue should begin at once.

"It seems to me," he said, "that those renegades didn't bring their horses up a sheer cliff face, so there must be another way down from this mesa. To prevent their escape, I suggest we attack right away."

"That's real good thinkin', Sir John," I said. "Johnny Blue will drop maybe half a dozen in his first fusillade, an' you boys can easy nail the rest."

The Englishman, whose good breeding had up until this time allowed him to studiously ignore the Gunfighter's choice of headgear, now raised an eyebrow and said: "I say, old chap, shouldn't you . . . er . . . change to your sombrero before we embark on this formidable venture?"

The Gunfighter set his little straw bonnet at a jaunty angle and adjusted the pink ribbon under his chin. "Nah,

I like this hat," he said. Then his eyes narrowed and he added ominously: "You got some kind of problem with that?"

Sir John, who didn't seem in the least bit intimidated, shook his head. "Not at all, dear boy. I once knew a gallant brigadier general who wore a silk top hat into battle. He got a Zulu assegai through the thing at the Battle of Isandlwana, and of course, needless to say, the hat—and his head—were never quite the same after that, poor chap. But live and let live, I say. A man's choice of chapeau is his own."

"Just so that's plain," observed the Gunfighter. "As I said, I like this hat."

"Right, let's quit this jawin' and get going," Doc said testily.

I gave Johnny Blue my gun and that pugnacious puncher gingerly climbed onto the handlebars of the Flyer. "Now, just you study on what I told you," he said. "I mean about shootin' them boys up the ass. I won't stand for it."

"An' like I told you, Blue Boy, I ain't got no gun," I retorted right sharply.

As the others followed closely, I started to pedal the Flyer.

Johnny Blue hadn't found his balance, especially since he was holding on to them two pistols, so we wobbled perilously all over the place for a few moments until he finally got the hang of it and allowed me to build up a good head of steam as I charged for the rim.

"This is gonna be great," I yelled at Johnny Blue as the edge of the mesa came closer and closer. "It's the best idea I've ever had."

"You're a luuuunatic," yelled that doubting drover as we hurtled over the rim and into the void.

The Flyer gamely held to the slope, wheels squeaking and protesting, and our speed built up very quickly.

Too quickly.

As we charged down the mesa the bike rolled faster and ever faster. Boys, up until then, I don't think human beings had ever moved at the speed we reached on the Flyer that day. My hat blew off in the passing wind we made, and so did Johnny Blue's.

"Slow down! Slow down!" screamed that nervous Nellie.

"No brakes! No brakes!" I screamed back.

All thought he may have had about using them Colts of his was now forgotten as Johnny Blue reached down and hung on to the handlebars of the Flyer like a tick to a pup's ear.

"Too fast! Too fast!" Johnny Blue hollered and when he turned his head to look at me, his eyes were bugging right out of his head with fear.

"Hang on!" I yelled. "We're almost there! Get ready to blaze away!"

We hit the ledge of rock like a runaway freight train and in maybe one single split second I saw the bearded, startled faces of them bandits flash past me.

The level shelf didn't slow the Flyer in the least, and we hurtled across its width fast as a cat with its tail on fire and then right over the yawning edge of the cliff.

"*Eeeeeiiiieeeeiiiii* . . ." Johnny Blue screamed horribly all the way down, until he landed with a sickening thud on his back more than twenty feet later.

I was lucky because my landing was softer. I slammed into Johnny Blue's belly and heard him gasp "*Oof!*" before I rolled off him and into the cloud of dust he'd kicked up when he hit the ground.

Shots from the top of the cliff began to thud into the sand around us and I knew right then that we were in a heap of trouble.

Johnny Blue sat up clutching his stomach and groggily shaking his head. There was a large boulder just a few feet away and I grabbed him by the shirt collar and dragged him to its welcome cover.

A bullet whined off the rock, then another, and to attempt a move from our present position was certain death.

More shots sounded—the steady fire of our gallant companions up on the mesa rim. But just as quickly as it had begun, the shooting stopped. Then I heard the pounding of many hooves and realized that the bandits, not knowing how few in number our party was, had made good their escape—taking with them poor Lady Agatha.

Gasping for breath, Johnny Blue was frantically reaching for his gun and found only empty leather.

"It's okay," I said, "they're gone."

"I'm gonna plug you," returned that cantankerous cow chaser. "I'm gonna shoot you right through both lungs. You're a dangerous lunatic and it ain't safe to let you live."

A quick, wary glance told me that our Colts lay half buried in the dust about fifteen feet away, so I said right sharply: "Blue Boy, you got no call to be sayin' stuff like that. You're always the same, gettin' real mean an' threatening to plug folks when things don't go your own way." I shook my head at him. "I swear, sometimes you act like a spoiled, bratty little kid."

Now Johnny Blue's eyes lighted on them Colts about

the same time mine did, so there's no telling what might have happened with him being in such a testy mood and all, had not a voice from the cliff top arrested our attention.

"Hey, you down there! Are you alive?" It was the Gunfighter.

"We're about half dead, does that count?" Johnny Blue yelled back.

"Stand aside, something comin' down!" the Gunfighter yelled.

Suddenly a man's limp body was thrown over the edge of the cliff, cartwheeling through the air before it landed with a thump about ten feet from where we stood.

I walked over and looked at the dead man, turning him faceup with my boot. He was about my age with black hair and a mustache and his gray eyes were wide open, staring into nothing.

The Gunfighter cupped his hand to his mouth and yelled: "That there is the Gallatin Kid. I shot another Gallatin Kid up Denver way about a year ago, but he wasn't a patch on this one."

As it happened, the unfortunate Kid was the only casualty among the bandits, and he'd fallen to the Gunfighter's deadly revolvers.

Doc came to the edge of the cliff and beckoned to me and Johnny Blue to come on up there. He swept his arm to the west, showing us that there was another, easier route to the ledge. Johnny Blue was still a shade tetchy, so I picked up both our guns and made my way to the other side of the mesa and I didn't give him his Colt back until we reached the ledge and were with civilized folks.

The reason Clemente Perez had chosen this site to

make camp was obvious: a large rock tank full of sweet, clear water.

"At least he didn't poison the water," I said, after drinking my fill.

The Gunfighter shook his head at me. "Out here a man doesn't poison water tanks, even the Apaches didn't do that. Perez knows he'll be heading back this way and he'll need water."

"The chap's deuced confident," Sir John said, the strain of failing to rescue his wife evident on his face.

"Oh, he's confident, all right," the Gunfighter allowed. "By this time he knows there's only five of us and the only reason he's not shooting at us right now is because he wants to be first to the gold. After he gets it, he and his men will head back to the border country where they can spend their money an' enjoy their woman."

Sir John seemed to grow many years older in an instant. His face crumpled and he bowed his head, sinking to the ground as he whispered: "Agatha, my darling, beloved little Agatha . . . "

Doc, who more than any of us understood the Englishman's loss, put an arm around the old man's shoulder and said: "Love is short, my friend. It's the forgetting that's long."

"An' I got more bad news," the Gunfighter said—like we hadn't heard enough already. "Hun Larrikin is runnin' with Perez an' them."

"Who's he?" asked Johnny Blue, building a smoke.

"He's a hired killer out of El Paso. Me an' him, we almost had it out in Dodge a few years back, but it came to nothing so the thing still lies between us. He shot a deputy sheriff last year in Del Rio an' later a named man in Uvalde. Since then he's been runnin' wild in the Big

Bend country, robbing and raping and doing whatever he has a mind to."

"Is he good?" asked Doc, his arm still around Sir John's shoulders.

"One of the best—maybe the very best," the Gunfighter replied. "Lightning quick and accurate with a Colt."

"You mean he's better than you?" Doc asked, a look of stunned disbelief on his face.

The Gunfighter shook his head. "I don't know. Like I said, the thing still lies between us. We'll settle it one day soon."

All this melancholy intelligence filled Sir John with fresh fears and he seemed weighed down by fatigue and wretchedness. But after a few moments' contemplation he suddenly freed himself of Doc's comforting arm and sprang to his feet, declaring in angry tones that he was setting out in immediate pursuit of Perez and his cohorts.

"I will rescue my wife or die in the attempt," he cried. "At least I will perish like a British officer and a gentleman."

I opened my mouth to speak, but it was Doc who once again stepped into the breach. "Sir John, that will do you no good," he declared. "Perez or Larrikin or one of the others will just shoot you down like a dog an' your wife will still be an unhappy captive. No, we will camp here through the heat of the day an' renew our pursuit by night." Doc nodded his head as though he had just made a profound statement and laid out the case most expertly. "After all," he added, "we know where Perez is going, for we follow the same map he does."

Sir John was mute, so Doc pressed home his argument.

"Be assured, sir," he said, "that our priorities have changed. Our first order of business is to rescue your lady wife from a fate worse than death, and then recover the gold."

The Englishman found his voice again and allowed that this was indeed a handsome "beau geste" on Doc's part, and the two men fell into each other's arms with many a tear and backslap and whispered word of encouragement. This was such a touching and at the same time triumphant scene that I was moved to cry out a loud "Huzzah!"—and soon the Gunfighter and even Johnny Blue joined their voices to mine.

Thus it was that by the time we had recovered the horses and brought them to our camp we were a happy and determined band of brothers and we later made merry over a meal of broiled salt pork and good hot coffee.

Indeed, Sir John's spirits were soon so restored, he willingly answered Johnny Blue's endless questions about his tea with old Queen Vic.

"As to the tea itself, it was Earl Grey," Sir John observed. "That's a mildly scented blend from India, don't you know."

"Ah, mildly scented," repeated Johnny Blue, nodding wisely. "I think I'd like that."   .

"And we had little cucumber sandwiches."

"Cucumber? What's cucumber?"

"I suppose it's a sort of vegetable. You peel it, then slice it very thin—a slice looks rather like the face of the full moon—and put it between little triangular slices of bread and butter. It's jolly good, you know."

"I've never seen a cucumber," said Johnny Blue.

"Well, when it's sliced wafer-thin it's tip-top. You do need the bread and butter, of course."

And so it went on, until one by one we sought what shade there was from the heat and dozed away the hours until day finally shadowed into night.

We filled our canteens and prepared once again to take to the trail, though Doc had one more melancholy task to perform—his last farewell to the bent and broken Fortune Flyer.

As he stood over the mangled wreckage of his machine, it took Doc a few moments before he found his voice, but finally, in the most somber tones, he said: "The Flyer is no more, but I vow that another will rise from the flames like a veritable phoenix." He turned to the rest of us and declared in a ringing voice, throwing his arms wide: "The Fortune Flyer will live again!"

Once more we gave voice to many a heartfelt "Huzzah!" and then we mounted and again headed toward the high peaks of the inner Sierras, where we hoped to find both the buried treasure of the dead bandit Pablo Olguin and Sir John's unhappy wife.

Fourteen

Me and Johnny Blue's Montana-bred American studs had so far stood up well to the desert heat, but now they were carrying an extra load, since Doc rode behind me and Sir John behind Johnny Blue.

As you boys probably figgered by now, neither of these parties was particularly keen to double up with the Gunfighter—before or behind—so unencumbered he again took the point and scouted far ahead of us.

For the next couple of days we holed up during the day and rode at night, mostly to spare the horses and conserve our dwindling supply of water.

By the standard of the Rockies, the mountains of the Sierras are not high, but crossing them is just as difficult and we kept to the valleys and canyons whenever we could, only riding higher up boulder-strewn slopes when there was no other way. A few hardy pine trees grew at the higher elevations and once we came on a small stand of mixed aspen and oak and camped in that welcome shade during the worst of the heat.

After four days, both riders and horses were suffering and we were down to a few drops of water in our canteens. Sir John wore the Gunfighter's sombrero, but his pink English skin was beginning to burn and blister from the sun and I could see the man was in obvious distress, though he uttered not a single word of complaint.

We had made camp just before dawn when the Gunfighter rode up and said he'd found tracks across a dry riverbed about a mile ahead.

"Perez?" Sir John asked hopefully.

The Gunfighter shook his head. "Moccasin tracks, two sets of them. Judging by the size, I'd say a man and a woman. The man favors his left leg, drags it a little."

"Apaches?" Doc asked. "Surely not."

"Ain't likely," the Gunfighter said. "Lots of folks wear moccasins besides Indians."

The mystery was solved a short time later as our salt pork was broiling for breakfast. A thin old man astride a burro rode down a shallow, rocky ravine about a hundred yards away from where we sat and hailed us. "Hello the camp."

I rose from beside our hatful of fire and took up my Winchester. "Come on in," I hollered. The man rode closer, holding upright a rifle in a fringed and beaded buckskin cover, the butt resting on his left thigh. "Smelled your cookin'," the man said. "Didn't smell no coffee, though."

"Us, we ain't got no water for coffee," I said.

The man reached behind him and found a water bottle. He tossed it to me and I heard its contents slosh. "Bile that."

"Step down," Doc said. "We're right poor folks but any man who rides open an' friendly into our camp is welcome to share what little we have."

The man wore a stained, collarless shirt and faded striped pants stuffed into knee-high moccasins. He stepped off the burro, turned, and beckoned with his arm at someone hidden among the scattered rocks of the ravine. Soon a slender young woman in a knee-length buckskin dress stepped into the open and slowly began to make her way toward us.

"She's Lipan Apache," the man said. "Got no reason to trust white folks." He stuck out a hand to Doc. "Name's Shorty Harris. I been prospectin' in these mountains man an' boy for the past forty year, off an' on."

The woman came up and stood behind Shorty, peering at us suspiciously over his shoulder. "This is my woman," he said, "an' her name don't matter. It's Apache anyhow."

Shorty squatted by the fire and accepted a piece of broiled salt pork on a stick. I made to offer a piece to his woman but he stopped me. "She won't take it, an' if she takes it, she won't eat it. You're a white man an' she'll take nothing from you."

Shorty grabbed the salt pork from me and handed it to the woman. She accepted it from him and began to eat, her solemn face betraying not the merest hint of feeling.

"Seems to me you're a white man," I said. "How come she took it from you?"

"I am a white man as you astutely noticed, sonny, but I'm also Chiricahua Apache. Ol' Naiche hisself told me so, and if Naiche said it, it is a natural fact."

"An' you've done your share of killin', old man," the Gunfighter said without rancor. "You ain't no bargain. I can tell."

"Seems to me you've done your share your ownself, sonny," Shorty said, his hard eyes revealing his opinion. "Any man who'd wear a woman's hat with a pink ribbon is got to be right handy with a gun."

"I get by," the Gunfighter said.

"I just bet you do," the old man said. "Anyhoo, you're

right—I done my share. Done the killin' an' done my share of scalpin', too. Rode with the Apaches an' then rode agin them. I was with Crook in eighty-six—my God, is it already two years ago?—when Geronimo surrendered at Skeleton Canyon right here in the Sierras. Me an' Geronimo, we never could get along. His hatred for the white man ran too deep an' he never could see past the color of my skin."

Shorty quickly turned on Johnny Blue. "You know what I'm talkin' about, don't you, boy?"

"Maybe," casually returned that taciturn rider, building a smoke. "I'm a black man in a white country an' it's been noticed a time or two."

The old man studied Johnny Blue's face closely for a few moments then said: "You favor somebody I knew. A woman, I think. Yeah, now that I study on it, she was a woman. Maybe around twenty years old when I knowed her. Called herself Mattie Dupree. She wasn't quite as dark-complected as you and she was a whole sight prettier."

At this, Johnny Blue exclaimed in much agitation: "That's my sister's name! When did you last see her?"

"Whoa, hold on there, sonny," Shorty said. He reached into the pocket of his greasy buckskin jacket and took out an old and battered pipe. "Give me time to think."

The old man stretched out, picked up a burning juniper twig from the fire, and began to light his pipe. Talking around the stem without looking at Johnny Blue, he said from behind a cloud of ill-smelling smoke: "She was Juh's woman—he was a great war chief an' cousin to Geronimo. Only problem he had was he s-s-spoke l-l-like th-th-this. He took your sister, if that's who she is, from a cantina on the Mexican side of the Rio Grande."

"Where is this Juh feller now?" Johnny Blue asked.

"Dead," replied Shorty. "Five year ago he was return-ing from a raid into Mexico with Geronimo an' his hoss slipped an' fell into the Casas Grandes River canyon in Chihuahua. When the others got to him, he'd already breathed his last."

"Bad way for a warrior to go," I said. "I mean, a fall like that."

"Wasn't the fall kilt him, sonny," Shorty said, smiling real thin. "It was the landin' that kilt him."

"And my sister?" asked Johnny Blue, now convinced that he and Shorty were talking about the same Mattie.

"In Florida," the old man said. "With Geronimo an' the rest of them."

This dolorous intelligence only served to further in-crease Johnny Blue's agitation and he cried out in a loud voice that he must travel to Florida right away and find Mattie.

But Doc said: "Not so fast. First you have business to complete here."

Shorty Harris smiled slyly. "Could it be that the busi-ness you speak of concerns gold coins buried hereabouts by an outlaw named Pablo Olguin?"

"How the hell do you know that?" exclaimed Doc, wringing his hands in the highest state of anxiety. "That's known by very few people."

"Could be that just yeste'dy mornin' a certain old man an' his Apache wife saw a strong party of horsemen led by an outlaw of their acquaintance named Clemente Perez headed in the same direction you are," Shorty said. "Could be that ol' Clemente is after the gold, too."

"But—but," stammered Doc, "there are only two maps

that show the location of the gold. How do you know about it?"

"Word gets around," replied Shorty. "Been a lot of folks lookin' for that gold in the past twelvemonth, including me, an' some have left their bones in these mountains. There was even a company of Mexican infantry poked around up here for a while. The soldiers left empty handed I think—or maybe they didn't."

"You speak in riddles, old man," the Gunfighter snapped. "What do you mean, maybe they didn't?"

"Just this," said Shorty, unfazed, "that entire company, with their officers, deserted right after they marched out of the mountains. Now, maybe they was afraid to tell Porfirio Díaz they'd failed—or maybe they found the gold an' didn't want to share it with no damned gub'mint, so they just split it up atween them an' lit out for Texas."

"These are dolorous tidings indeed," quoth Doc. "Unlike the fabled Jason who went in search of the golden fleece, we may find that when we arrive at our destination the sheep has already been sheared."

I handed Shorty a cup of coffee since it had now boiled and he accepted it gratefully. "'Course, I ain't sayin' all this is so. Maybe them soldiers found nothing."

"Even so, Clemente Perez is now a full day ahead of us," said Doc gloomily. "I fear he will reach the gold first."

Sir John, who had been sitting silently through this exchange, now spoke up for the first time. "Mr. Harris, did you see a young woman with Perez?" he asked.

The old mountain man nodded. "Sure did. She was ridin' with Clemente. Know her?"

"She's my wife," returned Sir John miserably. "Lady Agatha."

"Ah," said Shorty, but he offered nothing further. But what was left unsaid spoke loudly to the Englishman, who buried his face in his hands, perhaps seeing images in his mind that cruelly tore at him.

Shorty drank some of the scalding coffee, then handed the cup to his wife, who began to sip what was left.

"Could be an old friend of mine could help you get to the gold afore Clemente," he said, wiping his mustache with the back of his hand. "The outlaw is slowed down by a woman and he's still got a lot of bad ground to cover—if'n the gold is cached where I suspicion it is."

"Who is this friend?" asked Doc, ignoring Shorty's pointed reference to the whereabouts of the gold.

"Her name is Li'l Emily an' she can take you to the gold a lot faster than Clemente Perez and his boys will get there."

"Will you take us to her?" asked Doc.

"Well, maybe so," the old man replied. A sly look crept over his face. "That is, if you boys will do something for me."

"Name it," said Doc, who thought nothing of making rash promises.

"You got to help me get somewheres, is all," Shorty said. "It ain't too much to ask."

"Of course, my good man," said Doc, even more breezily than before. "Where do you want to go? Texas? Mexico?"

The old man shook his head. "None of them places."

He turned and pointed to a mountain peak that rose almost vertically behind him, so high its summit seemed to scrape the lemon-colored sky of the morning. "I want you to help me get up there," he said. "Today, afore it's too late."

Fifteen

"Old man, you're daffy," said the Gunfighter. "Why in God's name would you want to climb that mountain?"

"I'll answer that question," Shorty said, "but first I got to tell you something, an' then tell you a story."

"Then tell away, an' be damned to ye," said the Gunfighter irritably.

"Thankee," said Shorty. "Your patience and understanding does you credit." He took a deep breath and continued: "The first thing I got to tell you is that I'm dying."

"Dying, you say?" said Sir John in surprise. "What in the world ails you, man?"

"Are you a doctor?" the old man asked.

"Yes, I am. Come now, what ails you?"

"I have this pain, all over here." Shorty rubbed a hand over his stomach. "There's somethin' growin' in there an' it's eatin' me alive. It spread—the pain I mean—down my right leg about a year ago an' I've been walking with a limp ever since. I broke that leg about three months ago, an' it still ain't even fully healed yet."

A look of concern crossed Sir John's face. He rose and kneeled beside the old man. "Let's take a look at you, old chap," he said. "I do know something of these things."

The Lipan woman angrily said something in her own language and slapped Sir John's hand away from Shorty's stomach. But the old mountain man just smiled at her and said a few reassuring words in Apache and she reluctantly stepped back.

Sulkily the woman watched as Sir John carried out his examination.

After several minutes, the Englishman straightened up, his face grave. "I believe you have a cancer in your stomach," he said. "I believe it to be very deep-seated and very advanced. It's metastasized. That is, it's spread to other parts of your body, most noticeably your right leg and probably into your colon and bowel and I have no doubt there are tumors elsewhere."

"How long have I got?" Shorty asked without apparent concern.

Sir John shook his head. "Poor fellow, you don't have long. A few weeks. Maybe less."

The old man nodded. "I figgered as much. That's why I've got to get up the mountain today. If I leave it any longer I won't have the strength to make it up there, an' if I falter or fall, my woman won't be able to get me there alone."

"Why do you want to get to the top of that mountain so bad?" asked Doc. "There ain't nothing up there but rock, more rock, an' the sky."

"That's what you think," Shorty said slyly. "There's something precious up there an' I got to get to it while I'm still able."

"Is it gold?" the Gunfighter asked, his eyes suddenly greedy.

"Nah," Shorty said. "It's something worth its weight in gold, though. At least to me." His pipe was out and he lighted it again, then sat back, puffing contentedly. "'Member that story I said I'd tell you? Well here it is."

The old man took his pipe from his mouth and for the first time I realized just how sick he looked. His cheeks were sunken, his skin a strange yellow color, and his blue eyes looked hot and feverish.

"Back in the late fall of eighty-one I was in Tombstone, Arizona," he said. "Figgered to do some silver minin'—never did, though."

"Been there," interjected Doc. "Didn't cotton to it much. Had to shoot a—feller, only winged him as it happened—but the law ran me out of town."

Shorty nodded. "It's a tough town. Anyhoo, when I was there the law was mostly in the hands of three brothers, called themselves the Earps. Ever heard of them?"

We looked at the old man blankly and he continued: "Well, they was pretty famous at the time, at least in that neck o' the woods. Had another feller with them, a gambler named John Holliday. He was always sickly an' I heard he died a couple of years back."

"I've heard of him," the Gunfighter said. "I was in Leadville, Colorado, when he got into a saloon shooting scrape. From what I heard, he wasn't much."

Doc, who'd been sitting pensively as though trying to recollect something, suddenly exclaimed, "Wait, I did know a feller called hisself Earp. Wyatt Earp. I figgered nobody could be born with a name like that an' he must have made it up. He was a policeman in Wichita when I knew him—I guess it was way back in seventy-five—and me an' him did some goldbrickin' an' thimbleriggin' together, figgerin' to fleece the rubes. But he wasn't much of a hand at it. See, he was just off the plains, where he'd been buffalo huntin', an' he was as green as they come."

"Yeah, well, he didn't show green in Tombstone when I was there," Shorty said. "He an' his brothers an' that Holliday feller had a street fight with some drovers. When the smoke cleared three of them cowboys was dead as they were ever gonna be. An' now I'm gettin' to the point of the story."

"About time," said the Gunfighter sourly, not having much of an attention span.

"Yeah, well," continued Shorty, "them three punchers was buried the next day in the purtiest durn coffins you ever seen in your life. I mean, they was all polished black wood, kinda like ebony, and there was silver all over them, real fine silver from the mines in the Dragoons.

"Well, when I saw them beautiful coffins go past me in the hearse, I figgered to myself that a man deserves to spend eternity in something real fine like that. So I went an' spoke to the feller who made them coffins an' made him do one up for me, silver an' all.

"Then I brung it all the way here and ol' Juh and them, even though they was real superstitious of coffins an' sich, helped me get it up the mountain."

Johnny Blue shook his head at Shorty. "Why'd you take your nice new coffin all the way up that mountain? It don't make no sense."

"Oh, it makes sense all right," replied the old man. "See, one time when the Mexican so'diers were huntin' me an' the other Chiricahua in these mountains, I went up there to hide. There's a cave up there, damn near at the top of the peak, an' from there a man can look out and see the whole Sierras, almost all the way to Californy.

"I remembered that place, an' that's where I put that purty coffin. I reckon when I'm dead I can lie in it all warm and cozy, and when it's got a mind to, my spirit can get up an' look out over the mountains an' remember the good old days. I don't want to lie like the Apache dead, wrapped in a ragged blanket with a cold face in a dead place, that's no good endin' for a man. No, I want to rest content in my fifty-dollar coffin up there on the mountain. A man can't choose when he'll die, but he can choose where."

"Begging your pardon, old man," the Gunfighter said, "but in case you haven't noticed, you ain't dead yet, an' ain't likely to be for a while yet."

"That's very true, but I will be soon." Shorty turned to Sir John. "Ain't that a natural fact?"

"Poor chap," returned the Englishman, saying all he had to say.

"Well, I ain't taking you up that mountain," the Gunfighter said. "So my advice to you is to close your eyes an' die right where you are."

"I won't do that," Shorty said. "I need my mountain. Down here, I'm just a speck of dust. Up there, I'm a rising mountain peak an' maybe one day there will be snow on it." The old man picked up the empty coffeepot from beside the fire. "Down here, I'd soon be forgotten like the grounds in this pot. Up there, well, someday I'll come back down again—only I'll be molten lava, white-hot an' flowing an' alive." Shorty put the pot back down again. "I believe these things."

The Gunfighter shook his head, grinning. "Old man, you're nuts."

"Hell," said Johnny Blue suddenly, "I'll take you up there. You said if we do it, you'll have your woman take us to this Li'l Emily gal. I don't want to spend any longer in these mountains than I have to, an' if Emily can get us to where we're going faster, I'm all for it."

"Oh, she'll get you to where you're goin' faster," Shorty said. "Depend on it."

I rose to my feet. "I'm goin' with you, Blue Boy."

"How come," asked Johnny Blue, "I don't find that reassuring?"

"Because you lack trust," I said. "That's always been your problem an' it always will be."

It was still a ways before noon when me and Johnny Blue, Shorty, and the Lipan woman set off to climb the mountain. Shorty told us he'd stashed all manner of canned beans and meat and peaches in the cave and that nearby water trickled from a natural spring. "I won't send you boys away hungry," he said.

Doc, who was always much affected by such things, wept copiously and declared that death was always the saddest parting, and would have insisted on singing "Auld Lang Syne" again had not Johnny Blue told him he didn't understand a single word of that song and that he'd enjoyed about all of it he could stand.

Sir John, more practically, told Shorty to keep his rifle close to hand.

"Toward the end, the pain will be more than you can bear, old chap," he said. "I think you know what I'm telling you."

Shorty nodded. "Thank you for your concern. I know what you're saying an' I'll keep my ol' Henry close by."

On this melancholy note, we headed up the mountain slope; me—brave, handsome, and intrepid as always—leading the way.

At first the climb was relatively easy going, and despite his ill health and obvious weakness, Shorty was still spry. In the days before he became sick, him and his

Apache *compadres* must have climbed around these peaks like mountain goats.

As the sun rose higher in the sky it got hotter and hotter and soon we were all drenched in sweat. Only the Lipan woman seemed undisturbed, her face expressionless as she climbed. The slope was steep and in places we had to navigate sheer walls of burning rock using the slenderest of ledges as hand- and footholds. It was a terrible place to fall from, and as Shorty said, that wasn't the worst part—the landing would be the real problem.

At midday we stopped and sheltered from the sun under an overhanging slab of rock crowned by a stunted juniper, and shared the last of the water in our canteen. This time the Lipan woman took the canteen from my hand, so I guess she figgered we were helping her man and were friends.

After a few minutes' rest, we climbed again, heading upward into a colorless sky that hung above our heads like a sheet of white-hot steel.

Shorty was now gasping for breath, because we were maybe six thousand feet above ground level and the air was getting thinner. The old man's face was ashen gray, but his jaw was set and determined and there was no give in him.

Johnny Blue scrambled up beside me as we were navigating a ridge of rock that jutted maybe thirty feet right out from the side of the mountain and said: "I'd never have guessed that a man can catch the lunatic disease from another lunatic."

I opened my mouth to speak, but he held up a hand and said: "Next time I volunteer for something like this, shoot me."

"Where?" I asked.

"Anywhere but up the ass."

The higher we climbed, the more I wondered how ol' Juh and them other Apaches had gotten Shorty's coffin up this mountain. They must have been a tough bunch of Indians, and that's a natural fact.

Boys, if you ever take the notion to climb a mountain, lie down on your bunk until it goes away. It's no way for a good Christian to behave.

By the time we reached Shorty's cave, the day was shading into late afternoon and the air was thin and hard to breathe. My hands and knees were scraped raw from the climb and my new shirt and pants were torn and stained.

The old man lay flat on his back for a long time and for a minute I thought he was a goner, but he rose unsteadily to his feet and, after a few moments' pause, beckoned me and Johnny Blue to follow him into the cave.

The coffin was exactly as the old man described, and apart from a few dings and scratches, it looked as good as new, its silver fittings still bright and shiny.

"Ain't she a beaut?" Shorty asked proudly. "A man can go in style in somethin' like that."

"Sure enough," I said. "A man can go out in high fashion in a fancy buryin' crate like that."

I looked closer and read a little square plate attached to the coffin lid. It said:

Ebenezer Harris
Born Baton Rouge, Louisiana, 1827
Died

"Now I can finally finish that," Shorty said. He took his bowie knife from his belt and after the word "Died" he scratched with the point:

Mexico, real sune

All this was the work of a moment, and afterward the old man stepped back to admire his handiwork. Satisfied, he smiled and said: "I'm shore much obliged to you boys for being here."

"Hell," exclaimed Johnny Blue, "you didn't need us. You did it your ownself."

"I know, but it was a comfort to know that you two was there if'n I needed he'p."

I didn't want Shorty to think he was beholden to us, him coming up here to die an' all, so I said I was real hungry and Shorty said, "We can fix that," and so he did.

There were plenty of cans of food in the cave and a coffeepot and even some firewood. The old man had the Apache way of making a fire out of a couple of twigs and faith, and despite the thin air, he quickly made a tasty stew of corned beef, beans, and peaches and boiled up a pot of coffee.

After we'd eaten, the old man put his hand on my shoulder and said: "You boys better be startin' back now afore it gets dark. Take my woman with you an' see she comes to no harm. She's young and she still needs teachin'."

At this, the Lipan woman, who obviously understood American, began to chant in a low, slender voice, her face upturned to the sky.

Shorty looked at the woman and nodded. "She's singin' my death song. She's been a good woman to me this past ten year an' this is the last thing she'll ever do for me."

After the death song was over, it truly was time to leave.

Johnny Blue, who could on occasion be a kindly soul, took Shorty by the arm and said: "Now, you pay heed to what that English doctor told you. When the pain gets too bad, lie in your coffin then take up that Henry an' blow your brains out through the back of your head. Old-timer, them's words of wisdom."

Now these sentiments, so tenderly spoken and so sincerely meant, started tears in Shorty's eyes and in mine, too. I put my arm around the old man's thin shoulders and we stood there and blubbered like babies, each of us leaning into that hot afternoon with an overdose of woe. I thought I caught the glint of a single tear in the eye of the Lipan woman and even Johnny Blue looked downcast and kicked at the loose gravel under his feet.

As we left, me and Johnny Blue looked back and saw Shorty raise his arm in farewell. Moved as we were, we gave that brave old man three hearty "Huzzahs!" and so we left him.

I recollect hoping that his spirit would stay up there, looking out over the high Sierras, a-thinking about the good old days. I figured maybe Cottontail would join him up there and tell him about her whoring days and maybe they'd have many a laugh together.

I didn't know if it would happen exactly like that, but I surely hoped it would.

"Someday, maybe a hundred years from now, some feller who can write down words on paper will come across Shorty's rotted coffin up there on the mountain and wonder at it and decide to tell the old man's story," I said to Johnny Blue, a lump in my throat. "I don't know if it will happen that way, but I kinda like to think it might."

Johnny Blue grunted and said: "Maybe so."

But little did we know that this wasn't the end of Shorty's story, and that after many trials and tribulations, we'd live to see a dead man walk again.

As we started down the mountain, the Lipan woman trailing behind us, Johnny Blue said: "Maybe we should have waited until mornin'. I sure wouldn't want to be stuck on this mountain come dark."

I shook my head at him. "Nah, it's a lot faster goin' down than it is climbing up. We'll be back at camp afore dark."

Doubt clouded Johnny Blue's face and he said, all things considered, especially me being a lunatic an' all, he wasn't too sure about that.

"Trust me," I said.

Sixteen

The farther west you go in the Sierras, the rarer thunderstorms become, but when they hit, they hit hard.

And this one was a pip.

Me and Johnny Blue and the Lipan woman huddled in the lee of a massive rock that had rolled from the top of the mountain in ancient times, our shoulders hunched against the cold, pelting rain.

Around us lightning forged from blue steel flashed from peak to peak and the bare, rain-washed mountainside gleamed like a gun barrel. Thunder rumbled in the canyons as though colossal boulders were being bowled between their stone walls and the ragged, gusting wind smelled of burning sulfur like we were getting a whiff of hell.

We were in a miserable, dismal spot and we couldn't stay there. We had to make our way down to our camp or die up there of exposure or a lightning strike.

BLAM!

"What the hell—" Johnny Blue began.

"That ain't thunder, it was a gunshot," I yelled above the din of the storm.

BLAM! BLAM!

Shots bounced off the rock where we huddled, whining away into the night, angry and disappointed.

Lightning flashed. A man in a yellow slicker fired at us, cranked a round, and fired again. Another man was off to my right, laboring up the slope toward our position, rifle in hand.

I know most of you boys have been in a shooting scrape, but for them as hasn't, let me tell you that gunfighting is a lot different from shooting at empty bean cans by a riverbank.

When you're half-scared to death like I was that night, you just take the Colt in both hands, straight-arm it way out in front, point it in the general direction of them that's shooting at you, and cut 'er loose.

And that's what I did.

I didn't hit anybody and the muzzle flash blinded me so bad, my next shot went nowhere. Beside me, Johnny Blue fired, then fired again.

As far as I could tell, he did no execution among the oncoming outlaws, either.

"Who the hell are those guys?" Johnny Blue yelled into my ear.

"They must be Clemente's boys," I yelled back. "We was so sure they was racing ahead to get at the gold, we never figgered they'd double back an' hit us."

"They got us pinned here. We can't go back up an' we sure as hell can't go down," Johnny Blue said. "What do we do now?"

I shook my head at him, though it was so dark I doubted he saw it. "I don't know," I said.

"Oh great," said my somber sidekick. "This is just peachy."

Johnny Blue fumbled at his shell belt and then fed

rounds into the cylinder of his Colt. If anything, the rain had gotten heavier—a shifting curtain of gray that had closed over the mountain and hissed like an angry snake.

"One thing I do know," I said after a few moments, "is that we can't stay here."

I turned and looked at the Lipan woman. Her eyes were wide and frightened, but she was trying real hard not to let her fear show. I smiled at her, but she just ignored me and didn't smile back.

"Where are they?" Johnny Blue asked.

"Out there, hunkered down an' waitin' for us to make a move," I said. "If we leave the shelter of this rock they could cut us down real easy."

"But damn it, you just said we can't stay here," Johnny Blue snapped angrily.

"I know," I said. "But we can't move, either."

"Then what the hell do we do now?"

"I don't know," I said.

"Oh great," said Johnny Blue.

It was the woman who came to our rescue.

She got so close to me I could smell her—a wild mix of desert sage, wood smoke, and harsh lye soap, combined with the musky odor of her soaked buckskin dress and long hair, which clung to her shoulders and back in thick wet strands.

The woman beckoned to me to follow; motioned downward with the palm of her hand that I should stay low. She crawled away, and I followed, Johnny Blue close behind me.

Now, as the lightning forked over the mountaintop, I saw where she was taking us. There was a shallow depression on the slope just above us that ran straight for about twenty yards, then seemed to curve downward toward the base of the mountain. It wasn't much of a depression—more like a worn deer track or ancient Indian trail—but it was all the cover we were likely to find. The Lipan woman was already in the track, creeping along on her belly, and I motioned Johnny Blue to follow her while I took up the rear.

I turned and caught a flash of yellow slicker among the rocks below and snapped off a quick shot.

A bullet hammered into the boulder where we'd been hiding, followed by another. I fired a second time, but I was again shooting blind because of my gun flashes, and I doubt that I hit anybody.

One day a real smart feller will invent a cartridge that doesn't blind a man every time he takes a shot at some ranny in the dark. When he does, it will be a blessing to all mankind, and that's a natural fact.

I Injuned after Johnny Blue and bellied along the depression, my belt buckles scraping along the rock underneath me. Behind me I heard a man yell, followed by a shot. Then more voices were raised, calling out to each other as they tried to figger where we were hiding.

The rain pelted down and I was soaked to the skin, shivering now as the chill of my wet clothes settled in on me. I followed the depression until it suddenly sloped downward, and then got to my feet. The hue and cry was still going on behind me and I guessed they still didn't realize how we'd given them the slip.

The downward slope of the narrow track was steep and I half walked, half slid my way down—that is, until I crashed into Johnny Blue's back.

That rash rider yelled, "What the hell!" then spun around, his gun coming up fast.

"Hold your fire!" I yelled. "It's me."

"Hell," Johnny Blue growled, "when I heard all the shootin' back there, I thought fer sure you was a goner."

"No," I said, smiling. "Good news! I'm alive an' pretty well."

"You sure you ain't shot through the lungs an' maybe don't know it yet?" Johnny Blue asked, and he sounded real hopeful.

"Good as new," I said.

"Well, ain't that a kick in the ass," said my compassionate *compadre*.

I started to say something real sharp, but Johnny Blue cut me off. "We got a problem," he said.

"What?"

"That!"

Johnny Blue pointed into the darkness. I saw a solid wall of rock rising into the night, running with rain, but little else.

"I can't see nothin'," I said.

"You will," Johnny Blue said. "Wait until the next lightning flash."

The way that storm was raging, I didn't have to wait for long.

The lightning lit up the rock wall that rose vertically for about three hundred feet. From where we stood it plunged downward another three hundred feet or so into a narrow, rock-strewn gully.

"We got to cross that," Johnny Blue said.

"The hell we do."

"It's either that or wait until those bandits figger out where we are and come down here and finish us off," Johnny Blue said. "The woman calls that down there Devil Canyon because the Apaches believed it was haunted by demons. She says even Geronimo, who was scared of nothin', wouldn't go near the canyon. In fact, he'd ride three days out of his way to avoid it."

"She talks to you?" I asked in surprise.

"Of course she talks to me," Johnny Blue said. "She just don't talk to white men."

I stood there for a while and studied on our problem, the rattling rain drumming on my hat.

Then I said: "How do we get across a sheer rock face? It can't be done."

"The woman says there's a ledge across the rock wall, only about a man's-palm wide," Johnny Blue said. "She says when she was a younker, she saw an Apache boy walk across, proving how brave he was an' all."

"Me, I ain't that brave," I said.

Johnny Blue nodded. "Never figgered you was. Well anyhoo, me an' the woman are headin' across right now afore Clemente's boys get here. You load up your six gun an' wait for them an' make a right good fight of it. An' listen—die game. I don't want to be hearin' from folks later that my pardner went down squealin' like a baby pig caught under a gate."

I swallowed hard, and after a few moments said: "Tell the woman to lead the way. I'll be right behind you."

Johnny Blue looked at me and shook his head. "Well, ain't that another kick in the ass."

The Lipan woman led the way to the rock face, then tested the darkness with her foot. Lightning flashed among the surrounding peaks as she stretched out and stepped onto the ledge, clinging to its narrow width with her moccasin-clad feet. Johnny Blue followed, slowly toeing along the ledge after her. Then I went. Rain hammered at me, pelting and remorseless, determined not to give me the slightest break.

This wasn't work for boots. Here and there the ledge was narrower than Johnny Blue had said, in some places only an inch or two wide. Handholds on the rock wall were few and far between, and those I found were slick with rain.

As I inched my way along, scared stiff as a frozen rope, lightning forked and thunder roared and I looked down now and then into the dizzying depths of the canyon below. That was a long way to fall and a man would be broken all to horrible pieces on the rocks.

After what seemed like five long minutes tippy-toeing along the ledge, I was so occupied with my thoughts of imminent disaster and bloody death that I didn't realize the woman and Johnny Blue had suddenly stopped. I sidestepped into Johnny Blue and started an unfortunate chain of events that could have killed all three of us.

Boys, you ever been in a train yard when the locomotive hits a freight wagon, and that wagon bumps into another, then that one hits another even harder and so on down the line?

Well, that's what it was like when I bumped Johnny Blue. He bounced away from me and hit the woman even harder, then they both teetered on the ledge, windmilling their arms, and Johnny Blue yelled: "*Yeeeeaaaaaaaa!*"

The Lipan woman, wearing moccasins, recovered her balance very quickly. She reached out real fast and put an arm around Johnny Blue's waist, helping to steady that panicking puncher. Johnny Blue swung back toward the wall and his clawing hands dug into the rock. I swear he must have poked ten holes an inch deep into that hard granite.

His eyes bugging, he turned his head to me and yelled: "Hell, man, are you trying to murder us?"

"It was a accident," I said. "No need to be so tetchy."

"Tetchy!" Johnny Blue yelled. "If you was ten thousand feet up the side of a mountain a-holdin' on to a ledge a inch wide with a dangerous lunatic trying his best to kill you, wouldn't you be just a mite tetchy?"

"It was a accident," I said stubbornly. "I was studyin' on what would happen if I fell when you stopped without warning, so you got no call to be sayin' bad things about me."

"I swear," said Johnny Blue, "if we ever get off this here mountain alive I'm gonna shoot you through both lungs an' then punch your head."

I was about to say something right testy along the lines of how he wasn't buffaloing me on account of how he couldn't shade me on his best day anyhow, and that he shouldn't always be threatening folks and shootin' them through the lungs an' sich. But I never got the chance.

A bullet *spaaang*ed off the rock above my head, then another clipped chips of stone from the ledge by the toe of my right boot.

I peered through the streaming rain, but it was too dark to see anything. Then I caught the muzzle flash of a rifle, and a bullet split the air above my head.

"They found us!" Johnny Blue yelled, stating what was right then real obvious to everybody.

"Not far," the woman called out to us. "Just a little more."

Time after time, lightning lit up the whole mountainside and the teeming rain battered at us, driven by a gusting wind that had sprung up out of nowhere.

Chewing on a mouthful of my own heart I toed along the ledge after Johnny Blue and the woman, desperately clinging to handholds that were often there only in my imagination and all the time knowing that just one slip would send me plunging to bloody, smashing death on the rocks below.

Clemente's men had stopped shooting, maybe driven to shelter by the rain that was starting in to be even heavier than before, but I wasn't about to stake my life on that possibility. They could be standing there waiting for the flash of a lightning bolt so they could take another shot at us.

Then Johnny Blue stopped suddenly and let rip a mighty oath.

"What's wrong?" I asked, dreading the answer.

"The ledge peters out, here," he replied, rain pouring off the brim of his hat. "We got to jump for it."

The Lipan woman, being as agile as a mountain goat, had already made the terrifying leap and she urgently beckoned to us to come across.

"How big a jump?" I asked.

Johnny Blue shook his head at me. "Dunno. Three feet, maybe."

Now, as you boys know, I'm just a little feller— though well-made and powerful handsome for all that— so for me a three-foot jump in the dark onto a ledge an inch or two wide was no bargain.

It seemed like Johnny Blue read my thoughts, because he said: "The ledge is some wider on the other side. So this is a cinch."

"How much wider?" I asked. But I was talking to thin air because Johnny Blue had already made the jump and was now standing on the other side, looking back at me.

Thunder crashed and a searing white bolt of lightning struck with incredible venom higher up the mountain, and my head and shoulders were suddenly battered by a shattering shower of shale and rock.

I desperately clung to the rock face, my toes barely holding on to the ledge, head bent against the pounding deluge of dirt and stone. Then, after what seemed like an eternity, a single small rock bounced off the brim of my hat and it was over.

"Jump!" Johnny Blue yelled. "Or you'll die for sure!"

"Will you catch me?" I yelled. "You better catch me."

"Sure, I'll catch you," returned my *compadre*.

Rainwater cascaded off the brim of my hat as I looked down at the terrifying leap I had to make. Three hundred feet below, death waited. Behind me, death waited. There was nowhere to go. I had to jump.

"Blue Boy, all them bad things you said about me, I mean, shootin' me through the lungs an' sich," I hollered over the roar of the storm, "did you mean them?"

"Nah," Johnny Blue hollered back. "Now jump!"

"Will you be sure to catch me?"

That dusky drover's teeth flashed white as he grinned. "Trust me," he said.

I jumped.

Seventeen

I was in the air for what seemed like forever, then the toe of my right boot was scrabbling for footing on the wet, slippery rim of the ledge.

I felt myself fall backward, but then a strong hand grasped me by the front of my shirt and hauled me to safety.

Johnny Blue had been right. Here the ledge was much wider, maybe by a foot, and beyond the rise of the rock face, just a few yards away, it broadened out into a wide trail that seemed to descend down the side of the mountain.

"I never want to do something like that again," I said. "As long as I live I'll never do somethin' like that again."

Johnny Blue grinned, rain streaming down his face. "You're lucky I was there. If I hadn't been, you'd be lying in the canyon right now, all bloody an' broken."

"I knew you'd catch me," I said sincerely. "I never doubted you for a second."

"Well," said Johnny Blue, "I had time to study on it for a spell while you was in the air. I mean, catch or no catch. But then I thought, well, what the hell, he's just a poor lunatic and he ain't to be blamed for what he does. So I caught you after all."

Now I didn't know if Johnny Blue was just joshing me or not, but I let the thing go. There are times when a man's better not knowing the truth.

That jump had frightened me so much, my knees were shaking and I had a bellyful of bedsprings. But I still had something else to do. I shucked my Colt and emptied it in the direction of Clemente's gunmen. I didn't know if they were still there, but just blazing away seemed like a little payback for scaring me out of ten years' growth.

As I reholstered my gun, Johnny Blue shook his head at me and said: "You're one mighty strange ranny."

Then, at last, we took the path down the mountain.

I dreaded what I was going to find back at our camp. Clemente and his outlaws had struck without warning and I doubted that even the Gunfighter's skills would have been enough to fight off a surprise attack.

As we drew closer to where we'd left the others my imagination was working overtime and in my mind's eye I saw Doc and Sir John lying dead, their white faces and staring eyes upturned to the pouring rain.

It was a worrisome thing.

"Step easy," Johnny Blue said. "Them boys are liable to be spooked an' they'll shoot first an' identify the dear departed later."

He walked with his arm around the slim waist of the Lipan woman, and if I was any judge, that young lady had lost no time in forgetting about Shorty. I'm not putting down the fairer sex. I mean, life goes on, but she could have mourned at least for a day or two, seems to me.

We rounded an outcropping of rock and approached

the camp, then froze in our tracks as Doc's voice hollered to stand right where we were or there'd be hell to pay.

"I got me a Sharps big .50," Doc hollered. "An' she don't miss."

"Doc!" I yelled. "It's me and the others. We just come down off the mountain an' we're orphans from the storm."

"Come ahead," Doc yelled, "but don't make no fancy moves. I can be almighty sudden."

We walked on slowly, our hands well away from our guns and Doc stepped into the open, his Sharps pointed right at us. A hard, slanting rain hammered off Doc's slicker and poured off the narrow brim of his plug hat, but he looked determined and mean as a cornered cotton-mouth.

"Oh," he said finally, "it is you."

"Of course it's me," I said. "Hell, man, didn't you recognize my voice?"

"Voices can be impersonated," returned Doc. "A man in my position in life don't take no chances."

"How are the others?" This from Johnny Blue.

"We're all alive, though Sir John got nicked on the arm. It ain't bad." Doc laid his rifle on his shoulder. "They scattered the horses to hell an' gone an' it's gonna take all day tomorrow to round 'em up. The Gunfighter says he ain't goin' nowhere without his white hoss, which is probably exactly what Clemente wanted. Now he'll be well ahead of us an' we'll never catch up."

"You get any of the bandits?" I asked.

Doc shook his head. "Nah. The Gunfighter was out of it. He was putting cream on his face when the outlaws hit an' his hands were so slick he couldn't hold on to his Colts. It was him who shot the Englishman, on account of how his guns kept a-twistin' around in his greasy mitts an' he was spraying bullets everywhere."

Doc looked at us shrewdly. "You three look like you been through the mill. What happened?"

Briefly I told him about our run-in with the bandits and our hair-raising descent from the mountain, and after I was done Doc nodded then said: "Get any of them?"

I shook my head at him. "I don't think so. It was dark."

"Man's got to learn to shoot in the dark," Doc said. "You get into a scrape in a saloon an' the first shots fired blow out all the oil lamps. Next thing you know, you can't even see a ranny standin' six feet in front of you." He pointed an accusing finger at me. "A man should learn how to shoot in the dark is all I'm sayin'."

I wanted to say, "Well, hell, you wasn't up that mountain," but I didn't. I just smiled and said: "Doc, I'll sure keep that in mind." Seemed to me Doc had enough worries right at that moment without me arguing with him.

When we arrived at the camp—if a dead fire and a sea of mud describes such—Sir John endeavored to smile at us, though his arm was bandaged and he seemed a little white around the gills.

The Gunfighter, on the other hand, had his brace of pistols buckled around his waist and was angrily uttering vile oaths, dreadful to hear.

"At first light we go after my horse," he said to me by way of greeting. "I set store by that animal."

I soon saw the source of his displeasure and it wasn't only the missing horse that was troubling him. His straw hat with the pink ribbon lay trampled into the mud by the passing of many hooves.

The Gunfighter followed my eyes and said: "It was shot right off my head. Hun Larrikin did it an' now me an' him has another score to settle." The Gunfighter bent and picked up the muddy, battered hat. "I'm gonna feed this to him straw by straw afore I kill him."

With another dreadful oath, the Gunfighter turned on his heel and splashed away from me through the mud.

Meanwhile, Doc had found the coffeepot. Thankfully it was still intact and this time there was plenty of water to fill it. Getting a fire going was a bigger problem, since it was still raining, though not near as heavy as before, and everything was soaked.

The rain had caused a flash flood in a gully to the south of the camp and a lot of wood from dead trees higher up the mountains had washed down with the torrent. Doc gathered the driest twigs he could find and coaxed them into a smoky fire he could cover with his plug hat. But there was enough flame to boil the coffee, and right at that moment hot coffee is what we needed.

Later, we sat around in the rain with our coffee and, now that Doc was doing nothing to protect it, miserably watched the fire sizzle into a single trail of smoke, then nothing.

"Them outlaws must have had a man posted somewhere watching our every move," Doc said, glaring at the surrounding mountains like a tired old wolf. "When we split up, I guess they decided to strike.

"They hit us just as the thunderstorm started," Doc continued gloomily. "They just come ridin' into the camp and started blazing away. But it became pretty clear that killin' us wasn't their main aim. They wanted to stampede the horses an' set us afoot.

"The Gunfighter, because of his face cream"—he cast an accusing gaze at the Gunfighter, but the man just gave an unrepentant shrug—"was out of it, but Clemente didn't know that. The bandits gave him a wide berth and that probably saved the rest of us from worse harm."

"I guess Clemente figgered we was gettin' too close," Johnny Blue said, trying to build a smoke with wet paper. "He's probably ridin' right now and figgers to get at the gold long before we do."

"If Clemente gets the gold, we could take it from him," the Gunfighter said. "Shouldn't be too difficult."

"Hell, man," said Doc irritably, "there's ten of them, all good with a gun, including that Hun Larrikin feller you're always talkin' about."

The Gunfighter nodded. "Hun is a problem. He's no bargain and best left alone." He winked at Doc. "But I don't intend to leave him alone."

"You're forgettin' something, Doc," I said.

"And what's that, pray?"

"Li'l Emily. Remember, Shorty said she'd show us a faster route to the gold an' that the Lipan woman here knows where she is."

Doc slapped the side of his bald head. "Damn me, I forgot all about that Li'l Emily gal." He turned to the Lipan woman, who was sitting hip-to-hip with Johnny Blue. "Can you lead us to her?"

The woman looked at Johnny Blue and said: "I can take you to Li'l Emily."

Johnny Blue nodded. "She says she'll take us to Li'l Emily."

"Hell," said Doc, his irritability growing by the moment, "I heard her fine. I ain't deef."

The Gunfighter blew on a nail he was filing, spread out his fingers, and tilted his glossy head to admire his handiwork. "At first light we'll round up the horses and then see this Emily woman," he said. "But if there's a shortcut through these mountains, I sure as hell don't see it."

"She's our only hope," observed Doc, looking so down in the mouth he could have eaten oats out of a churn. "I just trust that we reach the ol' gal in time else all our sacrifice has been for nothing."

"Well," I said, trying to cheer everybody up, "all things considered, it could be worse."

Right then the heavens opened and the pelting rain battered down on us. I watched as Johnny Blue took his tally book from his shirt pocket, sighed deeply, and chewed on the end of his stub of pencil, eyes turned upward like he was deep in thought.

"Don't think I don't know what you're doin'," I said, rain pouring off the brim of my hat in torrents.

"What am I doin'?" asked Johnny Blue innocently, cupping his hand over his book to shelter it from the downpour.

"You're a-settin' there, making a list of my faults."

That rueful rider nodded and allowed that this was indeed the case.

A few moments passed while Johnny Blue chewed on his pencil, deep in thought, so I said finally: "Well, how many have you got?"

"Just the one so far," returned Johnny Blue. "It's spelled l-u-n-a-t-i-c, an' the trouble is, it pretty much seems to cover all the others."

At first light we went out after the horses. Thankfully, they hadn't wandered far in the storm and by noon we'd rounded up me and Johnny Blue's mounts and the Gunfighter's white stallion and we'd taken to the trail again, following the rapid, sway-hipped walk of the Lipan woman.

We rode through a wide gulch between the base of two mountains the woman called the San Jorge Canyon and then skirted the shallow, much eroded Mesa de Chahal, holding to the bayonet grass and cactus-strewn desert country that surrounded it. The rain had stopped and the sun came out as the clouds parted, its heat drying our soaked clothes within minutes.

Once we'd left the mesa three miles behind us, we stopped in the meager shade of a creosote bush beside a narrow creek that still held a few inches of rainwater, then boiled up some coffee and ate the last of our supplies—a few strips of salt pork that smelled bad and tasted worse.

"The Lipan woman says another hour's ride and we'll come across an old wagon road the Spaniards used for years," Johnny Blue said. "We follow the road for two, maybe three miles an' it will take us right to Li'l Emily."

"Don't that Indian gal have a name?" asked the Gunfighter irritably. "Can't you call her something else besides 'the Lipan woman'?"

"Yes," said Johnny Blue, rolling a cigarette. He added nothing else, to the Gunfighter's obvious chagrin.

"We're getting close to my wife, I can feel it," said Sir John, who had been anxious to speak. Being no longer a young man, the harrowing and exhausting events of recent days—not least among them being shot by the Gunfighter—had taken their toll on him and his face was strained, ashen with fatigue.

"Be assured, Sir John," said Doc, "that once this Li'l Emily person has led us to the gold, we will spare no effort to free your wife and return her to the safety of your bosom and the security of the connubial bed."

"Most kindly said, sir," returned the Englishman, "and the tender sentiment is much appreciated."

"You are most welcome, sir," said Doc. "I, too—though only temporarily, I trust—am bereft of those marital delights that I've grown to enjoy to the very fullest extent. You have," continued Doc with a shake of the head and admirable sincerity, "my sympathy, sir."

"And you, sir, have mine," returned Sir John.

Thus mutually assured, the two men sipped their coffee and stared into the dying fire, and there they remained, each busy with his own thoughts, until it was time to saddle up and ride once again.

The Lipan woman was right about the wagon road.

It wasn't much, as roads go: just two narrow, parallel depressions worn into the floor of the desert by the passage of many wagons over long years. The Lipan woman told Johnny Blue that twenty years earlier the French had used this road. They had planned to mine silver in the mountains but it had come to nothing.

We followed this track for about two miles, then urged on our double-burdened horses as it rose gradually, winding around the side of a tall, stepped mountain built of alternating layers of red, brown, and dark gray—almost black—rock. To accommodate the passage of wagons, the French had taken advantage of the mountain's natural steps as a roadway, but here and there short stretches had been blasted out of the slope itself. In recent years talus had slid from higher up the peak in a series of inverted Vs and blocked the road in several places. Dismounting, we led the reluctant horses around the talus slides and climbed higher.

"Hell," said the Gunfighter, taking off his hat and wiping sweat from his brow with the back of his hand, "that Emily gal sure picked an out of the way place to call home."

Doc was worried and it showed.

"It don't seem right, a little gal livin' away out here," he said. He turned to Johnny Blue. "Ask that Apache woman if we're gettin' close."

Johnny Blue took the woman aside and they talked at some length. Then he walked back to Doc and the rest of us and said: "We're real close. She says Shorty Harris told her this road was built during the time of Napoleon the Third, whoever he was, an' it leads to an abandoned settlement on a shelf of rock just around the other side of the mountain."

Sir John cleared his throat. "If you will pardon my intrusion, some twenty-odd years ago, if I recall my history correctly, just after the end of your Civil War, Napoleon the Third of France made a determined attempt to control Mexico. He placed a puppet emperor on the throne—an Austrian archduke named Maximilian—and planned to rule the country through him.

"Unfortunately for Napoleon, in 1867 the United States enforced the Monroe Doctrine, which forbids European intervention in the Americas, and forced him to withdraw his troops. He was sent packing back to France with his tail between his legs.

"Meanwhile, the wretched Maximilian, deprived of French bayonets, was captured by the Mexican president Benito Juarez and shot by firing squad.

"I suspect," continued Sir John, "that this wagon road was built by Napoleon's confounded Frenchies, hoping the silver they found in the Sierras would finance Maximilian's war against Juarez."

Doc shook his head at the Englishman. "There ain't no silver in this part of the Sierras. Come to that, no gold either, except that which is hidden away by outlaws."

"I suspect," said Sir John, "the late, unlamented Maximilian may have learned that to his cost."

"Well," said Doc, "let us proceed on our way around the mountain and find this settlement and Miss Emily, if such exist. Time is now of the essence."

Leading the horses, we followed the road around the mountain, and after a few minutes saw the old French settlement the Lipan woman had described spread out below us.

An L-shaped notch about three acres in extent had been blasted out of the side of the mountain and the wagon road ran down a fairly steep incline to its base. But what took my breath away was the trestle bridge that began at the notch and spanned a wide gorge between this peak and the next.

As far as I could tell, there were other bridges built from mountain to mountain, fading into the distance, and beside me Johnny Blue whistled in admiration.

"Hell, look at them tracks. This was a whole railroad built through the mountains."

The tracks seemed to begin inside a dilapidated little engine shed and next to the shed stood a water tower, its timbers green with age but seemingly still functional. There were a few other shacks, their roofs sagging, and their empty windows and doors gaping at us in surprise. Scattered junipers threw what shade they could into a corral behind a barn of curling timber planks slanting crazily on its foundation.

One time when I was riding for the old Rafter-H brand in Texas I took part in a trail drive to Dodge. I was a younker then, no more than fourteen or so, and considerably less than man-grown. We'd just crossed the Kansas line and I was out after strays, hazing them back to the main herd, when I come across an empty town. There were no people, just dilapidated buildings gazing blankly at each other from either side of a single street. There was a false-fronted saloon with a sign that said THE CATTLE-MAN'S PALACE. The sign was still tacked to the saloon's front on one side, the other side slanting down, its corner on the boardwalk. Folks had moved in here, hoping the railroad would build a spur to their town. But it had never happened. When the railroad bypassed them, they just up and left, leaving the town behind. Now the buildings just waited in the sun, not falling down, but fading away into the prairie, the town growing fainter and fainter with each passing year, like one of them old daguerreotype pictures that fades and fades until eventually there is nothing left.

One of the drovers on the drive told me I'd seen a ghost town, and before I was much older, I'd see more. "Cow towns, some of them," he said, "but most times they're mining towns. The mines eventually played out and the miners left. Ain't nothin' remainin' but empty buildings and empty memories a man can hear whispered in the wind when he lies awake an' still in his blankets of a night."

Now I said to the others: "This is a ghost town. There ain't nobody here."

"Emily is here," the Lipan woman said to Johnny Blue. She pointed to the engine shed. "That is her home."

"Then I believe," observed Doc, "that we have at last discovered the ol' gal's whereabouts."

"Lookee," said the Gunfighter, "over there by the corral, there's a flag flyin'."

"What kind of flag is that?" Johnny Blue asked. "I ain't seen that one before. Is it Mexican?"

All I could do was shrug my shoulders in reply, but again Sir John stepped up and filled in the gap in my knowledge.

"It's the French Tricolor," he observed. "Much faded and tattered, but it's Froggy all right."

The Englishman stood there musing for a while, then added: "Good soldier, the Frog—very—I mean, when he's well led. But he's never cared much for the bayonet in the belly. That's why we beat him at Waterloo, you know. The British soldier, now, he can take the bayonet in the belly, doesn't bother him in the slightest. Fine chap, the British soldier."

"You mean that flag's been flyin' there since the French left?" inquired Doc. "Lemme see, that's nigh on twenty-five years ago."

" 'Pon my soul, it does seem rather strange," replied Sir John. "But there's no other explanation, unless this Emily person has taken care of it all this time."

"Well," said Doc, "let's go find out fer sure."

We led the horses down the grade into the settlement and when we were close enough to the engine shed, Doc cupped a hand to his mouth and hollered: "*Cooee*, Miss Emily!"

There was no answer.

"Maybe the ol' gal's sleeping," the Gunfighter suggested. "You want maybe I should put a couple of balls through that there shed an' wake her up?"

"You'll do no such thing," said Doc sharply. "She ain't

gonna show us no shortcut to the gold with a bullet in her."

Once again Doc cupped his hand to his mouth and yelled in the same manner as before. And once again his cry met with the same result. Silence.

"Hell," I said, "enough of this, I'm goin' in there."

"You be careful, boy," warned Doc. "She could be set-tin' in there with a rifle aimed right at your belly. Woman like her, alone in this wilderness, she's bound to have met plenty of enemies an' mighty few friends."

Made a mite uneasy by Doc's caution, I shucked my Colt and walked to the engine shed. I put my hand on the door and was about to push it open when a harsh, commanding voice stopped me in my tracks.

"Attention! Laches vos armes at rendez-vous!"

I turned my head slowly and beheld a strange sight.

A soldier in a ragged blue uniform, a battered kepi on his head, was advancing purposefully toward me. He looked like a comic character out of one of them Gilbert and Sullivan operettas I'd seen in Dodge and Abilene a time or two.

But there was nothing comical about the musket he held in his hands and the long, sharp bayonet at the end of it.

And like the French, right then I didn't much care for a bayonet in the belly, either.

Eighteen

"It's a Frenchy, by God!" exclaimed Sir John. "As I live and breathe it's a Frenchy here."

"A dead Frenchy, you mean," declared the Gunfighter, whipping out his Colts.

But Doc, throwing up his hands in alarm, interposed himself between the Gunfighter and the Frenchman. "No! No! Don't shoot him!" he yelled. "He could be a friend of Li'l Emily's."

The soldier turned to Doc, his bayoneted musket at the ready, a sly look on his little rodent face. "Li'l Emily? What do you want with Li'l Emily?"

"You speak American!" I exclaimed.

The little man nodded. "And Spanish and some Apache."

"We need Li'l Emily's help," declared Doc, cutting to the heart of the matter as he reached out a hand to gently push the bayonet away from his chest. "We were told we'd find her here."

"*Non!*" the soldier said vehemently, swinging the bayonet back toward Doc's brisket. "I am Li'l Emily's protector. I guard her day and night."

I could see understanding dawn on Doc and the others and it was Sir John who gave it voice.

"How long have you been keeping guard here, Corporal?" he asked briskly.

"Ah, you recognize my rank," the Frenchman said, ignoring the question. "Like me, you are a soldier I think?"

Sir John nodded. "Lieutenant colonel, late of Her Britannic Majesty's Fifty-third of Foot, at your service." His face softened. "Now, see here my good man, we mean this Emily person no harm. Will you introduce us to her like a good chap?"

"I am a soldier," the Frenchman said. He turned and pointed to the flagpole where the tattered Tricolor hung limp in the breezeless afternoon stillness. "There is my post, under the flag. I stand there from dawn until dusk— like this."

The little Frenchman—he was even smaller than me— smartly slapped his musket to his shoulder and crossed his right arm, palm down, over his chest.

"This is how I have stood every day since my captain told me, 'Corporal Deschamps, you will remain here and guard Li'l Emily until I return for her.' And this I have done. I am a soldier. This is my post."

"Hold on there, just a minute," the Gunfighter said, "you mean to tell me you've been standing guard over Li'l Emily since the French left Mexico?"

The little Frenchman looked like he'd been slapped. "What is this? What is this nonsense? The French will never leave Mexico. You are trying to play your little tricks with the mind of Corporal Jean-Pierre Deschamps."

"My dear chap," said Sir John, not unkindly, "the French were thrown out of Mexico more than twenty years ago. Maximilian is dead."

Deschamps looked at the Englishman in horror. "You are a British officer. You would not lie to me?"

"I wouldn't lie to anyone," returned Sir John stiffly. "Poor chap, you've performed your duty like a good soldier. Now you must see your duty clear to help us."

I saw the confusion in the Frenchman's face and it made him look like a befuddled little rat. He was still trying to come to terms with the fact that there was no longer a French army in Mexico and he kept shaking his head in disbelief.

"You wish to meet Li'l Emily," he said finally. "There were men here just yesterday who wanted the same thing."

"Wait!" Sir John exclaimed in the highest state of agitation. "Was there a woman with them?"

Deschamps nodded. "*Oui*, a beautiful young woman. They put her in that shed over there while they were here and took her with them when they left."

"That woman is my wife," Sir John said miserably. "Those men are bandits and they kidnapped her. I am here to get her back.

"You have my sympathy, *mon colonel*," Deschamps said. "But if it's any consolation, they got no help from Li'l Emily. They had no idea how to treat her. In the end, they tried to lead their horses across the bridge, but the horses refused to go, so they went down the mountain again."

"Where were you when all this happened?" the Gunfighter asked suspiciously.

"I hid," Deschamps said without apparent shame. "There were too many, and sometimes discretion is better than valor, though I am a brave soldier."

"Hell, man, why didn't the Apaches kill you?" the

Gunfighter asked. "Did you hide from them for twenty years?"

Deschamps shook his little shaved head. "When I stood at my post under the flag, sometimes they would come and laugh at me and throw stones." He pointed to a scar above his left eye. "That was a stone. But I stood firmly to attention and ignored them and after a while they'd go away."

"That's because you're nuts," Johnny Blue said helpfully. "An Indian won't kill a ranny who's crazy. It's heap bad medicine."

"Well," said Deschamps, taking no offense, "crazy or not, I haven't seen the Apaches in a long time."

I didn't feel this was the time to go into an explanation about the fate of the Apaches, so I said: "Well, if'n it's all the same to you, Corporal, can we meet Miss Emily now?"

The little Frenchman laid the butt of his musket on the ground at his feet and bowed his head, deep in thought. Finally he looked up and said: "Soon. You will meet her soon." He fished inside his ragged blue coat and produced an old nickel-plated watch with a yellowed dial. "It is now the regulation hour for dinner. We must eat first."

"What do you have by way of grub?" asked Doc hopefully.

Deschamps waved a hand. "The sheds are full of provisions. Even after all these years I've scarcely made a dent in them. You see, we planned to feed Mexican laborers working in the silver mines from here."

"Laborers," snorted Johnny Blue, who was sensitive about such things. "Slaves, you mean."

Deschamps shrugged and spread his hands. "Laborers, slaves . . . it is of no importance. There was no silver."

"And that's when everyone pulled out of here and left you to guard Li'l Emily," Doc said.

"*Oui,*" the Frenchman said. "This was my duty until my captain returned for her." He looked at Doc pleadingly. "*Mon Dieu,* was that really twenty years ago?"

Doc nodded. "You're a reg'lar glutton for work, Corporal Deschamps."

The Frenchman claimed there was plenty of food in the sheds, and he was right; but what it amounted to was square cans of army biscuit piled as high as the roof and a few boxes of condensed milk and corned beef, and there was some coffee in sacks.

At one time there was probably more, but Corporal Deschamps had been feeding on it for more than twenty years and the cupboard was getting mighty bare.

Me and Johnny Blue loaded up with biscuit and cans from the shed closest to the old barn and were about to leave when I noticed writing scrawled on the inside of the door with a piece of charcoal, of which there was a great deal scattered around. It said simply: JOHN—HELP ME, and it was signed, AGAT.

"Who the hell is 'Agat'?" I asked. "Another Frenchman?"

"It's Lady Agatha," Johnny Blue replied. "She didn't have time to sign her whole name before she was took from here."

"I guess we should show this to Sir John," I suggested.

Johnny Blue shook his head at me. "Don't you think he already knows she needs his help? All you'd do is upset him more, and all for nothin'. Right now there ain't a thing he can do about it."

"Do you think Perez an' them is abusin' that woman real bad?" I asked.

Johnny Blue looked at me like I was crazy. "From what I've heard, Clemente and most of his boys were Comancheros at one time or another. You know what Comanches do to captive women?"

"I can guess."

Johnny Blue nodded. "I reckon if Lady Agatha survives this, she'll never want a man to touch her again as long as she lives."

"Don't sound good for poor Sir John."

"No, it don't."

We joined the others, but kept what we'd seen in the shack to ourselves and hurriedly prepared a meal.

When the French had blasted a chunk out of the mountain, they'd uncovered a cavern inside fed by a deep underground spring. The water was brackish and smelled of sulfur, but it was sweet enough to boil for coffee.

Me and Johnny Blue pounded the army biscuit into crumbs with our rifle butts, then we mixed the crumbs with the corned beef and poured condensed milk over the mixture. Everybody agreed it made for a good meal, and even Sir John said he'd eaten worse in Africa at least once and maybe twice.

After we'd eaten and drank our coffee, which was French and good and strong, we were ready to meet Li'l Emily. Above us, the white-hot sky had become lemon in color, streaked with red, as day slowly shaded into night, and I could sense the growing impatience of Doc and Sir John as Deschamps daintily wiped at his mouth with a blue-checkered handkerchief he'd produced from a pocket.

Finally he smoothed his mustache and cocked an eyebrow in Doc's direction. "Now we have dined, I suppose you are eager to meet Li'l Emily?"

"Lead on," returned Doc heartily. "I am indeed most anxious to make the lady's acquaintance."

"Then come this way," said the Frenchman, rising to his feet. "She awaits us."

We followed Deschamps to the engine shed, where he stopped. "She awaits within," he said.

"She lives in the engine shed?" asked the Gunfighter.

The Frenchman nodded. "*Oui, mon ami*, this is her home."

There was a double door on the side of the shed and Deschamps walked over and threw it wide. He stood there looking inside for a few moments, nodded, then turned to the rest of us, beaming.

"Gentlemen, I have the great honor of presenting La Petite Emily."

We crowded into the doorway, eyes straining in the half-light of dusk. And for the first time in our lives, beheld—just a-settin' there, pretty as a picture—the legendary Li'l Emily.

Nineteen

"Hell, that's only an old engine," the Gunfighter said, disappointment writ large on his face. "That ain't nothin'."

Sir John looked stunned and opened his mouth a time or two to speak but nothing came out. Only Doc seemed unmoved, and I could see by his expression that his always-nimble brain was busily working overtime.

Li'l Emily was an old narrow-gauge 0-4-0 engine, but preserved by the dry heat of the mountains, she was in almost perfect condition. Her once proud royal blue paint had faded to the color of old denim, but her brass was polished to a bright shine, no doubt the work of the faithful Deschamps.

As if reading my mind, that worthy spoke up and said: "She was built in Birmingham, England, and my brave comrades and I dismantled her when she came off the ship in Veracruz and carried her on mules, piece by piece, into the Sierras until we reached this place. My captain was an officer of engineers, and it was he who put her back together again," he added proudly.

"Well ain't this a kick in the ass," Johnny Blue grumbled, looking accusingly at the Lipan woman. "We came all the way up here for nothing."

Doc smiled and shook his head. "Not so fast, my young friend." He turned to Deschamps. "Can we get this old steam kettle up and running again?"

The Frenchman looked mortally offended. "But of course. *Mon Dieu*, I've taken care of her for twenty years. Why would she not run?"

"Why indeed," returned Doc, much heartened by this singularly optimistic intelligence.

"Corporal," he said, "how much track does Li'l Emily have?"

"Ah," said Deschamps. "Let me think." He beat a fist against the side of his head, his little rodent face screwed up in thought, saying over and over again, "Kilometers . . . kilometers . . . kilometers . . . no, no . . . miles . . . " After a few moments his face cleared and he yelped. "Yes, yes, miles! She has almost forty miles"—he extended his arm straight out—"in that direction."

"The map!" Doc said, in a state of the highest agitation. "The map!"

"You got it, Doc," the Gunfighter said.

"Ah yes," said Doc, "so I do."

He reached into his coat pocket and unfolded the map, laying it on top of a barrel just inside the door of the engine shed. Doc bent over the map and was soon deep in thought.

"Light!" he demanded, even more agitated than before, and Deschamps hurried away, returning with a lighted lantern, because it was now almost full dark.

Doc held the lantern above the map and studied it for a few moments, then yelled triumphantly: "Yes! Yes! This is perfect!"

"What's perfect, Doc?" asked Johnny Blue, sounding unimpressed.

"Don't you see?" asked Doc, and when the rest of us allowed that we didn't, he went on: "You boys didn't notice them when we rode in, but I did. I saw twin mountain peaks almost due west of where we are right now. The map calls them the Paps of Tecamachalco and it says the gold is hidden in a narrow canyon between them."

"How far away, Doc?" I asked.

"Well, that's the beauty of the thing, boy," said Doc. "I reckon the Paps are about thirty, forty mile away in that direction"—he pointed in the same direction as had Deschamps—"and Li'l Emily can get us there faster than any horse."

"She can," said the Frenchman, catching Doc's enthusiasm. "The track leads right through the mountains, mostly on a gentle upward grade. There are maybe five, six bridges to cross—from mountain to mountain, you see—but they will still be in good repair, I think."

The man thought for a few moments, then said: "The tracks into the mountains go through some very bad country, mostly towering pinnacles of rock split by great canyons. Even the Apaches did not roam that far. You must have a very good reason to travel in that direction, my friend."

"The best reason of all," Sir John interrupted. "To free my lady wife from the clutches of that foul fiend Clemente Perez."

The Frenchman shrugged. "There are many women and another can always be had. You have a more pressing reason, I think."

"Deschamps," said Doc, oozing oily friendliness, "a man of your intelligence must have guessed by this time that we're after hidden gold. If you can get the engine running and we find the treasure, trust me, you'll get all that's coming to you."

"A most generous offer," observed the Frenchman. Then his face saddened and he added: "But alas, that can never be. It can't be done."

"How come?" asked Doc, a mite less friendly than before.

"I am a soldier. I would be deserting my post."

"Hell, man, you don't have a post no more," the Gunfighter said, "Didn't you hear us? Napoleon's gone an' Maximilian is dead. You're as free as a bird."

Deschamps nodded rapidly in a most distraught manner. "*Quelle catastrophe!* Nevertheless, I was given an order and I must obey it. I was told to stay here until *mon capitaine* returns." He took off his kepi and waved it over his head. "*Vive la France!*"

Sir John, who now saw his best chance at rescuing his wife slowly slip through his fingers, said in a most soldierly voice: "Corporal Deschamps! Will you accept a direct order from a senior officer?"

"Of course, I am a soldier."

"Then as your senior officer, a lieutenant colonel in the army of Her Britannic Majesty, you are hereby relieved of this post and I order you to get to work on Li'l Emily. Now, Corporal, now!"

The little Frenchman thought this turn of events over for a few moments, then smartly snapped to attention. "*Oui, mon Colonel!*"

"About time," growled the Gunfighter. "I was gettin' mighty close to putting a bullet into the little rat."

"Good chap," said Sir John with a sigh of relief, but I couldn't tell if he was talking to Deschamps or the Gunfighter.

Above our heads the night birds were calling out to each other as they pecked at the first stars, but Doc declared "Time is of the essence" and said we must work until daybreak if need be to get Li'l Emily up and running.

"There will be plenty of time for sleep," he explained, "when the Fortune Flyer is in mass production and we're all rich men."

A quick inspection of Li'l Emily revealed that she still had cordwood, old and dry as tinder, stacked in her tender. Her firebox was clean and free of ash and the old girl looked to be in excellent shape.

Working in relays, we filled her boiler from the pool in the cave and Deschamps produced an oil can and lubricated all her moving parts.

Apart from a break for coffee around two in the morning, we worked nonstop until sunup and by that time cordwood was burning in Li'l Emily's firebox and she was hissing and steaming like a kettle on a stove.

"She is ready, *mon amis*," said Deschamps proudly as he stood back to admire the engine. "La Petite Emily is alive again."

"Yeah, if her boiler don't burst," said the Gunfighter sourly. He'd broken a nail carrying water from the cave and he was in a foul mood as a result.

A small V-shaped ore carrier made of steel was attached to the engine, and Doc declared that he, the Gunfighter, Johnny Blue, and Sir John should ride in that while I acted as fireman for Deschamps.

"The horses should be fine in the old barn until we return," he said. "And the Apache woman will be here to look in on them now and then."

We had indeed found a supply of oats, presumably for

the mules Maximilian hoped would carry silver ore down the mountain, and there was a corral where the horses could get outside and stretch their legs.

"I am of the opinion," said Doc as we ate a hasty meal before departing, "that Perez and his outlaws will be much slowed by the wild and uncertain nature of the terrain between here and the twin mountains. I am confident we will snag the gold and be on our way before he even realizes we're gone."

Sir John coughed, then after a few moments said: "Doc, aren't you forgetting something?"

"Ah yes," returned Doc. "Your wife." He made an expansive gesture, throwing his arms wide. "Fear not, dear sir, my word is my bond. We will rescue your distressed damsel from the clutches of the outlaws or die valiantly in the attempt. That, sir, was my promise to you and it still is my promise to you." He then added hastily and in a much quieter voice, "Time and circumstances permitting, of course."

If Sir John was disappointed by the latter part of Doc's declaration, he didn't let it show, but he sat very quiet until breakfast was over, his face troubled.

I had no doubt the Englishman would try to rescue his bride himself if it came to that in the end, but I guess he knew his chances of success were mighty slim.

To cheer him up, I said: "Doc will come through, he always does."

Sir John looked at me with bleak eyes and said only: "I hope so."

A few minutes later I was in the engine's cab, ready to act as fireman, and Doc, the Gunfighter, and Sir John clambered into the ore carrier.

But then we had trouble with the Lipan woman.

"I will not stay here, I go with you," she told Johnny Blue, clinging to his arm. "A woman's place is beside her man."

"Hell," the Gunfighter snapped, still smarting over his fingernail. "He ain't your man. Your man's on top of a mountain, waiting to die."

The Lipan woman ignored the Gunfighter, but she clung even more tightly to Johnny Blue and repeated: "I go with you. I will not stay here. There are oats aplenty in the barn and the horses can take care of themselves."

"Doc," said Johnny Blue helplessly, "she won't take no for an answer, an' that's a natural fact. It's not her to blame, it's just the effect I have on women."

Doc swept off his plug hat and made a gallant bow. "Well then, my dusky Don Juan, further argument is useless. Tell your inamorata that her carriage awaits."

Johnny Blue and the woman scrambled into the ore carrier, then Doc turned in the direction of the can where me and Deschamps waited, and waved his hat in the air. "Onward," he hollered, "onward to victory."

"*Vive la France!*" yelled Deschamps, opening Li'l Emily's throttle. "*Advancez mon braves!*"

"Huzzah! Remember the Alamo!" I cried, since I could think of nothing else.

Hissing, belching steam and smoke like a dragon with a bellyache, Li'l Emily chugged forward, faster and faster, into the heat of the dawning day.

I had a feeling our adventure was almost over, and that it would soon come to a successful and happy conclusion.

As it happened, I was dead wrong. On both counts.

Twenty

Li'l Emily was a tough and determined little locomotive and she proved her stuff as she clung to the rails, driving through a sun-hammered, barren landscape of majestic mountains broken up here and there by soaring spires of rock weathered into fantastic shapes and deep, narrow defiles. Now and again the iron rails curved around cramped rocky ledges and the little engine's wheels teetered on the edge of terrifying ravines, rattling loose showers of pebbles that bounced and plunged into the abyss below.

Rickety wooden bridges spanned the gaps between the mountains and Doc ordered Li'l Emily halted while he inspected each one before waving the engine across.

We stopped at the third of these bridges, a particularly flimsy-looking span, and Doc walked on ahead to check it out. I took the opportunity to leave the cabin to stretch my legs and ease my back, aching from the constant strain of feeding Li'l Emily's firebox. I was hot and sweaty and my face and hands were black with soot and ash.

"How's she lookin' there, Doc?" I hollered. "Will she hold us?"

Doc waved a hand but didn't reply.

I took off my hat and wiped the band with my fingers, looking around at the surrounding mountains that seemed to hem me in on all sides.

It was close to noon and the sun hung heavy above my head, burned into the sky like a smoking brand on a silver cow.

I caught something bright and fleeting out of the corner of my eye. Had it been a flash of sun on metal, or was I just imagining things?

I looked toward the top of a towering cliff face just beyond the bridge but saw nothing. Shaking my head, I cussed myself for getting so spooked. There was just no way that Clemente Perez could be ahead of us. Or was there? He was a daring and resourceful outlaw and he knew these mountains. Could he have ridden quickly through the passes and canyons and even now be somewhere in front of us, waiting in ambush?

My eyes squinting against the sun, I scanned the top of the ridge again. Nothing.

A few feet from where I stood, a rattlesnake made S-shaped undulations from one rock to another, then disappeared from sight. A lizard panted miserably on a railroad tie, done in by heat that threatened to set on fire the very air it breathed.

There was a hollow *thump, thump, thump* from the direction of the bridge and I saw Doc jump up and down, testing it with his weight.

"Will she hold?" yelled Johnny Blue, who had stepped to my side, the Lipan woman close beside him.

"She'll do," Doc yelled back. He cupped a hand to his mouth, waved his other arm, and hollered at Deschamps to bring Li'l Emily across.

The Frenchman pushed open the throttle and the engine's wheels spun as they sought traction on the rails, but she slowly picked up speed and chugged at a walking pace onto the bridge.

"Keep her slow," Doc hollered at Deschamps. "I don't want this old bridge vibrating too much." Li'l Emily slowed to a crawl, her boiler hissing in protest as gray smoke from her funnel made Indian signals in the air.

"Slow as she comes," Doc hollered, walking backward in front of the engine.

Sir John had abandoned the ore carrier for safety's sake, and he walked with me and Johnny Blue and the Lipan woman. The Gunfighter was tense and he constantly studied the top of the cliff where I'd seen the flash—if that's what it had been.

"Ease up there," I told him. "I swear you look as nervous as a whore in church."

"I feel something," the Gunfighter said. "There's something that ain't quite right around here."

A man in the Gunfighter's line of work must trust his instincts, so I didn't take what he said lightly. Neither did Johnny Blue, because he was carrying his rifle and was stepping wary. One glance told me the Lipan woman was frightened, so she sensed something, too.

"Man," I said to no one in particular, "it's gettin' mighty spooky around here."

"Just keep your eyes open," the Gunfighter said. "Like I tol' you, I'm feelin' something."

Li'l Emily and her attendant ore carrier were almost two-thirds of the way across the bridge when I heard a sudden and ominous *crreeeeak*, the sound of ancient, sun-dried timbers protesting the little locomotive's solid weight.

"Beware there, Doc, she could be goin'!" I yelled.

Even at a distance I saw the look of concern, not un-
mixed with sheer panic, on Doc's face.

Crreeeeak . . .

The bridge shuddered like an animal in pain. A few
small rocks tumbled from the ties and fell into the ravine
below. It took a long, long time before they hit bottom.

A low moan came from the old, dry beams as they
moved in unison, pulling away from each other, the iron
nails that held them shrieking out of the warped timber.

This time the whole bridge, all sixty feet of it, swayed
drunkenly to the left and a few beams worked loose to
tumble headlong into the rock-strewn, shadowed defile
below.

"She's going!" Sir John cried in the utmost horror.

Deschamps opened Li'l Emily's throttle and the engine chugged forward, her wheels spinning on the rails
for traction as she scrabbled desperately to make the
other side.

With a screech that sounded almost human, the middle
of the bridge buckled, the rail to our right rising straight
up while the other slanted downward, threatening to
plunge into the ravine. A dozen ties separated from the
rails and rained into the dizzying depths of the gorge, and
after a long while I heard them strike bottom, each thudding into the rocks with the sound of a sledgehammer hitting a tree.

Doc, nimble as a mountain goat, ran with short,
choppy steps across the ties and finally reached the safety
of the other side. Once there he turned and shouted words
of encouragement to Deschamps, who had Li'l Emily at
full throttle, the gallant little engine now only a few feet
from safety.

Crash!

This time the whole bridge let go, splintered timbers tumbling into the ravine like wood chips flying from a giant's ax. The center of the bridge straightened briefly, then lurched downward, the iron rails bending like bows.

Li'l Emily's front wheels were now on the other side of the bridge and Deschamps sounded the whistle in triumph. The ore carrier was hanging down at a steep angle behind the engine, but Li'l Emily's enormous power managed to haul it up and soon the carrier was on the level and in its accustomed place behind the hissing locomotive.

"Huzzah!" I cried. "*Vive la France!* Well done, Frenchy!"

Deschamps stepped from the cab and waved at me and the others, grinning.

He was still grinning when a bullet from the top of the cliff shot away half of his head.

Doc stood stunned for an instant, then he ran for the ore carrier and jumped inside. Soon he was banging away with his Sharps. A hail of bullets from the outlaw guns angrily whined off the steel sides of the carrier and Doc dropped from sight. No one needed to tell me he was in a heap of trouble.

"He's in a heap of trouble," Johnny Blue said.

"Sure is," agreed the Gunfighter, "and I don't reckon he can last much longer." He said it matter-of-factly, like he was discussing the preacher's sermon at a church social.

"We have to help him," I said. "He'll be killed for sure."

The Gunfighter nodded, then turned to Johnny Blue. "Send a round or two at the top of the cliff."

Obligingly, Johnny Blue cranked a round into his Winchester, fired, then fired again.

The Gunfighter, who had been closely studying the top of the cliff, shook his head. "Too far," he said. "We can't do no good from here."

"We could always head down this mountain, cross the ravine, then climb up to where Doc is," I offered, knowing it was dumb suggestion as soon as I uttered it.

"Take us too long," the Gunfighter said, stating the obvious as I knew he would. "We're at least a couple of thousand feet high up here. Take us forever, and by the time we get there Doc will be dead."

"Then we have to cross the bridge," I said. "Or what's left of it."

Sir John cried out in alarm. "We can't do that! We'd be under heavy, aimed fire all the way and we'd be slowed by having to pick our way across." He shook his head at me. "Young man, I admire your courage, but we'd be sitting ducks."

"I dunno about that," said the Gunfighter. "The little feller here is mighty spry. He could make his way across those rails while the rest of us give him covering fire. I don't think we'd hit anything at this distance, but we could worry them some."

"Well, maybe that wasn't such a great idea of mine after all," I said quickly, suddenly aware that my knees were knocking. "Truth to tell, I ain't much of a one for heights."

"You tryin' to tell us you ain't goin' across them bent rails with folks shootin' at you to save ol' Doc?" Johnny Blue asked.

"Nah," I said. "I don't feel up for it today."

"Well," declared that disgusted drover, "ain't that a real kick in the ass."

"Gentlemen, while we stand here arguing, Doc is in the greatest peril," Sir John said. "Since an attack across the ruined bridge under fire is impossible, I suggest we do what was first mooted by our redheaded friend here, and that is to proceed down this mountain and up the other one."

The Gunfighter inclined his head and clucked his disapproval. "Suits me, but I reckon by the time we get to where Doc is, he's gonna be dead meat. Believe me, Clemente Perez an' Hun Larrikin don't mess around."

On this despondent note, we started to make our way down the mountainside, each of us greatly fearing for Doc's life—and if truth be told, very much fearing for our own.

It took us all day and well into the night before we crossed the ravine and made our slow way up to Doc's position.

There was a bright moon and the mountains around us were bathed in silver as we stopped about fifty yards from the track and hunkered down behind some scattered boulders.

"They didn't take Li'l Emily," I whispered. "She's still there, but the bandits could still be around."

"They'd no reason to take the engine," the Gunfighter said. "They think we're already beat. Besides, none of them rannies of Clemente's know how to drive the thing."

"Maybe we are beat," Johnny Blue said miserably. "If'n they've killed Doc, I don't see no reason to go on."

"I do," the Gunfighter said, checking his Colts. "Listen, I can't be beat. It's taken me years to build up my reputation—some of it fact, some of it legend—but if Hun Larrikin spreads the word around that he buffaloed me good, well, my rep is gone forever and with it my status in the entire gunfighter community."

"Is a reputation that important to you?" I asked, trying to ignore Johnny Blue and the Lipan woman, who were snuggling close together, seemingly oblivious to our presence.

"Sure is." the Gunfighter holstered his guns and looked me in the eye. "You ever hear the story of the Battle of the Crab Apple Tree when I kilt the McPhee brothers?"

I shook my head at him. "Can't say as I have."

"You've lived a sheltered life, haven't you, boy?" The Gunfighter shook his head at me like I was a bucktoothed rube. "Well, anyhoo," he continued, "after I gunned them three brothers—they was just poor, hardworking sodbusters nesting on cattle range—this Kansas reporter feller comes around and says he'd like to write the story about how I done it. I was about to tell him how, but he puts up his hand an' says, 'You don't have to tell me nothin' except names an' places. I'll write the story, not exactly how it was, but how it should have been.'

"Well, he writes this story about how the McPhees took me captive and tied me to the crab apple tree, meaning to kill me at their leisure. But the reporter couldn't let it rest there. He wrote that 'with one bound the Gunfighter was free,' and that I then picked up my trusty Colts and 'though badly wounded, shot down all three vicious outlaws with flashing speed and unerring accuracy.' "

"I'd say that was a jolly good show," interjected Sir

John. "Accurate revolver work is most difficult. At least, it's always been for me."

"Is that how it happened?" Johnny Blue asked, interested in the story despite the amorous attentions of the Lipan woman.

"Nah, it didn't," the Gunfighter said. "But like I was telling you, it's how legends are made and reputations built. In actual fact, them McPhee brothers were up in the high branches of the tree because folks say the sweetest apples are always at the top.

"Well, I had me this Colt revolving rifle model of 1855, all set up with a sighting scope. So I just lay in a cozy spot in the grass about fifty yards from the tree and shot them three rannies right out of it. Seems I did those boys a favor, because crab apples can give a man a powerful bellyache."

The Gunfighter lifted his head above the rock and studied Li'l Emily and the surrounding area. "Anyhoo, you can see how fragile a thing a reputation is," he said. "It rests on more fancy than fact an' it takes a powerful long time to build, an' that's why I don't intend to ruin mine." He rose to his feet. "So let's go."

The Gunfighter led the way and the rest of us followed warily behind him. I gripped my Winchester tightly, at any minute expecting a murderous volley from the cliff top.

It never came.

The moon rode high in the sky and up there on the mountainside its light made everything look as clear as day but for the deep shadows brooding between the rocks, waiting for the night to pass and the hard dawn to melt them away. A hungry coyote yelped miserably in the distance, loudly complaining to the mountains that his was a tough way to make a living. If the mountains heard, they ignored his suffering with silent indifference.

One glance told us Deschamps was dead. Almost half his head had been blown away and his last grin was frozen on his blue lips, smiling into endless darkness.

"Poor little rat," the Gunfighter said. "He didn't have a chance."

Johnny Blue looked around. "Where's Doc?"

"I kinda think he's lying at the bottom of that ore carrier," I said. "I guess we'd better take a look."

"Just keep your eyes peeled," the Gunfighter said. "I think them outlaws are gone, but a time or two I've been known to be wrong about things like that."

We walked to the ore carrier, constantly searching the cliff top where the outlaws had lain in wait, but there was no sign of life up there.

I climbed onto the ore carrier and looked inside. A small pool of blood had collected in the V-shaped bottom, but of Doc there was no sign.

"They've kilt him for sure," I said. "Poor old Doc, they've done for him at last."

The Gunfighter shook his head at me. "I don't think so. See that blood down there?"

I allowed that I had.

"If he'd been gut shot there would have been a lot more blood, maybe a bucketful, and some of it would be almost brownish black in color as the contents of the bowel and the large intestine spilled all over into the belly. I'd also expect to see some piss down there. A bullet in the brisket loosens a man's bladder. Now, if he'd been shot in the chest, the blood would look bubbly, like the foam on the top of a glass of beer. That's because of the air in the lungs. There ain't no froth in that blood, so he wasn't plugged in the chest. If his head had been blowed off, there would be a sight of brains among the blood. You'll hear them as don't know say brains are gray, but they ain't. They're almost pure white and we'd see them fer sure. See some skull fragments, as well."

The Gunfighter rubbed his chin. "Nope, in my professional opinion, Doc was just nicked, maybe in the arm, then he gave up the fight right quick an' was took."

Since the Gunfighter was an expert on such matters, I accepted his diagnosis without question and suddenly found myself filled with the most exquisite melancholy. Now both Doc and Lady Agatha were in the clutches of the outlaws and I feared we'd never be able to rescue them.

"What will we do?" I asked the Gunfighter, wringing my hands in the highest state of anxiety.

"What will we do?" the Gunfighter repeated, a look of mad resolution on his face. "We'll do what we came here to do—claim the gold and rescue our two unfortunate hostages."

Twenty-one

"But—but how?" I stammered. "There's only the four of us against maybe ten bandits. An' besides"—to my mind this was the clincher—"who will drive the engine?"

The Gunfighter's smile was thin. "You will."

I opened my mouth to protest, but he said quickly: "You watched the little French guy. You must have picked up something."

"Well . . . maybe . . ."

"Then it's settled." The Gunfighter studied me closely. "As for the odds, I'll even them out right quick. It's my business. It's what I do."

Further argument was pointless, so I walked to Li'l Emily, got into the cab, and checked her wood supply. There was little left because the engine burned logs at a tremendous rate. But I figured there was enough to get us where we were headed, which probably wasn't going to be very far.

"You sure you can drive this thing?" Johnny Blue asked, looking up at me, doubt clouding his face.

"Sure I can," I said. "I watched Deschamps do it an' it's easy."

"You sure about that?" returned that doubting drover.

"I mean, with you bein' a lunatic an' all, it don't seem such a good idea."

"Trust me," I said.

Johnny Blue groaned, turned on his heel, and walked back to the Lipan woman.

His place was taken by the Gunfighter. "Got enough wood?"

"Plenty."

"How's her water?"

"She'll do."

The Gunfighter nodded. "Rustle up the grub and then get some sleep. We'll leave at first light."

I boiled up some coffee and we ate army biscuit spread with condensed milk, then turned in for the night.

I lay with my head against a rock and looked up at the silent stars, wishing I was far from this wilderness of heat and desert and rock. I longed to again hear the whispering pines of Montana and taste the winter wind blowing out of Canada, cold as iron on my tongue.

Somewhere in the tunnel of the darkness around me Johnny Blue and the Lipan woman giggled, then whispered urgently. Minutes passed, then the woman cried out—a single, fluttering butterfly of sound. Then silence.

"Hell," the Gunfighter muttered after a few moments, talking to Sir John and me, "I never could figger how a man can do that with a woman. I tell you, it just ain't natural."

Boys, it was easy for him to say. I lay awake half the night, mostly thinking about Daisy Mae's Emporium for Discerning Gentlemen in Austin and wishing I was standing under the red light a-knocking on the door, a five-dollar bill tucked down my boot and the musky-sweet smell of women making my head reel.

I made a vow that fevered night to visit Daisy Mae's place as soon as we got the gold and freed Doc and Lady Gray—if I lived that long.

Come dawn I rose gratefully and put on the coffee and when it was boiling the Lipan woman appeared, pushing her dress down over her pretty thighs, For the first time ever, she smiled at me, kinda knowing and sly, like a ten-year-old pickpocket. She knew what I'd heard last night, and she was telling me it didn't bother her none.

Johnny Blue poured a cup of coffee and rolled a smoke, just as surly and uncommunicative as he usually was of a morning.

But I had to hand it to him—that dashing drover sure had the power to cast a spell over women.

When the Gunfighter and Sir John joined us, we ate biscuit and drank coffee, then the Gunfighter rose and announced that were heading into harm's way and that we should all prepare for battle.

"I think," returned Sir John, "that we are probably now as ready as we'll ever be."

"Not I," the Gunfighter said with great solemnity. "This day I will engage in mortal combat with Hun Larrikin—once the proper proprieties have been observed, of course. That is, if he remembers them, for he is a low person and much given to loose women and strong drink."

Up until this time the Gunfighter had always talked like me and Johnny Blue, the rough and ready speech of the Western man. But now he sounded like Doc did at times, especially when that bald charlatan was on the make, goldbricking and sich.

"Bear with me," the Gunfighter said, "and give me thirty minutes to prepare."

He did not wait for a reply, but withdrew a little distance, removed his hat, and took out a small tortoiseshell box he'd stashed in the crown.

For the next half-hour the Gunfighter painted his face, using stuff from the box. He even had a little brush to blacken his eyelashes and a tiny sponge that rouged his cheeks with pink.

Me and Johnny Blue hadn't shaved for days and we were shaggy and bearded, but the Gunfighter never seemed to grow hair on his face, though he patiently sat there and plucked his eyebrows. Finally he combed out his long hair, arranging it over his shoulders in gentle waves. Lastly he carefully placed his hat dead-straight on his head and stepped back to the fire.

Boys, I don't rightly know what the Gunfighter was right then, man or woman, but whatever it was, it was painted perfect and mighty pretty.

"I am ready for this desperate endeavor," he said, his head held high like Christ come to cleanse the temple. "Let us now embark on what might well turn out to be our greatest trial."

The strange transformation in the Gunfighter was spooking the hell out of me and I was happy to leave and get a blaze started in Li'l Emily's firebox.

Johnny Blue stepped up into the cab and helped me throw wood into the fire. He had something on his mind, so I didn't talk to him, figuring he'd eventually get round to saying what he had to say.

"That gunfighter," he said finally, "chaps my butt. A man's got no call to paint hisself like a whore."

I slammed shut the steel door on Li'l Emily's firebox and nodded. "I reckon he's three pickles short of a full barrel."

"You figger that when it comes right down to it, we can depend on him?" Johnny Blue asked.

"You saw what he did to them bounty hunters," I answered. "He can shoot."

"He can that," returned Johnny Blue grudgingly. "But when we come up against Clemente Perez, I want a man at my side, not a painted pansy."

"I'm all the man you'll need, and then some, cowboy."

The Gunfighter was standing beside the cab, looking up at us—a strange, almost luminous light in his eyes.

"No offense," said Johnny Blue, though I heard him swallow hard.

"None taken," the Gunfighter said without rancor. "A man can't help the way he was born, but that doesn't make him any less of a man."

I opened my mouth to speak but the Gunfighter didn't wait to hear what I had to say. He turned on his heel and walked away.

"Touchy," Johnny Blue said.

"And dangerous," I added.

But just how dangerous the Gunfighter could be we wouldn't learn until later.

With Johnny Blue acting as fireman, I eased Li'l Emily into motion, steam hissing from her boiler as she chugged slowly away from the ruined bridge.

Sir John, the Gunfighter, and the Lipan woman rode uncomfortably in the ore carrier, since there wasn't room on the engine's tiny footplate for all of us. The sun was now climbing above the surrounding mountains and the day was already hot, dust thrown up from the track sifting over everything and everybody.

I opened the throttle and Li'l Emily responded at once,

her wheels singing happily on the iron rails as she chugged along at a spanking pace.

"I'm getting the hang of this," I told Johnny Blue. "It's real easy when you know how."

Johnny Blue wiped sweat from his face with his bandana and looked at me doubtfully. "I sure hope so," he said.

We entered a short tunnel, the first we'd encountered, and when we emerged I leaned my head out of the cab, checking the route ahead.

The twin mountains Doc had spoken about were much closer now, and at the rate we were traveling I reckoned we'd be real close to them in an hour. I opened the throttle wider and the little engine picked up speed, the rock walls of the mountains flashing past in a blur.

"Bridge up ahead," Johnny Blue warned.

I nodded and throttled back, finally slowing to a stop just as we reached the bridge.

The Gunfighter jumped out of the ore carrier and walked onto the span. He stood in the middle and, as Doc had done, jumped up and down. The bridge seemed solid and the Gunfighter beckoned at me to come on across.

This time we went over without incident and I stopped Li'l Emily in a cloud of steam on the other side.

It seemed the Gunfighter had also noticed the twin mountains were getting closer because he said: "I believe the track will go all the way to the mountains—what did Doc call them?"

"The Paps of something or other," I answered. "I can't quite recollect."

The Gunfighter nodded. "The closer we get, the more we're in danger. I think we'll arrive there before Perez and his men, but then we have to climb down into the ravine and search for the gold. Without Doc's map that could take time—maybe too much time."

"What do you suggest?" I asked.

The Gunfighter shook his head at me. "I don't have any suggestions. Just be sharp and stay alert. The outlaws may attempt to ambush us again."

He reached down and eased his Colts in their holsters. "Now you two pay heed to what I just told you," he said. "Stay sharp. Stay alive."

Johnny Blue, who didn't have much liking for the Gunfighter, swept off his hat and gravely intoned: "Yass, Massa. Anything you say, Massa."

"So mote it be," the Gunfighter said without blinking. Then he turned away and walked back to the ore carrier.

"Huh?" asked Johnny Blue, looking at me with puzzled eyes.

I shrugged. "That ol' boy's gettin' weirder an' weirder. Maybe it's the heat."

"It's something," Johnny Blue said. "Me, when I look at him, all I see is 'loco' camped out in his eyeballs." That rueful rider stood deep in thought for a few moments, then added: "You know, now that I've studied on it, I figger he's an even crazier lunatic than you are."

Boys, you know I would normally have made a right sharp reply to Johnny Blue, but I let it go because right then worry was eating at me like a caterpillar on a leaf. We had to rescue Doc and Lady Gray from the clutches of Perez, but with the Gunfighter as loco as he was, that task was looking more and more impossible.

Troubled by these mournful thoughts, I chewed on my bottom lip and opened the throttle on Li'l Emily once again. The little engine hissed steam and slowly began to roll forward.

The sun climbed into the sky so that it was right above our heads, adding to the intense heat in Li'l Emily's cab, and me and Johnny Blue were sweating buckets as we approached another bridge and, beyond that, a narrow cut blasted out of the side of a mountain by the French engineers.

"Wood's almost gone," Johnny Blue said as he slammed the firebox door shut. "I don't reckon we got more than three, four miles left."

"We're close to the Paps," I said. "I think another three miles will bring us there."

I slowed Li'l Emily for the bridge, but the Gunfighter yelled at us to keep on going.

I reversed the throttle and we picked up speed again and hit the bridge at a fast clip. I felt the span shudder and Li'l Emily jerked from side to side more than was usual. As we passed, ties came loose, tumbling into the ravine below, but above the noise of the engine I heard the Gunfighter yell to keep up our speed.

Li'l Emily rattled across the span, shaking more ties and support timbers loose, and the bridge was swaying so alarmingly to the right, I swear the engine had only two wheels on the track. Beside me, Johnny Blue's eyes were huge as he clung to the side of the cab, but I was sure his fear was no greater than my own.

Li'l Emily was now running at an angle, swayed way over on her left side, so that when I looked out the side of the cab all I saw was the ravine a long, long way below us. It was now or never.

I gave the little engine full throttle and she took the rest of the span at tremendous speed, finally clearing the bridge and onto solid bedrock. I glanced behind us in time to see the bridge collapse, raining hundreds of timbers into the gulch.

"Close," I said. "For a minute there I thought we were goners."

Johnny Blue, unable to speak, just looked at me, his mouth open and his eyes scared.

SPAAAANG!

A bullet whined off the front of the cab, then another hit the front of the engine and from somewhere I heard the urgent hiss of escaping steam.

"Look!" Johnny Blue yelled. "Ahead of us in the cut."

I followed his pointing finger. At least ten horsemen were crowded into the cut, some of them firing at us with rifles. The walls on either side rose sheer and high but the cut itself was very narrow, hemming in the riders so tightly they were only able to deploy three abreast.

Bullets cracked into Li'l Emily and whined off her steel sides, but she kept rolling. Here the rails were on a slight downward grade and she was gaining speed as we hammered straight for the cut. The little locomotive was going flat out and I felt her vibrate all over like a nervous Thoroughbred racehorse.

I felt a bullet tug at my sleeve and saw a bright splash of blood.

Johnny Blue had shucked his revolver and he was leaning out the side of the cab, banging away at the bandits, though he did no execution that I could see.

Helped by the grade, Li'l Emily was thundering down on the outlaws and I glanced quickly behind me and saw the ore carrier bouncing on the warped iron rails. The steel wagon was banging like a screen door in an orphanage and the three people inside were being thrown around like rag dolls.

Ahead was the cut, much closer now.

Then, with growing horror, it dawned on me that we were about to become the unwilling participants in a massacre, a massacre coming at us so fast that there was no way on God's green earth to stop it.

The horsemen in front milled around in confusion, suddenly realizing they were boxed in by the high, smooth walls of the cut and their companions behind them. Even their tough little mountain-bred mustangs, agile as goats, couldn't climb those slick walls.

"We're gonna hit them!" Johnny Blue yelled. "Oh Jesus!"

I sounded the whistle again and again and the little engine wailed like a banshee, her high-pitched scream bouncing off the hard stone walls of the cut, echoing in my ears like the cries of the damned.

A split second later all thirty tons of Li'l Emily, traveling at the speed of a swooping hawk, crashed into the bandits, who were trying desperately to ride clear of what they now knew was a death trap.

Horses and men screamed as Li'l Emily plowed into them, tempered steel and iron boilerplate against flesh and bone.

Blood and brains splashed over the engine as men and horses were smashed against the hard walls of the cut. There was barely room enough for Li'l Emily herself to get through, so the bandits had nowhere to go, nowhere to run. There was no escape from that ghastly trap. Some of the horsemen tried to gallop out of the cut, but were quickly overtaken by the engine, a remorseless, unstoppable killing force.

Terrible, fleeting images flashed in front of my horrified gaze. It was like I was seeing the cut and what was happening reflected in the hundred pieces of a shattered mirror.

Bloodied, bearded faces, mouths open in screams.

Men and horses pounded, crushed, shrieking as they died dreadfully.

The white, rolling eyes of the mustangs.

A severed head, still wearing its sombrero, spinning through the air before bouncing off the top of Li'l Emily's boiler.

Sudden gobs of scarlet gore and brain spattering high up the walls of the cut.

Bellows of pain.

Screeches of terror.

The shrill cry of horses, bewildered by this death all around them.

Blood. A bright red mist, like smoke against the sun.

Again and again Li'l Emily shuddered under the smashing impact of men and horses, then, mercifully, we were beyond the cut and once more hammering along into the open.

"Oh my God," Johnny Blue gasped. Like me, he was drenched in blood and his eyes were wild. "That was a thing no God-fearing man should ever see."

"Was Clemente there?" I asked. "Did you see Clemente?"

Johnny Blue shook his head. "I don't know. It"—he shuddered—"it happened too fast."

"I think we wiped them out," I said. "I think we killed every last one of them."

"I don't know," Johnny Blue said. "I don't want to even think about who we killed."

Behind us in the ore carrier, Sir John, the Gunfighter, and the woman were sitting very still, looking back toward the terrible scene of the massacre in the cut. Like me and Johnny Blue they seemed stunned, unable to believe what they'd just witnessed. And like us, their faces were spattered with blood and brain.

Up ahead there was a short bridge linking the mountains, one to another, and just beyond that, maybe a mile away, rose the twin, rounded peaks of the Paps of Tecamachalco.

"Better slow us up," Johnny Blue said. "We don't want to hit that bridge too fast."

I throttled back and slowly applied the steam brakes. Nothing.

"Slow her down!" the Gunfighter yelled from the ore carrier. "We got nothing to fear now." I tried again and again nothing happened.

"I think a bullet must have cut the brake steam line," I hollered at Johnny Blue. "I can't stop her."

That reckless rider's jaw dropped and he looked more stunned than frightened.

"Hold on!" I hollered. "We're almost there!"

Li'l Emily hit the bridge and rolled right over, smooth as silk. This time the timbers held.

"We made it!" I hollered. "Blue Boy, we did it!"

"You sure we're out of the woods?" Johnny Blue asked doubtfully.

"Trust me," I said.

Smiling, I confidently glanced at the track ahead—and saw with awful clarity that we were headed for disaster.

Twenty-two

A head, the tracks stopped abruptly at a wall of rock. Apparently, that was as far as Maximilian's mountain railroad ever got. His engineers had planned to blast a cut through this craggy, sheer-sided peak but had progressed only about a hundred feet before they were ordered home.

We'd maybe fifty feet of track left, then nothing—just a leveled stretch of mountain maybe twenty yards wide, and beyond that, a sheer wall of solid rock.

Li'l Emily hurtled toward her doom and I hollered to Johnny Blue: "No brakes! No brakes!" Then: "Jump!"

He went off the footplate to the left, me to the right.

I landed in a heap on the hard ground and all my breath was jolted out of me. But I looked up in time to see Li'l Emily slam into the wall. Her boiler burst in a mighty explosion of scalding steam, red-hot coals, and flying metal. Her front lifted straight up, like she was desperately trying to scale the mountain. For some reason her whistle shrilled—a scream of terror at her own violent death.

The little engine rose higher and higher, then crashed onto her right side and a moment later she was shattered by another explosion. Now she was unrecognizable as

Li'l Emily. She was just a pile of mangled, twisted metal, a wisp of steam rising from her shattered boiler like her departing soul.

A piece of debris that flew through the air when Li'l Emily first hit the rock wall lay close to my head. It was an oval brass plaque embossed with these words:

Churchward Steam Engine Company
Birmingham, England
1866

In her dying moments Li'l Emily had provided me with her own epitaph.

Boys, so much was happening all at once, it takes some time in the telling, so now let me describe what happened to the ore carrier and its unfortunate occupants.

Just after Li'l Emily ran out of track, the carrier's coupling separated. Instead of following the engine into the rock wall, it veered to the left, scraping along the wall of the cut, sparks flying from its steel side. I caught a fleeting glimpse of the Gunfighter and the others hanging on for dear life as they hurtled past—then the carrier disappeared behind the engine, the sound of its crash lost in the greater sound of Li'L Emily's shattering explosion.

I doubted that anyone inside the little wagon could have survived. They must have hit the solid rock wall at tremendous speed and the impact would have been devastating.

I rose unsteadily to my feet, my right shoulder and arm aching, especially where I'd been nicked by one of the outlaw bullets. I was sick to my stomach and my head ached.

Johnny Blue, his shirt and pants torn by rocks and debris, was staggering toward me, gun in hand, a wild, determined light in his eyes.

When he was still a few yards off, he stopped and yelled: "That does it! You're a dangerous lunatic an' can't be around civilized folks. I'm gonna shoot you through the lungs."

"No, you won't!" The Gunfighter stumbled through the engine wreckage, clutching his left knee. He had a Colt in his other hand, aimed right at me. "I will."

Now how all this would have ended I don't know, had not the unsteady but stalwart figure of Sir John Gray appeared and interposed himself between me and those two riled-up revolver toters.

"No cold-blooded murder!" he yelled. "My God, haven't we just witnessed murder enough?"

The Englishman's face was bruised and he had a cut on his forehead that trickled blood over his left eye and down his cheek.

"Gentlemen," he said, swaying on his feet, "think this through. We don't know if Clemente Perez and all his men died back there in the cut. We may still need to confront him to save my dear lady wife." He raised his arms in a pleading gesture. "My dear chaps, we require every man we have. We can't afford to lose any more."

He turned to the Gunfighter. "I implore you, sir, stifle your wrath, at least for the time being. You can," he pointed out reasonably, "shoot the damned little bounder later. I mean, at your leisure, as it were."

The Gunfighter pondered this suggestion long and hard, then finally holstered his Colt. He looked at me, his eyes cold. "We'll settle this at another time."

Johnny Blue, taking his cue from his fellow assassin, nodded and he too put his gun away.

"You're still a dangerous lunatic," he said. "You just ain't safe to be around folks."

Now those rannies were blaming me for something that clearly wasn't my fault. How could I help it if the steam line to the brakes was cut and I couldn't stop the engine?

I'd just launched into the justice of my cause—though both Johnny Blue and the Gunfighter weren't paying me the slightest heed—when the Lipan woman, her dress torn and stained, ran to Johnny Blue and threw herself into his arms.

They kissed passionately as I was saying: " . . . so any fool can tell that it warn't my fault an' anyhoo the brake line was all shot to hell and how was I to . . . "

But no one was listening, so I let it go. I'd keep my explanations for some other time, maybe for the future when the Gunfighter was aiming to plug me.

Since Johnny Blue was fully occupied with the woman and I didn't feel like talking to the Gunfighter, I asked Sir John how he and the others had survived the disaster.

"Providence, old chap, divine Providence," he replied with grave severity, wiping blood off his face with the bottom of his shirt. "The ore carrier was slowed considerably as it scraped along the side of the cut, and being of steel construction and quite heavy, it took the collision with the wall pretty well. We were thrown around inside, but I think no serious damage was done." He turned to the Gunfighter. "How is your knee?"

"It's nothing," answered the Gunfighter. "A mere bump. It won't hamper me much."

"Had the engine fallen the other way, I fear it would have gone much worse for us," said Sir John. "We would have been crushed or scalded to death. I believe only the intervention of the Divine saved us, so all praise to Him."

"Maybe so," said the Gunfighter. "If you believe in such things." He limped to the edge of the plateau and looked around. "There," he said, pointing. "Look over there."

Just beyond the mountain—and very close—rose the peaks of the Paps of Tecamachalco. We were maybe six hundred feet up the mountainside and the ravine below us headed almost due south for about a mile before curving to our right between the twin peaks.

"We'll get off this mountain and follow the ravine all the way," the Gunfighter declared. "Doc's map said the gold is hidden in the gulch between the peaks. It may be obvious where it's buried, it may not. But that's where we're headed."

Sir John nodded. "A sound plan. If Clemente Perez, that evil fiend, is still alive, he'll be near the gold and so will my sweet innocent—my dear wife."

We started down the slope of the mountain in the full heat of day.

The sun dominated the sky. It seemed like it had burned away every cloud that ever existed until only a hot, white glare was left. There was no shade and the rocks were blistering to the touch.

I opened another button on my shirt and wondered if any of the outlaws' little mountain-bred mustangs had survived the massacre in the cut. I doubted it very much. Nothing could be moving back there. Nothing living, that is.

When we finally came off the slope and reached the ravine the heat was even more intense. This was a small corner of hell in a shattered, unforgiving land long given up by God. Here even angels feared to tread, preferring to give the devil his due.

The bottom of the ravine was strewn with sand and ancient volcanic rock, but here and there among the tumbled boulders cactus grew: cholla, mostly and some prickly pear, but also the horizontally spreading Mexican mule clipper, used by *vaqueros* as a natural fence for cattle and horses because it's all hooks and spines, a vicious trap for the unwary.

A single canteen had survived the Li'l Emily disaster, and now when I shook it, a sluggish sloshing told me it was less than half full. We'd need water soon. Very soon.

In single file we stumbled through the ravine and soon my hands were raw and sore from the sizzling boulders and savage cactus spines.

After we'd been walking for an hour, the ravine curved to the right in front of us, heading between the twin peaks to the location of the hidden gold—and maybe also to Clemente Perez and what was left of his bandits, including the deadly Hun Larrikin.

My hands were in no shape for a gunfight, and I worried even more about the Gunfighter. He kept those mitts of his so soft and white, I figured they must be blistering even worse than my own, hardened as mine were from years of rope work.

The ravine outdistanced the slope of the mountain and angled across a wide area of open ground before disappearing between the peaks of the Paps of Tecamachalco.

Now that we were closer, the mountains no longer resembled the soft, rounded shape of a woman's breasts. For the first time I saw them for what they really were: towering pillars of rugged, jagged rock upthrust by earthquake and volcano from the middle of the earth millions of years ago with the rest of the Sierra Madre Oriental. When these mountains were born they must have glowed red-hot, later to hiss and steam in ancient rains like a pair of slowly petrifying dragons.

Now they stood there, tall and silent, looking over a brooding, unforgiving landscape. The open area spread out before us, about thirty acres of sand and rock, dotted by cactus and pressed in on all sides by mountains. As we walked into the flat, something white moved back and forth in the distance, half-hidden by a boulder that lay beside a dusty dry wash cutting across the clearing.

The Gunfighter threw up a hand and we stopped.

"What is it?" Johnny Blue asked, peering into the shimmering heat haze. "Can you make it out?"

"I don't know what it is," answered the Gunfighter. "But anything that doesn't naturally belong in this country is either dead or dangerous."

He shucked a Colt and nodded to me and Johnny Blue. "Let's go and take a look-see."

Johnny Blue pulled his own gun and I did the same, then we walked cautiously toward the white patch bobbing this way and that behind the rock. I thought it might be an animal's tail, but what kind of animal would be out here in the open in the heat of the day I couldn't imagine.

"If it doesn't look right, don't ask questions or start into a discussion, just shoot it," the Gunfighter whispered. "We can question it afterwards."

We stepped closer to the rock, and my knuckles were white on the handle of my .44. I was trying not to show my fear, but my heart was skipping more beats than a drummer with the hiccups.

As we drew closer to the boulder, the white patch disappeared behind it and I heard a muffled *"Mmm . . . mmm . . . mmm . . . "*

"What the hell?" Johnny Blue whispered.

"Mmm . . . mmm . . . mmm . . . "

"Well, here goes," the Gunfighter said.

He took a deep breath and dived to the left of the rock, rolled once, and came up fast on one knee, his gun pointing.

He stayed in that posture for a few moments then shook his head, smiling, and said: "Well, I'll be."

Figuring there was no danger, I stepped up to the rock—and my shocked eyes beheld the slim, graceful form of a young woman.

Her hands were tied and her mouth was gagged with a filthy bandanna. Around her neck, held by piggin strings, was a pencil-scrawled scrap of paper that read simply: TAKE HER SHES ALL YOORS.

I stepped closer to the woman and asked: "Are you dear Lady Agatha?"

"Mmm . . . mmm . . . mmm," the woman replied, unable to talk because of the gag in her mouth. But her flashing brown eyes were speaking volumes.

"Oh, sorry," I said. I leaned down and released the gag—and from that moment on was to wish a thousand times that I hadn't.

"How did you expect me to answer you with that thing stuck in my mouth, you ignorant oaf?" the woman snapped. She didn't wait for my reply, but added: "Of course I'm Lady Agatha Gray. Who the hell else would I bloody well be?"

She was right pretty, with a mass of flaming red hair and a right shapely figure. That she'd been badly treated was obvious. Her face was bruised and there were human bite marks on her shoulders and neck, angry and red. This woman had been used by Clemente Perez the way the Apaches used a horse, and it was not a pleasant sight to see.

I must admit, I'd expected Lady Agatha to say something like "Oh thank you, kind sir, for rescuing me, but I am undone," like the heroines do in the dime novels. In that, I was singularly disappointed.

When I helped her to her feet, she glared at Johnny Blue, who was gawping at her, and snapped: "What do you want, Darkie? Haven't you ever seen a white woman before?"

Johnny Blue was so taken aback, he opened his mouth to speak, but no words came out, just a strangled: "*Ug . . . ug . . . ug.*"

He didn't get a chance to speak, either, because Lady Agatha rounded on the Gunfighter and in that clipped, upper-class British accent of hers that could have ground an edge on a knife said sharply: "You there, nancy boy, where's my bloody husband?"

"Agatha!"

Sir John joyfully uttered her name with a loud cry as he ran toward his wife and took her into his arms.

"Oh, my darling," he whispered, holding her close, "my wonderful, beautiful, innocent darling."

"John," Lady Agatha said, "where the bloody hell have you been?"

Sir John, his face alight with happiness and relief, held his wife at arm's length and replied: "I've been trying to reach you, my love. Day and night, across mountains and deserts, I've been in search of you."

"Well, it's about bloody time," said the young lady, apparently unimpressed by her husband's gallant endeavors on her behalf.

"Agatha," Sir John began, his voice quavering, "what did he . . . what did they . . . "

Then, for the first and only time, I saw Lady Agatha's guard slip and her womanliness come through. "John," she said, "don't ask me that. As long as we both live, you must never ask me that again."

Sir John, who had perhaps read all he needed to know in his wife's haunted eyes and by the bite marks on her shoulders, merely nodded. "I never will, my love. I never will." He kissed her gently on the cheek. "As long as we both shall live."

Lady Agatha disengaged from her husband's arms and waved a hand at the rest of us, taking in me and Johnny Blue, dirty, ragged, and shaggy; the Gunfighter, who was looking down his nose at her like he smelled something bad; and the unusually bashful Lipan woman.

"John, I must say I'm surprised to see you in such low company. And—goodness gracious!—is that a . . . a . . . native girl?"

"She's Lipan Apache," said Johnny Blue, who had found his voice at last and made no attempt to make it sound friendly.

"Oh my God, we'll all be scalped in our sleep," returned Lady Agatha.

"My love, these people are my friends," declared Sir John sincerely. "They saved my life—not once, but several times. I owe them a great deal, much more than I can ever repay."

The Englishman stepped beside me and put a hand on the canteen. "May I?" he asked.

I nodded and slipped the strap off my shoulder, not

taking my eyes off Lady Agatha for a moment. I was fas-
cinated by the fact that even after the terrible ordeal she'd
endured and the loss of her honor, she could be so arrogant and, well . . . such a nag.

Sir John unscrewed the top and offered the canteen to
his wife. "Are you thirsty, my darling?" he asked.

One of the young woman's eyebrows arched and she
said: "Well, really, John. You could have gotten the native
girl to do this."

"She wouldn't do that," Johnny Blue said mildly. "She
doesn't cotton to white folks."

"Well," said Lady Agatha, shaking her glorious mane
of hair, "we don't ask natives to like us, do we? All we
ask is that they fear us."

"She's Lipan," said Johnny Blue stubbornly. "She
don't scare easily."

"She can be taught," said Lady Agatha, who now
showed good sense by taking the smallest sip of water.
"They can all be taught."

It was an awkward situation and Sir John did his best
to defuse it. He talked to his wife, but he meant the words
for the rest of us.

"You've been through a terrible ordeal, my dear," he
said. "I don't think you are quite yourself yet. It may take
many months before—"

"Of course I'm myself," returned his bride. "Only my
body has been outraged, John—my soul is still intact.
Even Clemente, that evil monster, couldn't reach that.
When it happened, as you know it did, I just closed my
eyes and thought of the empire. That," she added, "got
me through."

Lady Agatha grasped her husband's arm and said:
"John, Perez isn't human. He's a devil. I saw him shoot

down one of his own men because he touched me. All he did was touch me on the back and Perez shot him. He was smiling as he pulled the trigger. John, they didn't even bury the wretch. His body is still lying up on a mountain somewhere.

"Sometimes, when he was drinking his damned mescal, Perez told me about the people he'd murdered. Men, women, children—they're all the same to him. He told me that children run faster, so they're better target practice."

The woman swallowed hard. "John, he and that wild animal Hun Larrikin are further back in the ravine. Now take up your rifle and go kill them both."

"Hun is alive?" the Gunfighter asked, swallowing his obvious distaste for Lady Agatha.

"Of course he's still alive," she snapped. "He was nowhere near the ravine where you killed all the others. Neither was Perez." She held her chin high. "He . . . he was with me."

"The gold?" I asked. "What about the gold?"

"There is no bloody gold. That awful Doc person helped them go right to the place among the rocks where it was supposed to be hidden. It was long gone. Maybe the natives took it or the Mexican soldiers. Who knows?"

"Then we came all this way out here for nothing," I said, mostly to myself.

"How is Doc?" Johnny Blue asked. "Is he still alive?"

Lady Agatha shrugged. "He was still alive when Perez gagged and bound me and left me here. Personally, I suspect your friend Doc has more lives than a cat."

She turned once again to her husband. "Now, John, do your duty as a British officer and a gentleman. Take up your rifle and march right up that ravine and kill those two brigands. Avenge my honor, my darling."

"No," the Gunfighter said. "Hun Larrikin is mine. We have long had unfinished business and it must be attended to today."

"Then we'll all go," I said. "If Doc is still alive, we have to get Doc out of there."

This seemed agreeable to all parties except Lady Agatha, who looked at me like someone was holding a dead fish under her nose.

"The Lipan woman will stay here with you until we return, my love," said Sir John.

At this, the Lipan woman cupped her hand around Johnny Blue's ear and, giggling, whispered something, her black eyes slanting slyly to Lady Agatha.

Johnny Blue laughed, and Lady Agatha, her mouth tight, snapped: "What did that bold-faced thing just say to you?"

"Oh, nothing much," answered Johnny Blue. "She just told me the name she's made up for you."

"And what is that, may I ask?"

"Well, I can't quite get my tongue around the Apache, but in English it's 'Snooty Lady Dog.'" Johnny Blue grinned. "I guess you can work it out."

Lady Agatha said: "Well, really! I never! John, do something."

But to my surprise, Sir John was smiling. And he was still smiling as we headed across the open ground toward the ravine. We walked on, heads held high, a party of brave, good-looking and determined stalwarts stepping resolutely toward our destiny—a showdown with two of the most feared and skilled gunmen in the West.

Twenty-three

We were halfway across the clearing when a scattering of shots came from the ravine, kicking up sudden Vs of dust at our feet. There was a jumbled heap of boulders to our left and we took refuge there.

"Well," Johnny Blue said, "they got us spotted. We can't rush 'em. They'd drop us all afore we got anywhere near the ravine."

The Gunfighter looked at Johnny Blue for a few moments with his cold, hard eyes, but said nothing. He turned away, stuck his head above the rock, and yelled: "Hun, is that you?"

An answering call came from the rocks; a man's voice, sneering and seemingly amused. "Yeah, it's me. Is that you, Janice?"

"It's me, Hun."

"Seen you back at the mesa when them two idiots you have with you came down the slope on that contraption of theirs. Them boys was fortunate that day, Janice. Mighty lucky."

"Hun?"

"Yeah?"

"Those two are of no account. I believe this is now between you and me."

"I'll study on it some, Janice. Maybe this isn't the time."

"Hun?"

"Yeah?"

"Do you still gun women and children and get drunk as a pig and wallow in the gutter in your own stinking puke?"

"Sometimes. You still gun sodbusters out of crab apple trees an' wear women's dresses an' prance around like a great painted pansy?"

"Sometimes."

There was a pause as the Gunfighter figured his next move, then he said: "Hun?"

"Yeah?"

"We still have unfinished business from Dodge. It has to be settled sometime, so it might as well be now. Why wait, Hun?"

"Like I said, Janice, I'm studying on it. You can't beat me, you know. I think I'm maybe the best who ever lived. I've never seen anybody faster, even you, Janice."

"You could indeed be the fastest ever, Hun. That's a distinct possibility. But we've got to find out today. It's gone on too long, Hun."

"Let me study on it, Janice. I'll get back to you."

The Gunfighter slumped back behind the boulder and turned his hands palm-up, studying them, a disturbed scowl on his face. Both hands were blistered and swollen, the skin rubbed raw by cactus thorns and hot rocks.

"Hell," I said, "you can't hold a gun with those hands. Larrikin will kill you for sure."

The Gunfighter shook his head at me. "Even with hands like these I can shade him. Hun isn't nearly as good as he thinks he is."

"Let me see those," Sir John said.

I was surprised when the Gunfighter meekly complied, holding out his hands for the Englishman's inspection.

"Can you make a fist?" asked Sir John.

The Gunfighter tried, beads of sweat popping out on his forehead, but only the tips of his fingers curled a little. He relaxed his hands and tried again, with the same result.

Sir John shook his head and tut-tutted softly like doctors always seem to do. "I don't know how fast you are with your revolvers, young man," he said, "but with your hands in the state they are right now, your speed will be cut in half."

"Then I'll be fast enough," the Gunfighter said, that strange, luminous, and almost holy light in his eyes—eyes like one of those painted and suffering saints you see in Mexican cathedrals.

"My friend," Sir John said, not unkindly, "if you are determined to go through with this duel, I advise you to do it soon before your hands stiffen up, especially your left one, even worse than they are now."

"It will be soon," the Gunfighter acknowledged. "Hun Larrikin wants this thing settled every bit as much as I do. He's just a tad bashful, is all."

So saying, the Gunfighter drew his beautiful Colts. He reversed them in his hands and rubbed the smooth ivory handles against the rough surface of the rock. When the grip plates on both guns were well and truly scratched and gouged, he nodded his satisfaction and slipped the revolvers back into their holsters.

"That will help give me a surer grasp," he said. "Remember what happened the last time when my guns were slipping around in my hands?"

"Only too well," replied Sir John, touching his wounded shoulder—but his warm smile took the sting out of it.

The ivory handles on the Gunfighter's Colts cost as much as a puncher earned in a month, so the fact that he was willing to ruin them was a measure of his uncertainty at the outcome of the approaching shooting scrape. To my mind, he wasn't near as confident as he was pretending to be.

Larrikin's voice from the ravine: "Janice?"

"Yes?"

"I've studied on your proposition and you're right. It's time to settle this thing once and for all."

"Hun?"

"Yeah?"

"Tell Clemente to stay out of this. It's not for him. I have no quarrel with him today."

"I've told him. He won't interfere, at least until after you're dead."

The Gunfighter turned to the three of us. "Keep out of this. This fight is not for the likes of you. If Hun kills me, he walks free, you understand? He is not to be shot down by lesser men in hiding."

"Anything you say," returned Johnny Blue, though he looked less than pleased by the Gunfighter's speech.

"Then so mote it be," the Gunfighter said.

"Huh?" said Johnny Blue.

The Gunfighter rose and left the shelter of the rocks, and we all stood up and followed without really understanding why. Maybe it was because we knew this would be the last fight between two famous and named gunmen

that we would ever see. Both men were relics left over
from a wilder time in the West that even then, in the fall
of 1888, was rapidly fading into memory.

Then Hun Larrikin, a tall, hard-faced young man with
a single Colt stuck in his waistband, walked out of the
ravine and into the open space between us.

A few moments later Clemente Perez stepped out of
his hiding place but he went no further. The bandit, huge
and shaggy with a thick black beard falling over the
crossed shell belts on his chest, held a large and wicked
knife to Doc's throat.

Even at this distance I saw that Doc was mighty unhappy, and when I waved at him, he didn't wave back.
Doc could be right unsociable when he had a mind to be.
His shirt collar was soaked in blood, and it looked like his
neck had been nicked by a bullet during his battle from
the ore carrier. It seemed that after getting scratched ol'
Doc had quickly given up the fight and raised his hands,
having his own notions about what was brave and what
wasn't.

Without turning, the Gunfighter ordered us to stay
where we were. He then walked slowly toward Hun Larrikin, and the two professional *pistoleros* met in the middle of the open ground. Both men, each trying to outdo
the other, made the ritual display of fine manners and
good breeding such an encounter demanded. After ex-
changing many little bows, soft-spoken courtesies, and
inquiries as to the well-being of friends and loved ones,
they began the famous Gunman's Walk, pacing around
each other in a slow circle, neither man taking his eyes
off his opponent for a single instant.

Finally the Gunfighter said: "Who are you?"

"I am a named man, belted and armed," replied Larrikin.

"Then what is your name?"

"That is my own affair and is not for the asking."

"A man should not be ashamed of his name, unless he hides some shameful thing."

"I hide no shameful thing. My name is Hungerford Larrikin."

The two men circled each other like wary tigers for a few moments, then Larrikin said:

"Who are you?"

"I am a named man, belted and armed."

"Then what is your name?"

"I need hide no shameful thing. My name, used by many honest men, is Janice."

"Why do you come to this place?"

"To settle an urgent and outstanding matter between armed and named men who are regarded by their peers as equals."

"Where do you dwell?" asked Larrikin.

"In a house of brick among honest men. Where do you dwell?"

"In a house of wood among honest men."

"Will anyone else here present talk for you?"

"Um, ah, Hungerford, that should be 'speak,' " the Gunfighter said politely. " 'Will anyone else here present *speak* for you?' If you will recall, I say 'talk' later."

"I'm so sorry, you're right. Will anyone else here present speak for you?"

"No one else here present will speak for me."

"Then who will speak for you?"

"Only my guns will talk for me."

"Then let us immediately begin this debate."

"So mote it be," the Gunfighter said, bowing.

"So mote it be," echoed Larrikin with a similar bow.

And with flashing speed he went for the Colt in his waistband.

Twenty-four

Boys, thinking back on it now, fast as Hun Larrikin was, I believe the Gunfighter was a shade faster. But the range was very close and speed really didn't matter. In those old black-powder days a strong man could take a lot of hits from a .45 and keep standing, and as long as he was standing, he was shooting.

As Hun's Colt came up, the Gunfighter had already drawn. But immediately the revolver in his left hand fell to the ground, since apparently his stiff fingers couldn't hold on to it, and that unexpected turn of events surprised him and slowed him just a split second.

At a range of maybe five feet, Hun fired first and a puff of dust rose from the Gunfighter's left shoulder, turning him slightly. The Colt in the Gunfighter's right fist barked but I couldn't see the hit, though Larrikin gasped and took a single step backward under the impact.

"The ball has opened," the Gunfighter snapped. "Stand fast there and attend to your business."

Larrikin fired again, this time hitting the Gunfighter low in the belly. Shocked, the Gunfighter dropped to one knee, gritting his teeth against the pain, but he was still getting in excellent revolver work, and to great effect. His gun barked twice, and Larrikin shuddered as the bullets struck him square in the chest.

Now Larrikin steadied himself and returned fire once, and once again. A bullet hit the Gunfighter in the neck, but the other went wild. The Gunfighter swayed and for a moment I thought he must fall over. But he steadied himself and extended his arm straight out from the shoulder, aiming upward toward Larrikin's head, and thumbed off another round. The bullet crashed into Larrikin's skull just under his right eyebrow, beside the bridge of his nose, and with a horrible cry he dropped his Colt and crashed to the ground.

"Oh, I am killed!" Larrikin gasped. Then death rattled in his throat and he was gone.

The ominous presence of Clemente Perez forgotten for the moment, the three of us rushed to the Gunfighter, who was lying on his back, covered in blood. He waved us away weakly and said: "Give me air. I'm shot all to pieces."

The Gunfighter craned his neck, trying to find where Hun Larrikin lay, but couldn't see him. "Is he dead?" he asked.

"Dead as he's ever gonna be," Johnny Blue replied.

"Funny thing," the Gunfighter whispered. "I figgered to win or lose. Hell, I never figgered on a draw."

Now that his gunfight was over, the strange light had gone out of the Gunfighter's eyes and he had reverted once again to the rough and ready speech of the West.

"Boys," he said, "I've led a hard and sinful life, though I had a good mother. I just wanted you to know that."

Sir John stepped closer, kneeled beside the Gunfighter, and said softly: "Young man, your time is short. I suggest you make your peace with God."

But the Gunfighter reached up and grabbed the Englishman by the front of his shirt. "Listen," he said urgently, "when you bury me, don't let them two lunatics throw rocks on my face. I want to walk into hell as good-looking as I am right now." He tried to raise his head, his fading, unfocused eyes trying desperately to meet those of Sir John. "Promise me," he gasped.

"You have my word on it," Sir John said. "It will be as you desire."

The Gunfighter nodded. "Then it's time for me to throw the coffee on the fire an' saddle up." His eyes closed. Then, for the Gunfighter, there was only stillness and the cold loneliness of death.

"You down there!"

I looked up and saw Clemente Perez, his knife still at Doc's throat.

"What do you want?"

"I gave you back the woman. What she can give a man ain't worth her tongue. I thought about cutting her, but then I said to myself, 'Hey, what the hell, let them suffer.' That was a good choice, I think."

Clemente made a threatening gesture at Doc's throat with his knife. "I'm riding out of here. Don't take a single step toward me or I'll gut this man like a hog."

"Boys, he means what he says," Doc yelled, looking shrunken and miserable. "I would do nothing to antagonize him, no fancy moves and sich. He's tetched in the head."

I was sick of all the killing and I wanted no more of it. All I wished to do was get out of those damned mountains and back to civilization as quickly as possible.

"Go!" I yelled. "Just leave Doc alone and get the hell out of here."

"You!" Clemente hollered. "You, the little runt with the big red mustache who killed all my men. You and I will meet again—pretty damn soon, I think."

Now, Doc, for all he was starting to get on in years, was mighty spry for his age. I guess he figured Clemente was preoccupied at the moment hurling all those threats at me, because he suddenly jerked out from under the bandit's arm and lit a shuck out of there.

Perez swung at him with his knife, missed, and shucked his gun.

I threw my rifle to my shoulder and fired. The bullet *spaaang*ed off a rock about three feet from where Clemente stood, and I cranked another round and fired again.

Doc was running toward us at a fast clip, darting this way and that to confuse Clemente's aim, yelling all the time: "Shoot him! Shoot him!"

Johnny Blue joined his rifle fire to mine, and Perez, realizing that he was bucking a stacked deck, turned and ran.

"Get him!" Doc hollered. "Get after him! I want that ranny dead."

Me and Johnny Blue ran to the ravine, with Doc, who had grabbed the Gunfighter's dropped Colt, pounding right behind us.

We scrambled and stumbled over the rocks, getting torn up again by hidden cactus, but I figured we were right behind the fleeing Clemente. The ravine took a sharp right turn, and we followed it—only to see the bandit chief in the distance, running toward two mouse-colored mustangs ground-tied in a small open area.

Perez mounted and me and Johnny Blue stopped to fire our rifles at him. The outlaw shot the spare horse, then banged a few rounds at us before yanking on his pony's head and galloping down the ravine. His little mustang, bred and trained for these mountains, somehow found his way through the jumbled boulders and cactus, and soon there was only a thick cloud of dust drifting between the walls of the ravine, and the sound of the pony's receding hoofbeats.

Doc joined us a moment later, looked at the dust, and let rip with a vile oath. He shook his head at us in disgust and said: "Do you boys recollect me sayin' that you should learn how to shoot in the dark? Well, you also got to learn how to shoot in the daylight."

We walked back to where Clemente and Hun Larrikin had been holed up, and found a cache of food and three canteens that were full, or almost full.

"Well, Clemente won't get far without food and water," Doc said. "I reckon he'll die in these mountains, even if he eats his hoss."

He walked out of the ravine and into the clearing where we had a most melancholy task to perform: the burial of the Gunfighter.

True to his word, Sir John made sure we built a little protective cairn of rock around the Gunfighter's face before we piled on more boulders and buried him complete.

By the time we had laid Hun Larrikin to rest, the day was already shading into night. But Lady Agatha insisted that her husband say the Church of England service for the dead, or as much of it as he could remember, since she said their Bible had been in the baggage stolen by Clemente Perez.

When the prayers were over, we sang the Reverend Robert Lowry's crackerjack hymn "Shall We Gather at the River?" Sir John and his wife joined their voices in beautiful harmony:

> Shall we gather at the river,
> Where bright angel feet have trod,
> With its crystal tide forever,
> Flowing by the throne of God?
>
> Yes, we'll gather at the river,
> The beautiful, the beautiful river;
> Gather with the saints at the river
> That flows by the throne of God.

I really wasn't much of a one for singing, so when the hymn was over I raised a loud "Huzzah!" for the Gunfighter's gallantry and for the fact that he'd killed his man. Thus it was, much cheered and heartened by all this old-time religion and secure in the knowledge that we'd given the Gunfighter a right nice send-off, we made camp a little apart from the graves of the slain and prepared an excellent supper of coffee and broiled bacon.

At first light we were on the move, heading back the way we'd come, only this time there would be no Li'l Emily to make the trip through that wild Picacho de Zozaya mountain country shorter.

It turned out that water wasn't a major problem because of the rain that had fallen the night we took Shorty up the mountain to his coffin. Many of the natural tanks in the rocks were overflowing and we were regularly able to fill up our canteens.

But we did have one problem that grew worse with every passing day—grub.

The little amount of bacon and coffee we'd found in Clemente's stash was soon gone, and we were getting hungrier and hungrier—and a lot weaker.

Now, just making our way through those tortuous and blistering hot ravines exhausted us, and come nightfall we'd all just collapse wherever we were and fall into the sleep of the dead. Then daybreak would come, and we'd wake and yawn and have to live through another endless, scorching day.

Lady Agatha nagged at us constantly, demanding that "The native girl must go out and catch us something."

But the Lipan woman was just as hungry as the rest of us and had no more idea how to find food in that barren wilderness than did me and Johnny Blue and the others.

There was food where we were headed, at the place where we'd picked up Li'l Emily and left the horses, if we could hold out that long.

Then I had one of my brilliant ideas, the kind that later made me famous all over the West. Just before we prepared to move out on the fifth day after the Gunfighter's death, I assembled everyone together and said: "The way I see it, we ain't going to make La Lajilla without grub—at least some of us won't."

"We must," declared Doc, revealing the greatest anxiety. "We left my wife and child in La Lajilla, along with the Mauler and his son. Even though I am now a ruined man and the Fortune Flyer a vanished dream, I will not abandon them."

"Precisely," I said. "Now, we got two ways to go. We know there's food stashed where we found Li'l Emily. Okay, we ate all the meat an' peaches an' there's only hard army biscuit left, but it's food. But there is a better supply somewhere else."

"What's your drift?" Johnny Blue asked suspiciously.

"Only this: Do you recollect how much grub Shorty had stashed in that cave of his?"

Johnny Blue nodded. "Yeah, there was a lot of it: canned beef, beans—"

"Please," Sir John interrupted, rubbing his empty stomach. "No more, I beg you."

"Well, anyhoo," I said, "I suggest we head right for Shorty's mountain and get the better grub. Then, after we've eaten and rested, go back for the horses." I turned to Doc. "The horses had plenty of food, right Doc?"

Doc nodded. "They won't starve. The barn was full of oats."

"That's a fair piece out of our way, I mean doubling back like that," Johnny Blue said doubtfully.

"It's not so far," I said. "Hell, I'd rather have better grub that will stick to my ribs than iron-hard army biscuit. We won't get far on that. I don't suppose Shorty will mind. He must be as dead as a six-card poker hand by this time."

"I'd never have believed I would hear myself agreeing with the little man," said Lady Agatha, "because he's really not too bright, is he? But just study him for a moment. He's gotten so skinny, when I look at him all I see is a huge pair of haunted eyes and a scraggly red mustache. How he looks today is how we're all going to look tomorrow unless we get some decent food." She rounded on me. "Lead on, little fellow, I'm with you."

Although I welcomed Lady Agatha's support, there was much about her speech I didn't cotton to, but I held my tongue and said nothing. Once you got that woman started on a nag there was just no stopping her.

Boys, I won't burden you with the details of our terrible trek to Shorty's mountain. Let me just say that the Sierra Madres are no bargain and that any man with a lick of sense will do well to stay out of them. The ravines and gorges between the mountains are ovens by day and freezing cold by night. Everything that grows has spikes and everything that moves has a sting. Even when they were being hounded by Crook and Miles, the Apaches stayed out of that desolate country, knowing it had nothing to offer but hunger and thirst and a hundred different ways to die.

It took us the best part of three days to reach our destination, and by the time we got there we were in desperate straits, especially Sir John and Doc who, being older, were done in and could not have gone a single step further.

Even Lady Agatha, younger than all of us, collapsed against a rock and declared that if she didn't get something to eat soon she would surely perish.

Shorty's burro, which we had left to fend for himself, appeared and did what he could to welcome us, displaying his good breeding by choosing not to judge us by our dirty and ragged appearance. To me, the burro is the most refined, mannerly animal on earth, and how they manage to thrive in barren desert and mountain country is a mystery.

His face ashen, Doc took a sip of water from his canteen and nodded toward me and Johnny Blue. "You boys better get up that mountain and bring back some grub. I guess you know the way enough to get back before nightfall."

Now both me and Johnny Blue were pretty exhausted ourselves, but there was nothing for it but to climb up there in the full heat of the day. The Lipan woman, for reasons of her own, maybe just to see Shorty's body for the last time, volunteered to go with us.

"Don't dawdle up there, you people," Lady Agatha warned. "I don't wish to starve to death down here while you cow boys"—she carefully put a space between the words—"take in the sights." She waved weakly toward the Lipan woman. "If you are delayed for any reason, send back that useless native girl with the food."

The Lipan woman glared at Lady Agatha for a few moments, then said a few words in Apache.

"Well, really!" said Lady Agatha, this time needing no translation.

Twenty-five

B y the time we reached Shorty's cave high on the mountain both me and Johnny Blue were pretty much used up, and even the incredibly enduring Lipan woman was showing the strain.

The coffin was there in the cave, just where we'd left it—but of Shorty's body, there was no sign.

"Well," said Johnny Blue, "let's get to it an' load up. It's a long ways back down this mountain again."

My hands were raw and torn and my breath was coming in short, tortured gasps. Hunger had weakened me and the thought of scrambling back down the mountain carrying cans of food was horrifying, to say the least.

"We'll rest up awhile, maybe eat something afore we go," I said. "I think the others can wait just a little longer. We try to get down there without something in our bellies, we'll never make it."

Johnny Blue allowed that this made sense and we opened up some cans of Shorty's beans and the three of us ate ravenously. I felt some of my strength return and figured that, though still far from my normal robust self, I was just about recovered enough to very soon start down again.

Johnny Blue licked the blade of his jack-knife clean

and nodded toward Shorty's beautiful coffin. "I guess the old buzzard managed to crawl inside there before he gave up the ghost," he said.

I nodded. "Unless he fell off the mountain."

The Lipan woman superstitiously kept her distance from the coffin, though her eyes kept straying to it, a concerned expression on her face.

Johnny Blue noticed this and grinned at me. "Maybe she doesn't think ol' Shorty is in there her ownself."

"Maybe he is, maybe he ain't," I said.

"Should we take a look?" Johnny Blue asked.

I studied on this suggestion for a spell, then said: "Suppose he's lyin' in there an' he ain't pretty. I mean, he's been on a stoney lonesome now for quite a spell. He could be smellin' mighty bad."

"Hell," returned Johnny Blue, "what's the difference? He smelled mighty bad when he was alive."

He rose to his feet. "Well, I'm gonna take a look."

I stood and followed, though the woman held back, her eyes frightened. I was about as nervous as a hungry tick on a skinny dog myself, opening up coffins not being exactly in my line of work.

Me and Johnny Blue stepped up to the coffin, and that cautious puncher looked down at it for a spell, then said: "Go ahead. Open it."

"You open it."

"I ain't gonna open it. You open it."

I sniffed the air. "I don't smell nothing."

"Well, that means he's not in there," Johnny Blue said. "Dead or alive, you'd smell him, all right."

I took a deep breath and cautiously got my fingers under the lip of the coffin lid and slowly began to raise it.

Scrrreeech . . .

I dropped it right quick. "What the hell was that?"

"The hinges need oil, is all," Johnny Blue said. "Now quit being sich a fraidycat an' open the damn thing. I'm tellin' you, he ain't there. I bet you five dollars it's empty."

"You don't have five dollars," I said.

Johnny Blue shrugged. "My credit is good. Now, open it."

"Maybe we should just go an' leave ol' Shorty in peace," I said. "This don't seem decent."

"Open it."

"You open it."

"Oh hell, I'll open it."

Johnny Blue yanked open the lid—and there lay ol' Shorty, just as we'd seen him in life, kinda ugly and wizened and smelling real bad, but not rotted too much, considering.

"Would you get a load of that," I said. "He looks like he's asleep."

The corpse's eyes flew open and Shorty yelled: "I *was* asleep until you two idiots woke me up with all your cussin' an' arguin'."

Me and Johnny Blue almost tripped over each other scrambling to get away from there, and behind us Shorty stepped out of his coffin real spry as the Lipan woman screamed.

But there was nowhere to run except straight down the mountain, and I wasn't about to do that without the food we'd come up there for in the first place.

I stopped, my heart hammering in my chest, and yelled: "Shorty, you're dead. You just don't know it yet on account of how you ain't too bright."

"I ain't dead!" returned that ghastly cadaver. "How can I be dead when I'm a-standin' right here?"

"I don't know, but you are dead, oh dreadful apparition. It was us brung you up here, so we know. Don't we, Johnny Blue?"

"Shorty, you're as dead as a wooden Indian," Johnny Blue cried. He drew his gun. "Now, I'm gonna kill you oncet again an' make sure, because the dead shouldn't be roamin' the earth an' scarin' decent folks."

But before he could pull the trigger, the Lipan woman ran into Shorty's arms with a wild cry of joy and kissed him full on the mouth. Shorty returned her kiss with equal or maybe even greater enthusiasm.

"I've never seen a dead man do that," I said to Johnny Blue. "Never in all my born days. Have you?"

"No, I haven't," returned that shocked rider. "An' it's the first time I ever done lost my woman to a dead man."

"Well," I said, "seeing what's going on here, I don't reckon he's dead." Still keeping my distance, I yelled: "Hey, Shorty, how come you ain't dead yet?"

"Beats the hell out of me," he replied. "Every night since you left me up here, I'd lie down in that fancy coffin, thinking that day was my last, an' every mornin' I'd wake up lively as ever an' hungry for breakfast."

Shorty put his arm around the Lipan woman and walked toward us. "Now I've seen my woman again, I've decided I don't want to die no more."

"You're lookin' better, Shorty," I said. "You smell just as bad as you ever did, but you ain't limpin' so much."

"Feelin' better, too," Shorty returned. "An' a sight stronger."

He studied me and Johnny Blue for a few moments, then asked: "What are you boys doin' up here, anyhow?"

Quickly I sketched out the story of our battle with the bandits, the death of the Gunfighter, and the sorry plight of our companions at the bottom of the mountain.

Shorty listened to my story in silence, then said: "Well, let's load up. I'm comin' back down with you. I don't see no point in remainin' up here."

"What's about your coffin?" Johnny Blue asked, still smarting at losing his woman.

"The hell with it," Shorty said. "It ain't too comfortable an' the lid needs oil. Maybe someday I'll go back up there, but I ain't countin' on it."

So it was that we took a dead man off the mountain and long before day shaded into night were happily sharing a stew of beef and beans with our ravenous companions.

Later Sir John examined Shorty again and declared with much wise shaking of his head and tongue clucking that the little man did seem much improved.

"We in medicine are aware of a strange phenomenon in cancer called remission," he told Shorty. "That is, the cancer stops growing and actually seems to recede for a while. The symptoms become much less severe and the patient feels stronger and healthier."

"Hey, Doc, does that mean I'm cured?" asked Shorty hopefully.

Sir John shook his head again. "I'm afraid not, old chap. It just means that the cancer has retreated. It will return someday."

"When?"

The Englishman shrugged. "Who really knows? It could be months. It could be years. There's just no way of telling. I wish I could say more."

"Well, that's good enough for me," Shorty said. "I

thought I was a goner for sure, but it seems I got a new lease on life, at least for a spell."

"Good luck to you," said Sir John. "And let us hope you indeed have many years ahead."

On this happy note we all retired for the night, Shorty and his woman slipping off among the rocks after we'd bedded down.

And judging by the Lipan woman's giggles, that old mountain goat had a new lease on life, all right — much to Johnny Blue's obvious disgust. But since she'd been Shorty's woman in the first place, I didn't think my crest-fallen *compadre* had much of a beef.

Come first light, me and Johnny Blue went back for our horses, finding them in excellent shape, rested up and eager for the trail. It was kind of sad to see Li'l Emily's shed lying there empty and forlorn, because she'd proven to be a gallant little engine and she'd served us well.

Deschamps's flag still hung on its pole and we left it right where it was. As Johnny Blue said, it was a kind of memorial to the little Frenchman because he too had proven to be a brave and resourceful soldier.

When we returned, Shorty and the Lipan woman told us and the others that they planned to stay in the mountains together and eke out a living somehow.

"I recollect a year or two back seeing some color in a quartz seam at the base of a mountain due east of here," Shorty said. "Who knows? It might be gold."

"Fool's gold, you mean," muttered Johnny Blue sourly.

The sorry intelligence that the Lipan woman was staying with Shorty had made Johnny Blue even more glum, and I rubbed it in by telling him that if he had a way with women he must have mislaid it somewheres along the way.

"There's just no accountin' for women," mused that crestfallen puncher. "I just can't figger what she sees in that Shorty feller."

"Maybe you should buy yourself a coffin," I said.

A week later, in good health and high spirits, our little cavalcade rode into La Lajilla and a joyous reunion with Georgia, the Mauler, and the babies, who squalled even worse than they ever did before.

Me and Johnny Blue were dirty, ragged, and bearded, and when Georgia threw her massive arms around me and hugged me close she declared I was so scrawny there was nothing left of me but breath and britches.

"You was always a skinny little feller, but now you could stand under a clothesline in a thunderstorm and not get wet," she said.

The Mauler made pretty much the same observation, but Sir John laughed and said he would take care of that sorry state of affairs right away.

Accompanied by Doc, me and Johnny Blue followed Sir John and Lady Agatha into Michael O'Shaugnessy's store. It was typical of general stores of that time, smelling of just about everything under the sun: plug tobacco; fresh-ground coffee; tea in wooden boxes from India; the leather of belts, boots, and shoes; cheese; pickled and dried fish; and the tang of cloth in bolts and jeans and shirts stacked on the counter. From the rafters hung hams, great thick slabs of smoked bacon, and cooking pots. Just about every space on the floor was covered by kegs and barrels brimming with sugar, flour, vinegar, and molasses. Spices and dried fruit in canisters lined the shelves behind the counter, and beside them, glass jars bright with sticks of peppermint candy and pear drops.

"I must admit to being financially embarrassed at the moment," Sir John declared to the proprietor after he'd introduced himself and his wife. "But if you will extend me credit for what we need, I will draw on cash I have on deposit in a Laredo bank and send you what I owe."

O'Shaugnessy, who'd been in the general store business for a long time and knew how to judge whether or not a man was creditworthy, studied Sir John and Lady Agatha for a few moments, then said: "My store is at your disposal."

The Englishman turned to me and Johnny Blue. "Help yourselves, gentlemen," he said. "I believe this is the least I can do to thank you for saving my life. I fear by now my skeleton would be dangling from that rock had you not happened along."

He didn't have to ask us twice. We quickly outfitted ourselves with new pants, shirts, and cotton underwear, and even new boots that O'Shaugnessy said had been made by the famous Charles Garnet and J. Arthur Saddle Company, imported all the way from El Paso.

Lady Agatha browsed through the store's stock of ready-to-wear muslins and calicoes and threw up her hands in despair. "John," she said, "I can't possibly wear these rags!"

The Englishman frowned. "My dear," he said, an unusual note of severity in his voice, "we all have to make do. May I remind you that our ancestors, including your own distinguished father, didn't build an empire with that sort of attitude."

Lady Agatha looked shocked and she stood stock-still for several moments. Then she swallowed hard, and I thought I saw a gleam of tears in her eyes before she said meekly: "Of course, John. I understand. I had forgotten about the empire."

In the end, she chose a blue canvas skirt, split for riding, and some women's shirts, all of which became her well because she was a mighty shapely and pretty woman. In those days, the latest Western fashions were a year behind the East and two years behind Paris, but frontier women neither knew nor cared. But then, Lady Agatha was altogether a different sort of customer.

O'Shaugnessy had a Mexican boy who ran a bath house out back of the store and me and Johnny Blue soaked in a tin tub for an hour. Lady Agatha did the same, a curtain separating her from prying eyes.

The boy was also a barber and he carefully shaved me and Johnny Blue and cut our hair. By the time he'd slicked my hair down with pomade and waxed my beautiful cavalry mustache into two dashing points, I looked mighty handsome, and Johnny Blue didn't look too bad, either.

The Mauler and Georgia were camped on the edge of town, since there was no hotel, but they had done much to make themselves to home.

A canvas awning had been rigged by the Mauler from the top of the wagon, and as night shaded in, it was a pleasant place to sit around the fire and eat supper.

After we'd eaten, Sir John leaned toward Doc, who was then rocking one of the babies in his arms, and said: "You know, I've been thinking, old chap. I owe you a great deal, and I have a proposition for you."

"Do tell," said Doc, his suddenly greedy eyes glittering in the light of the fire.

"I am a poor man—"

"Oh," interrupted Doc, obviously disappointed and no longer interested.

"Well," continued Sir John, "at least I was a poor man. I mean, one doesn't get rich on a lieutenant colonel's salary, does one?"

"Not at all," returned Doc, who I'm sure had no idea what a lieutenant colonel earned. "The military life is hard indeed and not for the faint of heart."

"It's a vocation," declared Sir John vehemently.

"Indubitably," said Doc.

"But back to my point. As I said, I was a poor man, but my older brother recently died and left me his entire estate, so I am no longer, shall we say, poor, but in fact rather wealthy."

"Ah," said Doc, brightening as he scented opportunity like a hound. "And what does this . . . ah . . . estate entail?"

"Oh, a matter of some million pounds or so and a mansion house in Devon surrounded by several thousand broad acres. Sheep mostly, but some dairy cattle."

"A million pounds," repeated Doc, choking slightly. "And a mansion."

"Quite so," said Sir John. "Anyway, the point is this: I would love you and your family to come and live with me and Lady Agatha in England for a while. Think of it as my way of thanking you for your brave endeavors on our behalf."

"Sheep," murmured Doc. "You have sheep, Sir John. In fact, there's a whole empire full of sheep—sheep to be fleeced—is there not?"

"Quite so," smiled Sir John, thinking about an entirely different breed of sheep.

Doc passed the baby to Georgia and rubbed his hands

in glee. "Sir John, my dear friend, I am your man. I'm sure I speak for my lovely wife when I say we'd be glad to accompany you to England, that sceptered realm, that home of Shakespeare . . . and sheep."

"I hope it won't be too great an inconvenience for you?" said Sir John, his voice rising into a question. "I mean, old chap, I don't want to take you away from present commitments."

"Not at all," said Doc. "I have many pressing business matters that demand my attention, but I'm sure they can wait."

Lady Agatha, who had no great liking for Doc, had listened to this exchange with an expression of growing horror on her face.

"Of course you understand this would only be temporary," she said quickly. "My husband also inherited several coal mines in Scotland. I believe we could find you honest work in the coke and coal trade in those northern latitudes."

"Coals do not suit my husband's particular talents," said Georgia stiffly, looking daggers at Lady Agatha. "Besides, he is of a somewhat delicate constitution and not equipped for cold climes. No, I believe he is more suited to the banking trade, or possibly"—here she paused meaningfully—"estate management."

"Jolly good!" said Sir John, beaming. "Why, we might even get the Fortune Flyer up and running again."

"Yes," said Lady Agatha icily. "We might."

Georgia, her dark face shining, laid a hand on Doc's arm and said: "Oh, Doc, I always knew that one day you'd make me a fine lady and have me riding in a carriage drawn by four white horses."

"My love," declared Doc in an ecstasy of affection.

"Lord Doc Fortune and Lady Georgia Fortune. It has a nice ring to it." He turned to the Mauler. "Did you hear what Sir John said? Sheep, my boy, sheep."

The Mauler—who, we were happy to see, was slowly recovering from the grief of his wife's death—nodded, winked, nudged my elbow, and declared knowingly that fleecing sheep was his huckleberry, all right, make no mistake about that.

"Doc, I had no idea you had such a profound affection for sheep," wondered Sir John.

"Oh yes," returned that cheerful charlatan. "I love everything to do with the countryside. Also rubes. Deary me, yes, I do love rubes."

The Englishman nodded. "Ah yes, rubes. In Britain we call them yokels."

"Wonderful!" cried Doc, clapping his hands. "Yokels." He licked his lips. "That sounds even better."

Now, how this conversation might have ended, I don't know, because no sooner had Doc finished speaking than a bullet crashed into the fire, scattering hot coals and tipping over the coffeepot.

Another shot rang out, and this time the Mauler gave a horrible cry and slammed backward to the ground.

Twenty-six

As the Mauler fell, Doc stood and jerked the Gunfighter's scratched-up Colt from his waistband. He spared a fleeting glance for the fallen Mauler, then ordered the women and Sir John into the shelter of the wagon.

"Stay with the Mauler," Doc told the Englishman. "It looks like he's hit bad. You two," he said to me and Johnny Blue, "come with me."

The night was moonless and La Lajilla's single street was dark except for one lonely oil lamp on the cantina wall that splashed a pool of dirty orange light on the ground. A skinny coyote warily slunk around the wall of the cantina and then vanished from sight.

"This way," Doc said, running. "We'll head him off, whoever he is."

We followed Doc off the street and ran behind the nearest adobe house, where we paused for breath.

"Anyone see where the shots came from?" Doc asked.

I shook my head at him. "I saw nothing."

"Maybe near the church," offered Johnny Blue. "Someone could have fired from there."

"Let's go," said Doc.

We made our way past another adobe, but in the dark

I stumbled over a low chicken coop, fell on top of it, and smashed its fragile wooden framework. Chickens squawked and fluttered around my head, scattering white feathers everywhere, and a bullet split the air about an inch above the parting in my hair.

"Hell," I said, "this is gettin' personal."

"It could be," whispered Doc close to my ear. "I think the gunman, whoever he is, is trying his best to kill you."

"Who the hell is he?" I asked.

In the darkness Doc shrugged. "Who knows?"

A bullet thudded into the wall beside us, and this time we saw the flash of the assassin's gun. Doc fired and so did I, but the gunman had already moved. Whoever he was, he knew his business.

A door opened and a man came out, yammering something in Mexican. He saw his chickens running all around the yard, slapped his cheek, and cried: *"Aye! Aye! Aye!"*

Cussing a blue streak in Mexican, this ranny took off after his fleeing fowl and soon we were surrounded by fluttering chickens, their owner bent low, clapping his hands and clucking like a rooster. Now a stray dog, lean and hungry, his face full of ancient devilment, joined in the hunt, barking as he chased them birds around in ever diminishing circles so that I was sure he'd eventually disappear up his own ass. More doors opened and people rushed outside, some of them screaming for the law.

"Hell," Doc growled, picking a chicken feather off his eyebrow, "let's get out of here. We're causing a commotion."

We ran toward the back of O'Shaugnessy's store and pulled up when we saw the big Irishman himself standing there in a yellow rectangle of light from his door, a shotgun in his hands.

"What the blue blazes is going on?" he demanded. "What's all the shooting about?"

"Somebody took a shot at us, and he ran this way," Doc said, panting for breath.

"Who is the law around here, anyway?" I asked.

"I am," O'Shaugnessy said. "Hold on just a minute."

The Irishman ran inside, then reappeared a moment later, a tin star pinned to his stained undershirt. "Let's find this gunman," he said.

O'Shaugnessy led the way behind the remaining adobes, then he angled toward the small livery stable near the church where we'd left our horses.

"I'm betting he's around there someplace," the Irishman whispered. "If he hasn't left already."

"He could be over to the church," Johnny Blue said. "He'd have a view of the whole street from there."

O'Shaugnessy nodded. "Maybe, but I'm counting on him not being Anglo. If he's Mexican he wouldn't shoot a gun anywhere near the Church of the Madonna of the Gallows. They're a superstitious bunch when it comes to their religion."

The livery stable wasn't much: an adobe barn with a double wooden door and a single window to the front. Like all liveries, a lamp burned on the wall outside to guide late travelers, and a bench for loungers stood under the window. Illuminated by the circle of light from the lamp, a small tin sign was tacked to the wall, advertising DOCTOR ADOLPH TRUBSHAW'S TONIC FOR TIRED WOMEN. Why it was there of all places struck me as strange, but then La Lajilla was a strange town.

The four of us stepped closer to the barn. Inside a horse blew through its nose and stamped. On a wooden pole on the roof a crude galloping mustang cut from a piece of tin served as a weathervane and also advertised the livery stable's business.

The tin mustang moved slightly in the night breeze off the mountains, creaking softly. We were now about twenty yards or so from the barn, and Doc stuck out an arm to stop us.

"If there's shootin', you boys hold your iron in both hands an' push it out in front of you about chest-high," Doc whispered. "Don't put the gun up to your eyes or you'll be blinded by the flash an' hit nothin'." He peered at me through the gloom. "That's a crash course on shootin' in the dark. You got that, boy?"

I allowed that I had, but Doc seemed unconvinced. "Let's hope so," he said doubtfully.

Beside me O'Shaugnessy was white-knuckling his shotgun and his hands were trembling slightly, but whether from excitement or fear I did not know. I just hoped it wasn't the latter—for all our sakes.

Doc rubbed his mouth with the back of the hand that held his Colt, then stood from his crouched position. "Well," he said, "it's now or never. Let's surround that barn and move in on it from all sides."

We rose and followed after Doc—but hadn't taken more than half a dozen steps when all hell broke loose.

A horseman thundered out from behind the livery stable at breakneck speed, the rifle at his shoulder spitting gouts of orange flame. Bullets whined through the air around us and we dived for the ground. O'Shaugnessy yelled and fired both barrels of his shotgun, but where he was aiming I don't know—maybe straight up in the air, because his buckshot went nowhere.

The mounted man rode toward us, cranking his rifle as

he came. A bullet thudded into the ground near my face and another kicked up dust beside my head.

The assassin had us pegged and he knew it. He was coming straight for us, ignoring our own ineffective fire.

I raised up and fired my Colt, missed and fired again. Doc's gun barked, then Johnny Blue fired. The horseman kept coming. We were all standing now and the gunman was almost on top of us, close enough to allow his rifle do its deadliest work.

Boom!

A rifle slammed off to our right and the horseman screamed and somersaulted off the back of his horse, his Winchester spinning away from him. His wild-eyed mount, crazed by the gunfire, galloped past us and into the street.

"I got him, boys," said a voice off to my right. "I nailed him good."

I turned and saw the Mauler standing there, tall and terrible in the gloom, Doc's Sharps .50 smoking in his enormous hands. He was ghostly pale and blood splashed the front of his shirt. Boys, in that smoke-filled darkness, it was a horrifying sight to see.

The Mauler swayed, then the Sharps dropped from his hand and he crashed to the ground like a mighty felled oak.

Doc ran to the Mauler's side and Sir John appeared, panting for breath. "He wouldn't stay," he cried. "He insisted on coming to your aid."

Only O'Shaugnessy, in his capacity as sheriff, stepped slowly and carefully over to the rifleman's still body. The rest of us crowded around the Mauler, who looked to be in a bad way. He'd been shot high in the chest, and it could only be a killing wound.

"Hang on, boy," Doc whispered. "Don't leave me. I need you."

The Mauler smiled weakly. "Doc," he said, "it's been a real pleasure knowing you and I've sure enjoyed the play. They say you're a bad actor, but to me you've always been gold dust."

"Hang on, boy, hang on," said Doc, tears staining his cheeks. He looked up at Sir John. "Save him. You're a doctor and you know how. Save him."

Sadly the Englishman shook his head, saying nothing, his shoulders slumped in mute defeat.

"Doc?" asked the Mauler. "Doc, are you still there?"

"I'm here, boy, I'm here."

"Listen, take care of my son. When I meet Cottontail I want to be able to tell her that Doc's takin' care of our boy and all will be well."

"You'll take care of him yourself," Doc whispered. "You'll see, you're going to be just fine."

The Mauler smiled. "Doc, you're a one." He reached up a hand and grabbed Doc by the front of his coat. "Heed me, now. You take care of my boy."

Doc nodded and he dashed tears from his eyes with an unsteady hand. "I will, me and Georgia will. You got no worries on that score. I'll raise him as though he was my own."

"Doc," the Mauler whispered, "is Cottontail here? Doc . . . let her through. . . . "

Then the Boston Mauler—bare-knuckle prizefighter, the man who once fought the great John L. Sullivan to a draw—closed the curtain on the final act of his life and quietly and without fuss left the stage.

Doc stayed where he was for a few moments, then laid the Mauler's head gently on the ground. He grasped his

Colt and walked to where the gunman lay. O'Shaugnessy stepped into Doc's path and said: "He's still breathing, but barely. He needs a doctor real bad."

Roughly, Doc pushed the Irishman away and walked toward the wounded man, feeding shells into his revolver. He stopped beside the gunman, looked down at him for just an instant, then pumped six bullets into his jerking body, thumbing the hammer, pulling the trigger so fast his hand was a blur of motion.

As the racketing echo of the shots died away, Doc turned on his heel and walked into the darkness.

O'Shaugnessy looked at me, his face white with shock. "That was cold-blooded murder," he gasped. "He was lying there wounded, and he killed him."

I nodded. "Doc ain't a forgiving man." I jerked my chin toward the dead gunman. "Who was he?"

"I've seen him around the cantina here from time to time," the Irishman said. "His name is Díaz an' he had a reputation as a *pistolero*. Rode with Clemente Perez and them for a spell."

"He was good," I said, "real good. Only he didn't reckon on the Mauler."

"Didn't you tell me you left Clemente for dead back in the mountains?" O'Shaugnessy asked.

"He had no food an' no water," I said. "There was no chance he could make it."

"Well, I guess he did make it okay," O'Shaugnessy said. "It wouldn't surprise me none if he was the one who hired Díaz to kill you." The Irishman looked at me shrewdly. "You take care, boy, because Clemente Perez is a man to be reckoned with. He's a skilled gunman and he's killed more than his share. I've seen him in action, and in a close-range shooting scrape he's very fast and deadly accurate."

Mixed with my terrible grief over the death of the Mauler I felt a sudden stab of fear. I knew when it came right down to it, I was no match for Clemente Perez. And neither was Doc or Johnny Blue.

We buried the Mauler decent in the little graveyard behind the church, and the old Mexican priest who lived there performed the service.

Lady Agatha, who said she'd have no truck with popery, nevertheless attended, holding the Mauler's baby in her arms the whole time. Although she didn't like the rest of us very much, in the short time she'd known the Mauler she'd seemed to grow fond of him, perhaps because of the gentle way he had around her and his obvious love for his child.

After we saw the Mauler put to rest, me and Johnny Blue, Doc, and Sir John repaired to the cantina to drink to his memory while Georgia and Lady Agatha took the babies back to camp.

Doc, who had been very silent since the night of the shooting, looked old and tired, and my heart went out to him. He'd suffered a double loss with the deaths of Cottontail and the Mauler, and it had taken its toll on him.

We stood around drinking the raw whiskey of La Lajilla, each of us desperately thinking of something to say that would lift our spirits and draw Doc out of his terrible darkness.

But finally it was Doc himself who spoke. He stood there, his shoulders slumped, gazing into the bottom of his glass and said: "I've lost half of my family. I've lost Cottontail and the Mauler and I fear the fault is all mine."

"My dear chap, you can't blame yourself," Sir John said. "There is no blame to be laid here."

"But there is," returned Doc miserably. "The Fortune Flyer was an ill-starred venture from the start. Yes, half my family—I believe the better half—is gone. The Gunfighter, all those men who died so horribly in the cut...it was too steep a price to pay. I was charged dearly for my ambition and I paid the bill in full . . . with other people's blood." Doc poured himself another drink. "I'm just so sick of it all—the killing . . . the dying."

Doc drained his glass and filled it again. "Sir John," he said, "you've no way of knowing this, but I've killed six men in gunfights—seven if you count a ballet dancer I shot by accident one time. I don't want to kill no more. I'm through—through with the West. Through with all of it."

Sir John nodded, his eyes sympathetic. "That's all the more reason for you and your wife to come to England with Lady Agatha and me." Trying to sidetrack Doc toward a more pleasant topic, he added: "Have you ever visited England?"

Doc shook his head. "No, never have."

"It's a green and pleasant land. I believe there you'll find what you are seeking."

"Seeking?" asked Doc. "What am I seeking?"

"Peace, my dear fellow. Peace."

Doc studied on this for a few moments, then said: "You're right, Sir John. That's what I want—peace." He looked into the Englishman's eyes as if trying to find the answer there, and said: "Is that too much to ask?"

"No," answered Sir John. "No, it's not. I believe it's every man and woman's right."

"Peace," whispered Doc. And again: "Peace."

But standing in that quiet cantina, grieving for the Mauler, none of us knew that the peace Doc sought would not be quick in coming. Soon he and the rest of us would once more face the blaze of six-guns and hear the harsh roar of dying men.

Twenty-seven

Through the good graces of Michael O'Shaugnessy, Sir John rented horses for him and Lady Agatha from the livery stable, and the services of a Mexican boy to bring them back from Laredo. Doc and Georgia would ride in the wagon with the babies.

We were a much chastened company, not given to talk, and even Lady Agatha was mostly quiet for once. She fussed with the babies constantly and seemed to have found her true vocation as a stand-in mother.

We were still two days' ride from the ford over the Sabinas, near a place called Hidalgo Wells, when I first saw a column of dust rise in the air about a mile behind us.

The wagon road cut through a pass made between two saddleback hills, and the rock wall on the eastern side had a number of small tanks fed by an underground stream that gave Hidalgo Wells its name. There had been a stage station here at one time until it was burned by the Apaches, and all that remained of the buildings was a single stone wall eight feet long and about as high as a man's waist, and a few charred timbers.

A huge oak that once sheltered the main cabin still spread its leafy branches over the ruin, and I reckoned this must have been a cool and pleasant stop for weary travelers.

Doc suggested we make camp for an hour and boil coffee and water the horses. I didn't want to alarm the womenfolk unnecessarily, so I drew him aside and told him what I'd seen.

Doc put a hand over his eyes and peered down our back trail, but the dust plume was now gone.

"Could be honest pilgrims like ourselves," Doc said. "A lot of folks take this road, heading for Texas."

"Could be," I repeated. "But it could be somethin' else."

Johnny Blue joined us and I told him about the dust cloud. Like Doc, he studied the trail behind us, then said: "Maybe it was kicked up by antelope. There's a passel of antelope and deer around these parts."

"It could also be Clemente Perez," I said, voicing the unspoken fear that was within us all.

Doc nodded. "Him? Yes, maybe. Could also be bounty hunters. I think you boys have forgotten something, and maybe it's time to bring it back to mind."

"What's that, Doc?" asked Johnny Blue.

"You're still wanted men," replied Doc. "There's a ten-thousand-dollar price on your heads, dead or alive, for high treason and disturbing the peace an' sich. Maybe you've forgotten, but I bet there are others who haven't."

"Nah," I said, "that's all water under the bridge. The Rangers and the army must have finally figgered we didn't mean to poison the wrong Mexicans and it was just a unfortunate accident. It's all forgotten by this time."

"Hell, you almost started a shootin' war between Mexico and the United States, boy," Doc said, "an' one of our generals got wounded by a cannonball. That takes a whole heap o' forgetting."

I bit my lip, doubt creeping into my mind. "What do you suggest, Doc?" I asked.

"What I suggest is, as soon as the rest of us pull out of here, you boys kinda fade back and see who's following us. I don't want no unpleasant surprises—not when I'm travelin' with women and little babies."

"Yeah, but suppose it's Clemente?" asked Johnny Blue, not overly impressed by this suggestion.

"Then," said Doc, "you boys are gonna be in a heap of trouble, ain't you?"

"Hell, Doc," I said, "Georgia can drive the wagon. We need your gun."

Doc held up his hand. "No gunplay for me," he said piously. "I am a man of peace." He stepped away from us, turned, and added: "Now come get some coffee an' grub an' then do like I told you."

An hour later, me and Johnny Blue sat our horses under the oak and watched the others leave.

"Know somethin'," began Johnny Blue, "I've been sittin' here thinking that if you weren't such a lunatic in the first place we wouldn't be in this mess. None of it would have happened."

I opened my mouth to speak but Johnny Blue shook his head at me and held up his hand.

"Ah, ah, ah," he said. "This time I'll do the talkin'. See, first you took a notion to shoot everybody you met up the ass, an' if you recollect, that caused us no end of problems, includin' gettin' hung. Then you was so all-fired set on signing on with the Rangers—against my better judgment, I might add—that you poisoned a whole wrong village of Mexicans with fumigation bombs an' started a major war."

I tried to talk again, but Johnny Blue shushed me.

"Now we got the Rangers after us, the United States Army, Mexican bandits, bounty hunters and maybe half the border riffraff of Texas, an' that's just for starters. The aforementioned want us dead or alive—and for all of them, that means preferably dead."

He lifted his head and stared into the branches of the oak. "An' all because you're a dangerous lunatic who shouldn't be allowed near civilized folks."

Now I got the chance to speak, I said: "First off, when that Ranger captain told me he wanted them Mexicans fumigated, he didn't say just the *jacales*. Secondly—"

"Enough!" said Johnny Blue, dropping his head to his chest and shaking it slowly like he'd been talking more in sorrow than in anger. "Let's fade back down the trail an' see who else wants to take a shot at us."

We didn't have to wait for long.

We'd covered maybe half a mile and were riding close to a dry creek about fifteen feet across, spanned by a narrow trestle bridge, when half a dozen shots peppered the ground around us. At least three men were hunkered down behind the bank of the creek on each side of the bridge, firing at us.

I yanked my horse around, reaching for my rifle, but my mount suddenly reared and I went over his rump, thudding onto the ground on my back. Johnny Blue reined up beside and fired at the creek with his Winchester.

"Run for it!" he yelled. "They've got us cold."

I rose unsteadily to my feet and followed my trotting horse. Bullets kicked up puffs of dust around me as I ran, and behind me Johnny Blue was still cranking out shots at our ambushers.

He turned his horse and rode beside me at a fast lope, slipping his left foot out of the stirrup. I stepped into the stirrup with my right and we hightailed it out of there, Johnny Blue holding on to me by the back of my shirt as I hung one-legged on the saddle.

Behind us, voices were raised in shouts of derisory laughter and a few more bullets buzzed like angry bees through the air above our heads.

When Johnny Blue judged we were out of range, he let me go and I stepped down and caught up my horse. "That was close," I said as I mounted. "Them boys had us dead to rights."

"They wasn't tryin'," Johnny Blue said. "They wasn't even half tryin'."

"Yeah, they was," I objected. "Them bushwhackers was doing their darndest to kill us."

"No, they wasn't," Johnny Blue said with finality. "If they was, we'd both be dead by now. Like you say, they had us dead to rights, but all they did was put the fear of God into us."

"Why the hell would they go to all the trouble of bush-whacking us, then not kill us?" I asked.

"Beats me," Johnny Blue said. "I've studied on that an' I don't have an answer for it."

"Maybe it's a good sign. It could be a good sign."

My gloomy *compadre* shrugged. "Maybe good. But probably bad."

When we rejoined and told Doc what had transpired back on the trail, he was as mystified as we were, maybe even more so, judging by the worried expression on his face.

" 'Tis passing strange," he said. "We heard the shootin' and thought fer certain you were both dead. If it was Clemente Perez he would surely have killed you both. Ditto, bounty hunters."

"Ditto the army and the Rangers," added Johnny Blue sourly.

"And they laughed, you say?"

"Fit to bust a gut," I said. "They stopped shootin' an' just laughed at us."

"Practical jokers?" suggested Sir John. "It's been known to happen."

Johnny Blue shook his head at him. "Them rifles were no joke. Some of their bullets came mighty close."

"Well, let's be on the alert from now until we reach Laredo," Doc said somberly. "There's a mystery here and perhaps a hidden danger I don't understand."

We reached the Sabinas ford without incident— though the following dust cloud kept pace with us, never getting any closer, and at night we saw a campfire burn in the distance.

Two days after crossing the ford we splashed through the shallows of the Rio Grande and rode into Laredo.

The city was even busier than it was when we left, and for that I was much relieved. The more people around, the less likely me and Johnny Blue would be discovered by the law.

Sir John and Lady Agatha went first to the bank where they'd earlier deposited a large sum of money, then checked us all into the Cattleman's Hotel at their expense.

Me and Johnny Blue found a livery stable for our horses and rubbed them down with some pieces of sacking and gave them each a bucket of oats while Doc closeted himself with the owner, dickering over the price of his horse and wagon.

"I have no more use for it," he'd told us earlier. "Besides, it brings back only bitter memories that I'd soon try to forget."

Doc still struck a hard bargain, and left the livery with ninety dollars—eighty for the wagon and ten for the horse. "This is walking money," he told me and Johnny Blue, "and I insist that you share in my bounty by dining with me tonight."

But when we met Sir John at the hotel he insisted that we must join him and Lady Agatha for dinner at the Cattleman's restaurant—famous for its steak, but also for its lobster, brought down by the Katy from Houston.

Once more dressed in smart clothes, thanks to Sir John, I didn't want to spoil the effect by belting on a gun, so I stuck my Colt in the waistband of my pants and covered it with my new linen jacket. I didn't think our mysterious bushwhackers, whoever they were, would try anything around the crowded plazas of Laredo, where there were lawmen aplenty, but it didn't pay to take chances.

I slicked down my hair and curled my mustache into two fine points, and I cut a right handsome and impressive figure as I greeted Johnny Blue in the hotel lobby, then stepped into the dining room, where Sir John and Lady Agatha already sat with Doc and Georgia.

The babies were being cared for by a local woman with a dozen younkers of her own, though Georgia professed to being much concerned for their well-being and declared with a worried expression that she fervently hoped the woman knew her business.

"With all them kids, I would think she does," said

Doc, not in the least put out by it all. "If she's raised all them brats she must know what she's about."

Lady Agatha had obviously found clothes more to her liking in Laredo and she wore a brilliant blue dress of fine silk, her beautiful hair done up in gay ribbons of the same color.

"I believe, gentlemen," said Doc with a knowing wink, "that we are sitting at table with the two most beautiful women in Texas, if not the entire United States."

At this pretty compliment, Georgia smiled and squeezed Doc's arm, and even Lady Agatha gave a slight nod of her lovely head.

The waiter came and took our order, and after an excellent meal, Doc, who seemed to be in an expansive mood, lit a cigar and ordered with great flair, "Mumms all round."

Thus we were a happy and joyous company as the evening wore on and the dining room filled up with well-dressed people who had been attending one of the city's several theaters, or had been walking in the plazas.

Doc and Sir John then began to talk about the former's prospects in England, while Lady Agatha and Georgia began one of their endless discussions about babies.

Me and Johnny Blue sat in silence for the most part, both of us feeling a little uncomfortable in these glittering surroundings, being more used to the rough life of bunkhouse and camp.

Without trying to be obvious, I was studying a young woman at a nearby table—at least studying her naked shoulders and the swell of her breasts above her red dress—when out of the corner of my eye, I saw a small Mexican boy step into the restaurant. He looked around

quickly, saw me, smiled broadly, and walked straight for
my table.

"For you, señor," he said, handing me a small slip of
paper. "You are the scrawny little runt with the big red
mustache, I think."

"Who is this from?" I asked, but the boy was already
threading his way through the busy tables and was gone.

"What is it?" asked Doc. He smiled. "A *billet-doux*
from that pretty young lady you've been eyeing so sur-
reptitiously for the past half hour, perhaps?"

"I dunno," I said, "but let's find out."

I opened up a rectangular sheet of paper filled with
lines of small, cramped printing, but what caught my startled gaze were the words that had been scrawled across it,
obviously by using the soft lead of a bullet. It said simply: SUNE YOU DIE.

There was no signature, no indication of who sent it. I
passed the note to Doc, who studied it with great interest
and growing alarm.

"Let me see that," Lady Agatha said impatiently. Doc
passed her the note and she looked at it for a few moments, then passed it on to Sir John. "Do you recognize
that page?" she asked.

The Englishman didn't hesitate for a single moment.
"Why yes, darling, I believe that's a page torn from your
Bible. I'd recognize that thick, London bond paper anywhere. And look, by Jove, it's from the Book of Revela-
tion."

"May I?" asked Doc. He took the page from Sir John
and again studied it with care. Then he began to read
from one of the verses: " 'Behold, He is coming with the
clouds; and every eye will see Him, and every one who
pierced Him: and all will wail on account of Him.' "

"I say," said Sir John, "it's really bad luck to write a threatening note on a page torn from the Holy Bible."

"Yes, it is bad luck," agreed Doc. "But bad luck for whom?"

Twenty-eight

That night I locked myself in my room and jammed a chair under the doorknob. I took off my boots and coat, but otherwise lay down fully clothed, my gun close to hand on the table beside the bed.

Whoever had sent that note—and I was now convinced it could only be Clemente Perez, since Lady Agatha's Bible had been with the baggage he stole from her—said he'd kill me soon. And to me, soon could be tonight.

I dozed off and on for about an hour and woke with a start. What had wakened me? Ears straining, I lay in the darkness, alert for the slightest sound.

Outside in the hallway a board creaked. Then another. Careful footsteps sounded in the hallway. I sat up on the bed and picked up my Colt. It could be just a late reveler returning to his room after a night on the town, or—

The doorknob turned slowly.

"Who's there?" I yelled. "Speak up or you're a dead man."

Booted feet pounded along the hallway, then I heard them clatter down the stairs. Quickly I put on my hat, stamped into my boots, and opened the door. I ran downstairs and into the lobby. A drowsy clerk in a striped vest and black coat looked at me in surprise, rubbing sleep from his eyes, then did a double take when he saw the gun in my hand.

"Did somebody come through here?" I asked.

"When?"

I cussed that dozy clerk up and down. "Now!" I yelled finally. "Why the hell would I ask you if I didn't mean right now?"

The clerk shook his head. "I didn't see nothing."

I threw the clerk a disgusted look and stepped outside.

The plaza was quiet, the oil lamps along the sidewalks casting yellow pools of light, white moths fluttering around their fan-shaped flames. In the distance a man rode along a cross street, head down, nodding in the saddle, letting his plodding horse take him home.

I looked up and down the plaza again, then, crouching low, crossed to the other side. A cool breeze from the north heralded the arrival of fall. The breeze swirled and caught up a piece of paper, which rose high into the air, then wrapped itself around an awning post, flapping frantically like a trapped dove.

Whoever had tried my door had vanished completely into the night. I stepped inside the doorway of a hat shop and stayed there, my gun ready. There was just a chance he'd come back to try his luck again.

From a saloon the tinny notes of a piano dropped like shards of broken glass into the stillness. It was midweek and the saloons that were still open were quiet. It seemed most of the ten thousand citizens of Laredo believed in early bedtimes, and the hard-drinking hands from the surrounding ranches wouldn't be in until Friday night.

I stood in the doorway for several minutes, then decided my nocturnal visitor had made good his escape.

Shoving my gun back in my waistband, I was about to cross the plaza and return to the hotel when I heard the clink of a bottle and a man's muffled curse.

The man, whoever he was, had likely accidentally kicked an empty bottle in the narrow alley between the hat shop where I stood and the Masonic hall across the way.

It could be the man I was after.

Swallowing hard, I shucked my Colt again and cautiously entered the alley.

As you boys know, back in them olden days I was reckoned to be both mighty handsome and mighty brave. That I was handsome there was no doubt, but my bravery was tempered by a bushel basket of common sense, and right then, as I stepped deeper into the alley, my common sense was hollering at me to get the hell out of there, back to the hotel, and wake up Doc and Johnny Blue.

But there was something inside me demanding that I get to the bottom of this mystery, and despite the fact that the butterflies in my stomach had butterflies, I fought down my fear and kept on going.

The alley was littered with empty cans and bottles, and I reckoned the man who'd come to my room had been sneaking up on me when he'd kicked an empty bottle and the sudden *chink!* had given him away. He must have turned and hightailed it back the way he'd come.

Gun in hand, I kept going and reached an open space behind the hat shop and the Masonic hall. The alley didn't lead to another plaza, but to some waste ground, hemmed in on the other side by the backs of stores, saloons, and other buildings.

It was very dark and quiet, and nothing moved back there but the breeze. A dog barked a long distance away, then abruptly stopped and there was only the silence again.

"Is there anybody there?" I said, not yelling, but loud enough, my voice cracking on a high note of fear.

There was no reply.

That was it. Now the time for my reckless brand of bravery was over and the time for good ol' American common sense was at hand.

I turned to step back down the alley, when I heard something come squeaking at me in the dark.

The *squeak . . . squeak . . . squeak . . .* came closer, rushing at me very fast. Panicked, blind in that darkness, I aimed at the sound and cut loose with my Colt.

Three shots, very fast—then the squeaking thing, with a metallic clatter, crashed into me and fell over.

I looked down—and saw the Fortune Flyer.

Across the open ground a door slammed open and a man yelled: "What the hell!"

Lights were coming on in some of the buildings opposite, and a dog started to bark furiously. Fear rising in me, tasting like acid in my throat, I turned to run out of there—but way off, in the distance between the buildings, I saw the sudden glow of a candle. A man stood there, holding it at arm's length above his head. His long hair blew in the breeze, and I knew instantly who it was: the Gunfighter.

A heavy hand slammed down on my shoulder. I jumped three feet in the air and spun, my Colt coming up fast. A strong fist caught my gun hand and Johnny Blue yelled: "What the hell are you doing, shootin' up the town at this hour?"

A quick glance told me the Gunfighter and his candle

were gone. But borne on the breeze I heard a man's mocking laugh fade into the distance.

As people clustered around me and Johnny Blue— some mighty angry at being wakened by gunfire, some merely curious—I quickly explained what had happened, leaving out nothing, not even the Gunfighter's terrible apparition.

Johnny Blue listened in silence, then said: "You was seein' things, is all."

"Seeing things?" I repeated. I kicked the Fortune Flyer lying at my feet and said: "Is this 'seeing things'?"

Johnny Blue allowed that the appearance of the Flyer was passing strange. He bent over, picked up the machine, and studied it. "It's the Flyer all right," he said, stating what to me was pretty obvious.

The bicycle's mangled frame and wheels had been crudely straightened, probably by beating them with a rock, and someone had taken advantage of the darkness to roll it toward me. But why? I had the question, but no answer.

"Make way, there, make way for an officer of the law!"

A big man wearing only hat, boots, a nightshirt, and a mustache pushed his way through the crowd, some of whom held aloft guttering oil lamps.

The lawman, who said he was a duly sworn deputy, was holding fast to a Greener and a grudge. He obviously didn't enjoy being rousted out of bed at almost two o'clock in the morning.

"What's going on here?" he demanded.

I opened my mouth to speak, but Johnny Blue stepped in. "Deputy, this little feller here is an escaped lunatic," he said matter-of-factly. "He takes notions to shoot folks up the ass, especially when he walks in his sleep. He came into this alley, hoping to ambush folks, but thankfully there were none around."

"If there were none around, then what the hell was he shootin' at?" the deputy asked suspiciously.

"That," returned Johnny Blue. "They call it a bicycle."

"I know what they call it," the deputy said. "What I want to know is why he was shootin' at it."

"Well, you see," said Johnny Blue smoothly, "he took it fer a ghost."

"A what?"

"A ghost. He figgered to shoot a ghost up the ass, just to make a change."

The deputy thought about this for a spell, rubbing his chin, then said: "A lunatic, you say?"

"He's dangerous," answered Johnny Blue. "Just a poor, dangerous lunatic."

"I suppose I should take him into custody," the deputy said.

"That won't be necessary, Officer."

Sir John stepped into the circle of people surrounding me. "I'm his doctor. I will take care of him."

"You haven't been doin' a good job of it so far, have you, Doc?" the deputy said sourly. "A dangerous lunatic shouldn't be wandering the streets with a murderous revolver."

"It won't happen again, I assure you," returned Sir John. "By the way," he added, "I am a close personal friend of Governor Ross, and I plan to tell him how efficiently you've done your duty."

At this the deputy puffed up a little and said: "I'm glad I could be of service, Doctor." He waved his shotgun.

"Now, you people, clear a way there, there's nothing to see here. Clear a way for a dangerous lunatic."

As Sir John led me away, Johnny Blue flanking me on the other side, I turned and saw the deputy looking after us, rubbing his chin, his face puzzled like he was deep in thought. That, I thought, was a worrisome thing, since me and Johnny Blue was poor hunted creatures with every man's hand turned against us.

Alerted by all the fuss and my shooting, Doc met us at the door of the hotel and demanded to know what had happened. I told him of my encounter with the Flyer and of seeing the candlelit shade of the Gunfighter.

When I'd finished, Doc was silent for a few moments, then he said: "It seems to me that it can only be Clemente Perez who wants you dead. But there's one thing I don't understand."

"What's that, Doc?" I asked.

"Why doesn't he just shoot you? Why the hell is he trying to scare you to death?"

Twenty-nine

I returned to bed and slept fitfully until daybreak, then dressed hurriedly and walked downstairs to the hotel dining room. At this time in the morning the room was empty except for a couple of early-rising businessmen in black broadcloth suits who sat in a corner and read newspapers over their coffee and first cigars of the day.

A pretty young waitress took my order and I drank coffee until my breakfast arrived. I'd just finished eating when Sir John and Lady Agatha arrived, followed a few minutes later by Doc, Georgia, and Johnny Blue.

As she ate, Lady Agatha made it clear that the events of the night had left her "trembling like a reed." She insisted that Sir John obtain tickets on the Katy that very day for Houston, and from there they would make their way to New York and book passage on a steamer bound for Southampton.

I didn't blame her none. Lady Agatha herself had endured a terrible ordeal and borne up well, and besides, my troubles were none of her own.

Sir John listened to his young wife in silence, then said her suggestion was a tolerably good one, though he admitted he was loath to leave me and Johnny Blue, as it were, "in the lurch."

At this objection, Lady Agatha grew even more distressed. "John," she sobbed, "I am so sick of this country and I long for the green fields of my home. If you insist that I remain a single day longer, I shall die here"—she struck her forehead—"or here"—she struck her breast—"or wherever it is the soul of this most unfortunate of women dwells."

Sir John sprang to his feet in the greatest condition of anxiety, wringing his hands in a most piteous manner. "My darling, do not afflict yourself so. We will leave today, at once, if it is at all in my power."

Lady Agatha instantly brightened considerably. "John, your kindness and consideration were often much remarked upon by my poor papa." She tilted her beautiful cheek toward him. "You may kiss me for minding me so well."

After kissing his wife, Sir John regained his seat and said with the utmost sincerity: "There is another solution to our mutual problem." He regarded me and Johnny Blue with affection. "You two young men can come with us to England."

Johnny Blue, who was rolling a smoke, struck a match with his thumbnail and lit his cigarette. He shook out the match and placed it, smoking slightly, on the ashtray at his elbow.

"Sir John, them broad acres of yours you was talkin' about, you got sheep on 'em, right?"

The Englishman nodded. "Cheviot and Leicester crossbreds mostly, but I do have some Suffolks. Excellent sheep, the Suffolk, very."

"Well, see," said Johnny Blue, "I'm a cow man, always have been since I were a younker. I can't be around woolies. Can't abide them."

"I'm so sorry," returned Sir John, somewhat taken aback, "I had no idea."

Johnny Blue nodded. "Sheep will ruin your range, back there in England. They crop the grass too close an' then poison it. A cow won't walk where a woolie has been." He leaned toward the Englishman and said in confidential tones: "Get them woolies off your range afore they ruin your grass. Them's words of wisdom."

Sir John turned to me. "And you, my young friend, do you feel the same way?"

"Afraid I do," I said. "I can't work for a man who runs woolies on his range. It ain't fittin'."

"Then we must soon part our ways," Sir John said with much feeling. "After we've shared so many adventures together, it is indeed a melancholy prospect."

Doc, who up until now had been mute, suggested that he and Sir John now repair with all haste to the train station to reserve their space on the next Katy train north—Doc always being a believer in striking the iron while it was hot.

"Then," he continued, "if we have time ere we board our conveyance, let us say farewell to our young friends here over a convivial bowl of the best hot gin punch—which can be obtained at a small hostelry I know of close by—so that auld acquaintance be ne'er forgot."

At this pretty speech our company was much cheered, and we separately retired to our rooms while Doc and Sir John repaired to the train station.

The two returned within the hour and Sir John declared that their train would leave punctually at fifteen minutes after four o'clock, so we had now plenty of time to visit Doc's saloon and seal our friendship with a social bowl or two.

The ladies declined to come with us, saying that they needed to pack, and besides, the babies—now that they were back in parental custody—would require constant attention to get over whatever trauma separation from the maternal breast might have occasioned.

The four of us stepped outside, Doc assuring us that his hostelry lay in a quiet street just off a nearby plaza. He gave me his arm and Sir John did the same for Johnny Blue and thus linked we made our way through crowded Laredo, Sir John and Doc singing little snatches from Gilbert and Sullivan operettas as we walked.

The only sour note in the proceedings was a Mexican with the lean and hungry look of the outlaw about him, who attentively watched us leave the hotel, then quickly ducked into a nearby saloon, his eyes alight.

Boys, as you might guess, the saloon Doc led us to was like the man himself: seedy, run-down, but with pretensions to gentility. Most unusual for that time in the West, a U-shaped bar was in the center of the long, low-ceilinged room. The only windows were small and to the front of the building, and despite its being almost noon, the place was cool and dark, most of the lighting coming from a row of oil lamps hung above the bar.

There were some tables and chairs scattered around and some prints on the wall that showed mounted men in red coats chasing foxes with hounds. A few bent trumpets, which Doc declared were hunting horns, hung beside the prints, and a large sign in a glass frame on the bar asked the poignant question HAVE YOU WRITTEN TO MOTHER?

Doc, with an imperious air, ordered a bowl of the best gin punch—"Make it hot, mind."—and the elderly bartender was soon lost behind a cloud of steam as he busied himself with boiling water, gin, sugar, and lemons.

While we waited for the punch, Sir John, at Doc's request, regaled us with tales of his adventures among the wild Zulus of Africa, adding as he usually did that they were "fine, brave chaps, though no match for the Martini Henry rifle and bayonet in the hands of steady British infantry."

When the punch arrived, Doc poured us cups from the smoking bowl with great ceremony.

"Now," he asked, "everyone got a drink?" When we nodded our assent, he said: "Well, here's to us: we few, we happy few, we band of brothers."

"Hear, hear," said Sir John. "Jolly good show."

Smiling, Doc raised his glass cup to his lips, but it froze there as his eyes widened into a look of the most unbelievable horror.

I slid away from the bar and glanced behind me, and instantly fear spiked at my belly. Standing there, smiling evilly, stood Clemente Perez. And on either side of him, a gunman—one with long hair rippling in soft waves to his shoulders.

Thirty

"Well, well, well, isn't this cozy," Perez said softly. "I mean, us all together again like this."

Doc was the first to recover his composure and he said: "We want no trouble here, Clemente. What's done is done, and there's an end to it."

Perez—huge, shaggy, and bearded, two guns strapped around his hips—shrugged. "Trouble? I want no trouble with you, Doc. You and your English friend aren't in this. You're free to go and be damned to ye."

"I say," returned Sir John, outraged, "this just won't do. Now, speak your piece and leave."

Perez ignored the Englishman and nodded at me. "This is good, I think. You are very scared, little man. And I've tried very hard to scare you."

The longhaired man took a step or two closer, grinning with yellowed teeth, and I saw then that he wasn't the Gunfighter at all, just a two-bit gunman who fancied himself the new Wild Bill Hickok.

"It was you," I said to the longhaired man. "It was you who came to my room and then pushed the Flyer into me."

"Scared you pretty good, didn't I?" the man said. "Of course, you scare real easy."

Perez laughed. "You also scared pretty damn good when we ambushed you at Hidalgo Wells." He shrugged. "Of course, we didn't want to kill you, at least not then, though that idiot Díaz nearly ruined the whole thing at La Lajilla."

"Clemente," said Doc softly, his eyes glittering, "you killed one of our number at La Lajilla, a man who was very dear to me."

Perez spread his hands, grinning. "It was unfortunate, but he got in the way. The order I gave to Díaz was to scare the hell out of this little man." Perez's eyes narrowed as he looked at me, his grin slowly vanishing. "Yes, I wanted you to taste fear. I wanted you to taste it like green bile in your mouth. I wanted you to taste it the way my brother must have tasted it when he realized he was trapped like a rat in the railroad cut."

"Your brother?" I asked, surprised. "Your brother was there?"

"Yes," Perez said. "He died with all the rest. And it was you who killed him, little man. You and your black companion who now stands at your side."

"Well," I said, doing my best to sound breezy, "I'm right unhappy to hear that, Clemente, an' I hope it's all water under the bridge an' there's no hard feelings. Let bygones be bygones I say, an' have a nice glass of hot gin punch."

Perez grinned again, this time even more evilly than before. "Are you crazy, little man? I've come here to kill you, not to drink with you. The only reason I haven't done it before is because I want to look at you as you die. I want to see the fear in your face as my bullets hit and you die screaming. I want to enjoy it, savor every moment. In my day I've killed men, women, children, and puppy dogs, but I've never enjoyed killing anyone as much as I'm going to enjoy killing you."

Boys, that statement was a real conversation stopper, and maybe for the first time in my life I was suddenly at a loss for words.

However, Clemente stepped into the silence. "Doc, you and your friend can leave now," he said. "You and I will meet at another time, I think, but not today."

Doc, his face stiff and hard, nodded and drained his punch cup. He shook my hand, then Johnny Blue's, and said: "Well, boys, it's been real nice knowing you. All you can do now is die game an' don't let ol' Clemente here scare you too bad."

"Get out of here, Doc," Perez said, his voice flat and dangerous. "I don't want to kill you today. But depend on it, there will be other days."

"No shooting, Clemente," returned Doc. "I have recently become a man of peace and have forsworn all violence. I have put gunplay behind me."

Sir John made to protest, but Doc impatiently shushed him into silence and roughly pushed him toward the door.

Now, I don't know how many mistakes Clemente Perez made in his lifetime, but he sure got the wrong dog by the tail that day, and that mistake would be his last.

You just didn't trust a man like Doc. He was as slippery as an eel and could be as sudden and deadly as a coiled rattler. And he had a fierce and unshakable loyalty to them he counted as friends, and he wasn't—as I'd told O'Shaugnessy back in La Lajilla—a forgiving man.

Perez, confident in his own gun skills, didn't even turn his head as Doc walked past him, keeping his eyes on my scared face the whole time. I was stunned at Doc's betrayal but had no time to study on it. I had maybe seconds to live, and I felt my knees tremble and my hands shake—a bad thing when you've got to shuck a gun real fast.

Doc took a step beyond Perez and suddenly spun on his heel, drawing the Gunfighter's Colt from his waistband.

He rammed the muzzle of the revolver against Clemente's back between the shoulder blades and fired. Shocked, his backbone burst asunder, blood spurting in a scarlet stream from his open mouth, Perez staggered, then drew as he turned to face his assailant.

Doc shoved his gun against the bandit's belly and fired again. Perez screamed, his shirt smoking as it caught fire. He took several steps backward, and Doc followed, shooting into him again and again until Clemente sprawled on the floor in death.

"That," said Doc, coldly looking down at the dead bandit, "was for the Mauler."

As Doc had once predicted, the concussion of his gun had blasted out most of the oil lamps above the bar, plunging the saloon into almost total darkness.

After Doc gunned Perez, everyone seemed frozen in place for a few moments, then Johnny Blue drew his gun and yelled at me: "Sam'l, right!"

I shucked my Colt and through the gloom saw a gout of orange flame as the longhaired gunman fired. His bullet cracked past my ear and shattered the punch bowl on the bar. Johnny Blue's gun and mine roared at the same time, and the gunman crashed into a table behind him, then slid off onto the floor, the table tipping over on top of him.

The third bandit, not liking what he was seeing, bolted

for the door. I sent a quick shot after him and heard him yell: "*Yiiiii!*"

He stumbled, picked himself up off the floor, and staggered outside, leaving a trail of blood behind him.

The saloon was full of smoke and the windows near the door looked like lanterns shining dimly in a gray fog. I was trembling like a leaf all over, stunned by the sudden and shocking violence and scarcely able to comprehend the unbelievable fact that I was still alive.

Doc stepped up beside us, his smoking Colt hanging from his right hand. "Are you boys okay?" he asked. "Is anyone hurt?"

I nodded. "Reckon we're just fine, Doc. You had me fooled for a spell there. I figgered you was walkin' out on us."

"How little," replied that smiling charlatan, "do you know the mind and the heart of Doc Fortune. I would not abandon my friends, or let the Mauler die unavenged."

The bartender was relighting the oil lamps, and now I could see Sir John's face in the gloom, his eyes wide, his cheeks totally drained of blood.

"Doc," choked the Englishman, shaking his head in disbelief, "you . . . you shot that man in the back."

Doc shrugged. "Couldn't do nothin' else. His back was the only part of him facing me."

The saloon door burst open and the deputy I'd seen earlier that morning stomped inside, only this time he was flanked by two more lawmen, a couple of hard cases holding shotguns.

"What's going on, here?" he demanded. He glanced at the bodies of Clemente and the longhaired gunman and added: "This looks like bloody murder, by God."

"Not murder, deputy," observed Doc coolly, "but self-defense. That there," he said, nodding toward the fallen bandit, "is the vicious outlaw Clemente Perez. He came here to kill us but we got the drop on him."

"I'll be the judge of that," the deputy said ominously. He shoved the toe of his boot under Perez and rolled the bandit over on his back. "That's ol' Clemente, all right," he said. "Looks like you boys done for him fer sure."

"I don't know the one over there," said Doc, pointing with his Colt to the body of the longhaired gunman.

The deputy walked over and glanced down at the body. "I know him, called hisself the Ponca City Kid. Killed a man in Abilene awhile back an' another in McAllen. He wasn't much."

After pondering the situation for a few moments, the deputy called over the bartender, a man in his seventies with white hair and a thin, sallow face. "These gents are calling this self-defense," the lawman said. "Is that how it played out to you?"

The bartender nodded. "Threats were made against the lives of the little gentleman and the colored man. Seemed like self-defense to me, an' no mistake."

"Well, ol' Clemente was wanted for rape an' murder on both sides of the border," the deputy said. "But we'll let a judge decide the right or wrong of this thing."

"But that's impossible," declared Sir John urgently. "We're leaving for Houston on the Katy this very afternoon."

"That's no problem," the deputy said. "We'll go see Judge Ryan right now. By the way," he added, "there's a wounded man outside by the name of Happy Jack Ronco. He's a tinhorn gambler by profession but he's done his share of killing. Was he running with Clemente?"

"He was in on it," declared Doc. "But he fled once the shooting started."

"Well, Happy Jack ain't so happy no more, on account of how somebody shot him up the ass." He looked hard at Johnny Blue. "Didn't you tell me this morning that the dangerous lunatic here had took a notion to shoot folks up the ass?"

I felt Johnny Blue's eyes boring into me, so I said quickly, "There were bullets flying everywhere, Deputy. It could have been any one of us."

"Maybe so," the deputy said. He studied me and Johnny Blue real close. "You sure I haven't seen you boys around here before? You, the lunatic, did you make the newspaper one time, maybe on account of something dangerous you done to folks? No? Well, it seems to me I've read something . . . " He shook his head. "Ah well, it'll come back to me. Now, let's all walk down to the courthouse an' see the judge."

Thanks to Sir John's being a rich foreigner and the fact that Clemente Perez was a wanted man, Judge Ryan was quick to pass a verdict of self-defense and told us we were free to go.

"There may be reward money involved," the judge said, "so drop off your names and addresses with my clerk as you leave and we'll be in touch."

Needless to say, me and Johnny Blue was a mite uneasy when it came to the touchy subject of reward money, so we let that go and stepped around the clerk's desk real quiet before lighting a shuck out of that courthouse.

The rest of the day passed uneventfully and all too soon it was time for me and Johnny Blue to accompany

Sir John and Lady Agatha and Doc and Georgia to the train station.

Doc hugged me and Johnny Blue, his face stained with tears, and hugged us again.

"I just want you boys to know that you did handsomely in that shootin' scrape," he said. "It just goes to show that when the chips are down, you can shoot pretty good, an' I'm proud of both of you."

Then, his excessively tender and often overly sensitive nature much overcome by a tangle of emotion, Doc hugged us both again and declared in a halting voice that he could speak not another word since this parting was such a bitter pill to swallow and he was quite used up and undone.

For his part, Sir John cried out earnestly that he had found no truer and more steadfast comrades even among the ranks of his fellow officers in darkest Africa, and that, midst the deepest of his slumbers, he was quite sure he'd dream of me and Johnny Blue.

"That makes us powerful glad, Sir John," was my answer, "an' it's been right nice a-knowin' of ye."

Georgia—tears running down her round, brown cheeks—held me, then Johnny Blue, close to her great bosom and insisted we kiss both babies, who were squalling unmercifully, not once, but twice.

"How many adventures we three have been though," she said with passion after we'd performed our duty, Johnny Blue somewhat distastefully. "When I'm a fine lady riding in my carriage, I know I'll wish you were running beside me in your footman's livery of blue and gold." Then, quite overcome, she sobbed into her little lace handkerchief and said she must surely die of grief at our parting.

Lady Agatha, looking devastatingly beautiful in a gray traveling outfit, merely gave me and Johnny Blue her hand and bade us coolly to "Take care."

Then the conductor cried, "All aboard," and we watched as the Katy train took away our friends to foreign climes, and as for me, I was downcast and much disheartened, fearing that I'd never see Doc and Georgia again.

Thirty-one

Me and Johnny Blue returned to our hotel, but that canny rider was much distressed, saying that the deputy had a suspicious mind, and that he was sure he'd read our wanted poster and would remember sooner or later that we were desperate and hunted men.

"I suggest we hit the trail right away an' head for Florida," he said. "We ain't gonna be able to rescue my little sister if we're rotting in a jail—or dead."

I thought this over for a while and decided that this was sound advice, and said we should get our horses from the livery stable and ride as fast as we could out of Texas.

The trouble was, we were both flat broke as usual, and that was a worrisome thing. But our worries on that score were soon ended—by a loud knock on my room door.

Johnny Blue shucked his gun, standing poised and alert, as I slowly opened the door. The clerk in the striped vest stood there, a brown paper package in his hand.

"For you," he said sulkily, and left.

I opened up the package on the bed, Johnny Blue looking curiously over my shoulder, and there were seven items inside: the Gunfighter's scratched-up Colt, five gold double eagles, and an envelope embossed with the name of the Cattleman's Hotel, addressed to "The Cow Boys."

"Open it," Johnny Blue said impatiently.

I thumbed open the envelope and took the letter from inside. It was in a fair copperplate hand and had been written by Lady Agatha, obviously sometime before she left to catch the train.

> Dear Cow Boys,
>
> I have relieved Mr. Fortune of this, his murderous revolver, since he will have no further need of it when he arrives on the more civilized shores of Great Britain.
>
> Since they have shown little interest in the coal and coke trade, I plan to find him and his wife honest employ by throwing down the gauntlet, as it were, to the influential friends of my late papa.
>
> Since many of these men have business interests in the remote Highlands of Scotland, notably in forestry and barley growing, I believe Mr. and Mrs. Fortune might find a situation more to their liking, possibly in the manure and fertilizer occupation.
>
> In the meantime, you may write to them in care of Colonel Sir John Gray, K.G., Huntley Hall, Devon, England, and I will see that your letters are sent on to Scotland by post coach.
>
> I remain,
> Your Obed't Servant,
> Lady Agatha Gray
>
> P.S. Thank you.

"What does she mean by that?" Johnny Blue asked. "I mean, saying thank you."

I shrugged. "She never said thank you before."

"Well, anyhoo," returned Johnny Blue, shaking his

head, "the hunnerd dollars is welcome, an' that's a natural fact."

We checked out of the hotel and walked to the livery stable, where we saddled our horses and rode out of Laredo with many an uneasy backward glance, because that suspicious deputy was very much on our minds.

I planned a route that would take us northeast toward the Nueces, then we'd bypass Houston and head due east to New Orleans, where we could maybe board a train or a steam packet bound for Florida.

Johnny Blue allowed that this was an excellent plan, so long as our money held out. But we planned to shoot most of our chuck along the way, and in that way make our hundred dollars go a lot further.

We were three days out of Laredo and still a fair piece south of the Nueces when we climbed a shallow saddle-back hill near Los Olmos Creek and looked back at the plain spread out behind us. The nip of fall was in the air and we both wore our ragged mackinaws against the morning chill.

"Well," I said to Johnny Blue, "would you just look at that."

Below us on the plain, a cavalry regiment, pennons fluttering, hove into view in column; then, as we watched, deployed into a long, glittering line of blue.

Two galloping batteries of horse artillery followed, and they pulled up in a cloud of dust and rearing horses and unlimbered their cannons on both flanks of the cavalry.

A party of civilian horsemen—maybe fifty strong, led by a couple of Indian scouts—soon arrived, and as we watched, formed a line near the cannons on the western flank of the cavalry.

It was a martial and gallant display that gave me a lump in my throat and made me feel all a-tremble. I was glad me and Johnny Blue had once saved the U.S. Army from destruction, else we would never have seen such a thrilling sight.

"Makes a man proud to be an American, don't it?" I said to Johnny Blue.

But that puzzled puncher's face was scrunched up in thought as he watched the valiant and warlike scene unfold before us.

"Don't those guys down there with the cal'vry look like Texas Rangers to you?" he asked suspiciously. "And I swear the big bearded ranny on the gray hoss is that Captain Frank Jones."

I shook my head at him. "I don't think so. What they're having down there is called maneuvers. It keeps the troops sharp by pretending they're making war on somebody."

"Then who are the guys in the go-to-prayer-meetin' clothes?" Johnny Blue asked. "They sure as hell look like Rangers to me."

"So what?" I asked right back, too enthralled by the martial marvel below to listen to Johnny Blue's constant complaints.

"Remember that deputy back in Laredo?" Johnny Blue pressed on. "You don't suppose he suddenly recollected where he'd read about us an' alerted the army and the Rangers?"

"Nah," I said, "that's all forgotten. All that high treason stuff is water under the bridge. Hell, I don't think they ever meant it in the first place."

"You sure about that?" Johnny Blue asked nervously. "All those boys down there are a-lookin' up here. I mean, some of them officers have field glasses on us and they're studying us right close."

"Trust me," I said.

Boooom!

Both batteries of cannons fired at the same time, and balls whistled over our heads to burst in mighty explosions just twenty yards behind us.

"They're firing at us!" Johnny Blue yelled, desperately trying to control his terrified horse.

"Nah," I said, "can't be. It's a mistake."

More shells burst around us, and a shelf of rock that had stood a few yards to our right suddenly disappeared in a cloud of fire, jagged chunks of red-hot metal and slabs of rock flying through the air perilously close to where we stood.

Down on the plain I heard an officer bark an order, and the cavalry regiment drew sabers, transforming themselves into a glittering ribbon of steel. Then a bugle sounded the charge, and them horse soldiers galloped right at us, closely followed by the Rangers, who were already firing their rifles.

"You were right, Blue Boy, and I was wrong," I yelled. "I guess they really did mean that high treason stuff. Let's get out of here!"

We rode hell-for-leather off the hill, and behind us the bugler kept sounding the charge again and again and the cavalrymen roared and waved their sabers over their heads. Bullets spat through the air from Ranger rifles as the quiet morning was shredded apart by shot and shell.

"How many are chasin' us?" Johnny Blue asked, his face scared as he galloped beside me.

I glanced back. "Do you want I should include the horse artillery?"

"All of them!"

"Including the Rangers?"

"Damn it, all of them!"

"Oh, about eight hunnerd, give or take a few."

"Then we're dead fer sure," Johnny Blue wailed. "Dead as flies in molasses."

More cannon shells burst ahead of us in fans of orange flame, throwing up great clods of dirt and rock, and we rode over trembling ground cratered and broken by the explosions.

"Know somethin', Blue Boy," I said as we galloped though a thick cloud of cordite smoke. "When we get to Florida an' rescue our little sister, we should spring ol' Geronimo, as well."

Johnny Blue glanced behind him at the oncoming cavalry and frantically spurred his horse.

"I don't know about that—he's a wild Injun an' not to be trusted around white folks." He looked over at me quickly. "Why'd you want to spring ol' Geronimo, anyhow?"

I shrugged—or as nearest I could get to a shrug, since I was bent over the neck of my horse, the brim of my hat flattened against the crown.

"Oh, I dunno," I yelled. "Just for fun, I guess."

"Well, we ain't springing that Apache," Johnny Blue yelled back, shouting over the cannon fire and the warlike cries of the cavalry. "He ain't to be trusted with a tommyhawk in his hand, an' that's an end to it."

But it wasn't, not by a long shot.

It was still a fair piece to Florida, and I'd talk him into it.

Hell, I always do.

Historical Note

By 1888, the Texas Rangers was no longer a hard-riding, straight-shooting frontier battalion set up primarily to defend against marauding Indians, but was well on its way to becoming the modern law-enforcement agency it is today.

In July 1901, the governor of Texas was authorized "to organize a force to be known as the Ranger Force for the purpose of protecting the frontier against marauding or thieving parties, and for the suppression of lawlessness and crime throughout the state."

One of the duties of the new Rangers was the eradication of the virulent smallpox epidemics that flared, like clockwork, each spring along the Rio Grande.

More on the effects their compulsory fumigation had on the indigenous and long-suffering Mexican population can be read in the excellent history of the Rangers by Walter Prescott Webb, *The Texas Rangers, A Century of Frontier Defense* (University of Texas Press).

The adventures of Li'l Emily are based on the exploits of the gambler Henry Arbuckle, the only man to use a train to rout an Indian war party.

Arbuckle won an 0-4-0 engine named Little Emma during a Fourth of July craps game in Pueblo, Colorado, in 1882, and promptly had the old locomotive freighted to Clifton, Arizona, where he used her to haul silver ore for the Lazensky Mine Company.

During one of his trips, Arbuckle spotted a large Apache war party filing through a narrow cut right in his path, intent on raiding Clifton. The gambler didn't hesitate. He opened Little Emma's throttle wide and plowed into the unfortunate warriors.

Trapped within the sheer rock walls of the cut, the Apaches had nowhere to go and the result was a complete rout.

That this was no hunting party became evident when Little Emma chugged triumphantly into Clifton and the front of the engine was found to be smeared with yellow, blue, and red war paint and other, much more gruesome reminders of her charge.

To order call: 1-800-788-6262